The Haunted

Hope A. C. Bentley

Golden Light Factory
East Burke, VT

This is a work of fiction. All of the characters, organizations and events portrayed in this novel are either products of the author's imagination or are used fictitiously.

Published by
Golden Light Factory
East Burke, Vermont
www.goldenlightfactory.com

ISBN 978-1-7327645-2-1

To James

The best thing to come
out of boarding school

Chapter One

Lydia Boswell zipped her backpack and looked around her room one last time. Her folder with the two lists was in the front pocket of the backpack, and she patted it to reassure herself before heading downstairs. She was not usually the kind of person who had folders or lists, but then very little was usual about her life anymore.

In the kitchen Emily was dropping some yogurt cartons into a cooler and pouring coffee into a travel mug.

"Ready, sweetie?" she asked.

"Yup."

"Abilene dropped this by yesterday." Emily held up a bag of Cool Ranch Doritos and a loaf of homemade pumpkin bread. "I'm sure she would have liked to say good-bye in person, but it's so early. . . ." Emily trailed off and gave Lydia a smile that was more of a wince.

Lydia shrugged and smiled back at her mom. They both knew that Abilene had other reasons for not saying good-bye in person.

The fact that Lydia was leaving made the kitchen seem unfamiliar. Did the refrigerator always hum like that? Had they always had curtains? Where was the picture of her and Matthew that used to be by the sink? In it, they were toddlers, dressed as bowling pins for Halloween, and were both frowning mistrustfully at the camera. Or had it been the one of them sleeping in a sticky pile in the backseat of Abilene's car?

Outside, the light was the pale lavender of predawn and the birdsong was deafening. Lydia looked down the road and across the street to Abilene's house. It was shadowed and still. She imagined for a moment that Matthew might jog down the front steps with his long, flopping limbs that always seemed to have an extra joint, imagined the white of his grin in his dark brown face. She imagined what it would be like if they were going to Claybourne together.

She turned and looked over her own home. *I'll be back,* she promised herself.

Lydia and her mom drove north and east for six hours and then wiggled their way through small, winding roads in rural Maine. Lydia was just beginning to think that they'd never get there when they crested a steep hill that was like reaching the top of a roller coaster. Lydia's stomach dropped as the car plunged down the other side.

The long, steep slope was smattered with houses, peppered with tall, narrow pines and large gray boulders. Below, the ocean spilled out in front of them like a sheet of hammered metal.

"The sea," Emily breathed out reverently. She slowed the car to take in the view. "Look at it, Wid. John Banville, Ian McEwan, Colm Tóibín; no wonder they all write so beautifully about the sea." Lydia's mom was slightly nuts about books. "Or maybe it's Maine. *Cider House Rules, Empire Falls, Olive Kitteridge.*"

"Stephen King," added Lydia, then, "Look." Down below, one of the houses had a widow's walk on the roof. The figure of an old man was leaning against the seaward railing. "Is he real? Or do they pay some old guy to look rustic all day?"

"It looks like a postcard. The whole town does."

Emily drove slowly down the hill past cheerful window boxes and a steep, haphazard sidewalk made of big granite slabs.

Every house was built of the same components: worn picket fence, gables, dark green shutters, and white or graying clapboards. Emily reached the bottom and had to turn either right or left along the water. She went left and passed a church with a very steep graveyard, a general store, and a hardware store. Lydia looked up at the long, sagging porch. At first she thought it was a scarecrow seated in a rocking chair, but then the face turned to follow Lydia as she passed. Lydia looked away and sank down in her seat. The scarecrow was really an old lady wearing dark, round sunglasses. Her stare left two warm spots on Lydia's cheek.

There were a few more buildings, and then Emily spotted a small gray-and-crimson sign with the Claybourne seal on it and an arrow pointing toward the ocean.

Emily steered the car carefully down the narrow lane to a small parking lot and a modest boathouse with the words "CLAYBOURNE FERRY," also in crimson. The parking lot was half full; mostly regular old cars except for one dark gray limo and something else low and sleek. Matthew would have known what it was, but all Lydia could say was that it reminded her of James Bond.

Emily parked the car and squeezed Lydia's hand.

"All right, sweetie?"

Lydia offered her mom a grin and a nod. She studied the other people in the parking lot. They looked surprisingly normal, but Lydia knew they weren't.

If you took all the students who had been accepted to top-tier high schools and asked them to apply to the Claybourne Academy of Excellence, only one in thirty would be accepted. Take a random sample of Claybourne alumni and you'd have the top experts in any given field, Pulitzer Prize winners, Nobel Laureates, heads of state. Claybourne alumni wrote theorems, and poems for presidential inaugurations. They discovered particles and cures. They conducted orchestras and nuclear experiments. They were, in short, the very last people that Lydia felt any kind of kinship with. Lydia, with her better-than-average grades and good recommendations, would have been a squeeze to get into Andover or Hotchkiss, but Claybourne? She shifted in her seat and glanced at her mom. Emily flashed her a reassuring grin.

"Ready?" she asked.

"I guess."

"I still can't believe you got in."

"Mom! Jeez." Lydia rolled her eyes and pretended to be insulted.

"I mean, *I* think you're amazing and a genius and everything, but *wow*. You got into *Claybourne*."

"So did Matthew."

"I don't know how *either* of you got in."

Lydia looked out the window at a barrel of flowers. She was pretty sure she knew how she and Matthew had gotten in, but she didn't know what it meant. She had applied, of course, because of Matthew. What he'd written.

I am not me.

But what if she did turn out to be a genius? Matthew had.

The flowers in the barrel were also crimson. The ones that were alive, anyway. For some reason Lydia felt comforted by the dying flowers. Claybourne was not so perfect after all.

Lydia and Emily got out of the car and stretched. The air here was cooler than it had been at home and had that salty musk that told you you were close to the ocean. Lydia fished her sunglasses out of the front seat. They'd be useful for watching the other students unobtrusively.

Next to the white boathouse was a gray wooden dock, several luggage trolleys, and one large rack, which would presumably be loaded onto the boat when it came. Lydia knew that most days the Claybourne ferry ran back and forth just twice between the small coastal town of Stillbay and Fortmouth Island, which was where the school had been built. Today it would run every two hours. Lydia and Emily had plenty of time to find a luggage trolley and unload Lydia's stuff from the back of the car. Lydia spent the time studying the other families from behind her sunglasses.

Most students were there with just one parent. Only one boy, the one from the sleek black car, had both parents, but they just leaned up against their car in a row, all tapping on their smartphones. The second thing people knew about Claybourne, besides that it produced geniuses, was that it didn't allow tech of any kind.

The James Bond family were not the only ones trying to get in one last burst of cyber activity. Over by a bright yellow car, a girl with a mane of tawny curls took selfie after selfie with a gold iPhone, while her father attempted to balance her mountain of luggage on one trolley.

Lydia dismissed Selfie Girl and looked around. There was a girl with very erect posture who was carefully standing leather instrument cases in a row at the edge of the dock. She had at least five instruments and was getting more out of the back of a minivan. Lydia's skin prickled. Her first encounter with a genius?

A boy with short, dark hair approached Selfie Girl's dad and gestured to the luggage rack, clearly offering to help.

Lydia looked away and saw another girl, very tall, fiddling with a piece of paper. By the time Lydia and her mom had all her stuff stowed on the big luggage rack that would be loaded onto the boat, the boy had organized Selfie Girl's trolley so that everything fit. Genius number two.

Paper Girl stood at the end of the dock and tossed the folded paper into the air. Her paper airplane inscribed three corkscrew curls into the brilliant sky before skidding along the dock in a graceful landing. Genius number three.

Lydia's neck flushed with self-consciousness. She thought about taking out a notebook to scribble into so that people might think she was writing something brilliant. At least she wasn't making fish faces at an iPhone.

The ferry was visible for a long time before it bumped into the heavy pilings at the edge of the dock, which meant that Lydia's nerves had a long time to scrabble at the inside of her rib cage. The ferry was smaller than Lydia had imagined and had all the charm of a barge. After it slowed and bumped into the dock, three porters knocked out a section of the stern, which acted as the ramp. Each porter had easy, bowlegged strides, and they all lit up cigarettes the moment they got ashore.

Behind them, two middle-aged women stepped off. Lydia guessed they were mothers of students. Everyone on the dock surged forward, but then another woman appeared at the end of the ramp holding up her hands. She was shaped like the boat, solid and rectangular, and she had the leathery complexion of a person who had spent most of her life outside. When she opened her mouth to speak, her voice came out like a foghorn.

"All right here, folks! This is the Claybourne ferry! We make one stop and one stop only! If you do not want to go to Claybourne Academy of Excellence, do not board this ferry! If you do not have a Claybourne pass, do not board this ferry! If you are surgically attached to your smartphone, do not board this ferry!" Here she paused, and Lydia heard a few chuckles and a few groans. "Cell phones, smartphones, digital cameras, iPads, laptops, iPods, radios, walkie-talkies, beepers, Fitbits, ANYTHING that is forbidden in the Claybourne pamphlet should be left in your car or surrendered in the boathouse locker!"

The woman shifted her weight and crossed her arms over her chest. "Parents!" she barked. "That means you, too! If the world will stop spinning because you cannot answer an e-mail, then do us all a favor and stay here!" She glared into the crowd. "Students! We will be passing a very powerful magnet over the luggage rack! If you do not want everything on your devices to be fried, leave your devices in the car!"

Two students sheepishly scuttled over to the luggage rack and started digging into duffel bags. The woman smirked and continued.

"If you have a pacemaker, please inform me! We have several methods to deal with unwelcome tech, and some of them might interfere with a pacemaker. If you have metal plates or screws in your body, please let me know!"

Two parents detached themselves from the back of the crowd and hurried to their cars. Lydia guessed they had just realized that sneaking their iPhones on board would be very risky indeed. Lydia had to fight the feeling of proximal guilt that crinkled her shoulder blades. Her phone was at home, waiting like an abandoned puppy on the corner of her desk, but she checked her pockets one last time to make sure it hadn't somehow stowed itself away.

The woman paused and glared at the small crowd, making sure that everything she'd said had sunk in. "I am Captain Martha Whelk! Welcome aboard!" With that, the woman turned and strode through a heavy door, which clanged shut behind her.

One of the porters waved everybody into a line, while the other two pushed the baggage racks up the ramp. Posture Girl was overseeing the inspection of her instrument cases and demanding several promises that they would not be subjected to the magnet.

Lydia turned to her mom and smiled. Emily had decided not to come across on the ferry because of the long drive ahead of her. She and Lydia had been saying all sorts of good-byes for a week now, and Lydia was actually relieved that this was the final one. Well, hopefully not *final,* but the last one for a while.

"Love you, Mom."

"Oh, sweetie!" Lydia's mom crushed her in a hug. "I love you, too. I am going to miss you so much!"

"Me too," mumbled Lydia into her mom's shoulder. "I'll write you every week."

"You *have* to write once a week, so make it twice," said Emily.

"We'll see," said Lydia, smiling.

"Oh, my baby." Emily was doing the thing where she opened her eyes as wide as she could so that no tears spilled out. It almost never worked. Lydia wiped her mom's cheeks and hugged her again. The ferry blasted its horn, and Lydia and Emily both jumped.

"Love you," called Lydia over her shoulder.

"Love you, sweetie!" Emily waved and wiped her face alternately. "Have fun! Be safe!"

Lydia thought, *I'll try.*

Chapter Two

Lydia found a spot against the railing near the bow of the ferry. Had Matthew stood here on his first time over? Had he felt the same cocktail of emotion: nervous, hopeful? A small voice added *fraudulent* in Lydia's mind. She straightened her back and shook the thought away. She wasn't a fraud; she just wasn't really certain she belonged at Claybourne. Matthew had at least had Abilene's complete conviction that he was exceptional in every way. Lydia thought of Matthew flopping back on his bed with a groan. "She thinks I'm the first coming of black Jesus," he'd complained, gripping the slightly-less-than-perfect report card that had triggered a half-hour lecture on potential from Abilene.

The familiar heat of anger pricked at Lydia. *He should be here.*

Lydia gripped the railing harder and leaned forward to peer over the edge. She and Matthew had grown up watching *The Twilight Zone* on VHS in the library where Emily worked, then had graduated to scarier stuff in middle school, but Lydia still loved the old Alfred Hitchcock movies. She imagined that, standing at the rail of the ship, she looked a little like the heroine of a Hitchcock movie, the wind tousling her straight brown hair, her face turned resolutely forward with tears drying on her cheeks. She wondered: If this were a movie, would she toss a pebble into the water? Would it be the kind of movie where the camera followed the pebble down into the depths of the ocean? Would the pebble pass an old shipwreck or maybe some grisly human remains?

She was imagining the dim green light and the blackness, the last wink of the pebble before it disappeared into murk, when a voice near her ear startled her.

"You find it yet?"

Lydia looked up. A boy with a spray of fine blond hair that flapped in the wind was grinning at her.

"What?"

"You've been staring into the water for about seven minutes. You find what you're looking for?" He made a face of exaggerated stupidity staring over the side. Lydia glanced around. The clownish face seemed like the kind of thing a popular kid might make for an audience. He was alone, but definitely cute and confident enough to be used to an appreciative crowd.

"Oh." Lydia grinned hesitantly. "I guess I don't look much like genius material."

The boy laughed a wonderful bray of a laugh, and Lydia relaxed a little bit. "Don't worry!" he said. "You will be."

Lydia frowned. "How do you know?" She directed her gaze pointedly at Selfie Girl. Selfie Girl was biting her lip and batting her eyelashes at an old-fashioned camera on the end of what appeared to be a modified selfie stick.

The boy laughed again. "You're new here, right? But you'll see. By the end of orientation you'll all be geniuses of some kind or another."

"Orientation must really be something," said Lydia. Selfie Girl was having trouble aiming the heavy camera, which was the kind with film, and maintaining a sufficiently sultry smile.

The boy looked at her seriously. "Orientation is the best. Honest. It's like you've been floating around in darkness and then suddenly . . ." The boy made a motion like an explosion with his hands. "You're alive! What are you going to declare for?"

"Uh, I don't know yet."

"Oh." The boy gave her the look you give someone who's just announced she loves boy bands: sort of pitying and sort of curious.

Lydia wondered if she should have made something up, said she was here for writing maybe, but then he shrugged, dismissing the whole thing. Lydia plunged onward. "I'm Lydia," she said, trying to decide if she should offer her hand or not.

"I know," said the boy. "Lydia Boswell of 726 Eastern Court."

"How do you know that?" asked Lydia.

"Maybe I'm a genius." The boy waggled his eyebrows at Lydia. "Or maybe you have a luggage tag stuck on your backpack." He pointed to the white tag with Emily's neat handwriting on it.

Lydia rolled her eyes and smiled. "My mom labeled everything," she groaned.

"So did my grandma," laughed the boy. He pulled up the back of his shirt collar so that Lydia could read SETH FINN on a neatly sewn name tag.

"Nice to meet you, Seth," said Lydia. "So, uh, what kind of genius are you?"

"The hungry kind," said Seth. "Come on, I'll take you to the finest vending machine in town."

The Claybourne ferry had a flat deck at the stern and then an indoor section that was about the size of Lydia's house. Inside, the center of the large room was walled off and presumably held the mechanics of the ship and was where the captain and crew stayed. You could walk a lap around the center part and go out any of the four doors onto the deck. Everything, from floor to ceiling, was done in crimson and gray. At the back was the vending machine and a few rows of benches, and it was here that Seth led Lydia.

They found a small group of students that included Paper Airplane Girl and the boy who had helped Selfie Girl's dad with the trolley.

"Finn!" shouted the trolley boy, standing up to hug Seth. "Where've you been?"

Seth grinned and slapped hands with another boy, then bumped fists with Paper Airplane Girl. "I barely made the ferry. My grandma drove, like, eight miles an hour the whole way. Plus, I was just talking to a new girl." Seth straightened and half turned back to Lydia. "Everyone, this is Lydia."

Lydia smiled and fluttered her fingers, then immediately wished she hadn't. Everybody else nodded at her in a way that was much more genius than waving.

"All right, this is Sorcha Metcalf, engineering." Seth pointed to Paper Airplane Girl, who nodded. "Jay Grant, architecture." Trolley Boy grinned. "Marin Blodgett, writing, and Kit Orban, physics." The girl and boy both gave slight nods.

Sorcha flopped back against the bench. "What will you declare for?" she asked. Everyone else looked up expectantly.

Lydia glanced at Seth. It was too late to make something up, since she'd just told him she didn't know. "I, uh, haven't quite decided, uh, yet."

The grins fell.

If Seth had introduced her as the school's new chalkboard wiper, she might have gotten more interest. Lydia's neck burned with embarrassment.

"New kids never know," said Marin with unmistakable derision. She had a long, narrow face and hair that was pulled back into a ponytail so tight that the skin on her forehead looked like it was one firm brush stroke from splitting open.

Every person Lydia had just met turned their eyes back on Seth without so much as another blink at Lydia. If new kids never knew, why did they ask her?

"Anybody have any quarters?" said Seth. His back was to her, so Lydia took a breath to soothe herself.

Lydia searched her pockets and found a quarter. Kit dropped a handful of coins into Seth's open palm. Together, she and Seth had two quarters.

"Can we get anything for fifty cents?" asked Seth.

"I got you." Sorcha stepped forward to the vending machine. "What do you want?"

Seth tipped his head to Lydia to indicate that she should pick. She studied the machine. It was old-fashioned looking and had two rows of candy bars. Each candy bar had slots for four quarters below it. Evidently, you put in the quarters, pushed in a knob, and the candy bar dropped out the bottom.

"Reese's," said Lydia, handing her quarter to Sorcha.

Sorcha took two barrettes from her thin light brown hair and then inserted the quarters into two of the slots below the Reese's. She pushed in the knob and said to Lydia, "Hold that in for a second." Lydia kept the knob pushed in while Sorcha jiggled her barrettes into the two empty quarter slots. After a minute Lydia heard a mechanical thump and the sound of the quarters dropping inside the machine. The Reese's peanut butter cups dropped to the bottom, and Sorcha motioned casually for Lydia to get them.

"Impressive, Metcalf," drawled Seth. "You've just given me an idea."

"Boat prank?" asked Jay.

Seth grinned.

"I am not getting in trouble," declared Marin. She picked up her bag and looked at Lydia. "You should leave if you don't want to get in trouble."

Lydia hesitated.

Marin shrugged. "They don't need *your* help." Marin weighted the "*your*" perfectly. There was just enough emphasis for Lydia to hear the insult, but not so much that she could take offense. Marin held Lydia's gaze briefly, then threaded her way along the bench and left.

For a moment Lydia waited to see if anyone would contradict Marin or invite her to join them or apologize for Marin's rudeness. Instead they all turned to look at Seth, whose back was still to Lydia.

"All right, listen . . . ," said Seth.

Lydia quietly placed the unopened Reese's on the end of the bench and left, going the opposite direction Marin had taken. She walked out the door onto the side deck of the ship and bent against the wind to get up front. There was a bench in the shade up against the cabin, and she settled there, eyes stinging in the wind. She tried not to feel too wounded about her first exposure to Claybourne students, but she felt a sort of limp hopelessness overtake her.

She wished Matthew were here; the old Matthew, who had been so *not* cool that he was cool, not the new Matthew, who had been moody and quippy and painfully aware of himself.

She remembered the first time she thought he had changed. It was his first year at Claybourne, and he was home for Easter. Lydia heard from her mom that he'd written a hundred pages of a novel, and when Lydia saw him, she was a little alarmed. Matt's skin was usually the exact color of a brown crayon, but now it was gray, with dry, ashy spots on his arms. It looked as if whatever life he put into his writing were coming directly from him. Abilene worried that he was working too hard at school.

"Even at home he's been up every night until two, three in the morning just scratching away."

"Scratching?" asked Lydia's mom.

"Yeah, pen and paper. I hear it through the wall of the bedroom like rats."

"Well, it's probably better for him than being on a computer all the time." Lydia's mom shot Lydia a meaningful look.

"It's weird, is all I'm saying. What fifteen-year-old writes a novel, and what fifteen-year-old writes with pen and paper?"

"Genius ones," said Lydia's mom comfortingly. "Genius fifteen-years-olds do." She patted Abilene's hand. "Why don't you two come over tonight? We'll watch a scary movie, like old times. Eat popcorn. Spill soda on the couch."

Abilene mustered a smile. "It's been a while, I guess."

"I miss mopping cola off my cushions. You two come over after dinner."

If Lydia had thought to make a list of things that weren't quite right, it would have included the following:

1. Matt sat in Lydia's seat on the couch. It had always been her seat. His seat was on the other side. He didn't say anything or even seem aware that he'd taken her seat.

2. When the music started, the spooky music that let you know that these weren't just woods, but *haunted* woods, Matt looked puzzled when Lydia nudged him. Like he'd forgotten how many times they'd talked about sound tracks in scary movies.

3. When the clown dropped down out of the hayloft, making everybody jump and Matthew spill his soda like always, he didn't laugh like he usually did. He was genuinely embarrassed.

Lydia didn't miss *that* Matt, but she was in no position to be picky.

Selfie Girl was sitting on the back of a bench facing a small group of students. Lydia had to admit that the girl was stunning to look at. Her skin was a golden-brown color and looked as smooth and plush as suede. Far back in her ancestry there must have been an Ethiopian princess who was responsible for the thick curls that corkscrewed through her honey-colored mane and for her wide, pouty lips. The wind kept lifting glinting locks of hair, so that they batted at Selfie Girl's neck and breasts in a way that made her seem naked. The wind also brought snatches of her voice over to Lydia.

"I thought of this invention myself. . . ." She lifted the selfie stick with the old-fashioned camera on it. "Supposably, you need at least a thousand hits a day to get a sponsor, and I don't want to miss out just because I'm here, so I'm mailing film to my dad."

It was catty, but Lydia smirked. *Supposably.* Good luck making a genius out of *her*.

Chapter 3

The new students were separated from the returning ones as they stepped off the boat. *Like the third-class passengers on the* Titanic, thought Lydia. One of the porters waved a sort of wand over Lydia's backpack and nodded at her as he returned it. He didn't say what the wand did, and he had a sort of blank fish-eyed gaze that didn't encourage questions.

A young woman dressed in a spotless white lab coat met the new students at the end of the dock. Her hair unfurled down her back like a shiny black tongue, and she wore deep red lipstick. As she waited for the new students to assemble, she sucked her teeth as if she were deciding which of the new students to eat first. The boy next to Lydia looked like he hoped it would be him.

"I'm Dr. Kennedy," she told the group. "Apparently, you need to be shown where the dorms are." It was extremely clear that Dr. Kennedy considered the job of tour guide to be well beneath her.

After counting everybody, Dr. Kennedy cleared her throat and shook her hair back from her face. "Yes, well, come with me."

Somebody asked, "What about our stuff?"

Dr. Kennedy pegged the student with flashing eyes. "That will be searched and then brought to your rooms."

A couple of kids murmured. *Searched?* thought Lydia. She pulled the straps of her backpack tighter. She had her lists with her. The fact that nobody protested was evidence that everybody was as nervous as Lydia.

Dr. Kennedy pursed her red mouth in a pucker of distaste and whirled on her heel. Without looking back to see if anyone was following her, she started striding into the trees. The new students were all frozen for a second and then scurried after her.

It was a steep five-minute walk up from the dock on a wide, sandy path that threaded through some tall pine trees. The pine needles were warmed by the sun and gave off a wonderful, clean smell. Lydia inhaled deeply and felt a bit of the loneliness lift off her shoulders. *It's beautiful here*, thought Lydia. *Maybe that's the secret to being a genius. Go somewhere beautiful without any tech and you just get inspired.*

Most of the students were breathing heavily but smiling when they arrived at the base of an elegant lawn across from the central entrance of the main building.

If the town of Stillbay had been charming in a haphazard and well-worn way, then the Claybourne campus was charming for its orderliness and clever layout. The main building was an imposing stone edifice that held the cafeteria, the auditorium, and all the classrooms. Near each corner of the main building was a white clapboard dorm, each different but all in the same classic style. Gracious shade trees created intimate compartments on the lawn, and there were late-summer flowers along the foundations of all the buildings. Lydia couldn't help but feel elevated by her surroundings. This was a place where people did great things. Lydia knew it.

"The main building was designed by Bronson," said Dr. Kennedy.

Somebody made a small moue of appreciation.

"Carson Kelly did all the dorms," Dr. Kennedy went on. "She and Bronson worked together, so that there is not even a broom closet on this island that is not built according to their terms." Dr. Kennedy swept her gaze over the students. "Try not to mess it up."

Dr. Kennedy pointed out the underclassman boys' dorm to the left and took the girls over to a white clapboard house that managed to look both stately and cozy at the same time.

A porch wrapped around two sides of the building, and there were already clusters of girls sitting in Adirondack chairs and porch swings. Lydia noted that a group of girls rose like a flock of startled seagulls to descend on Sorcha, but that Marin slipped inside without notice. It made Lydia feel better. Maybe she wasn't the only one who'd been insulted by Marin.

Dr. Kennedy checked her clipboard again, then studied a sturdy-looking girl in the front of the group.

"These are your room assignments," she said, her voice sharp and impatient. "You can figure it out." She gave the clipboard to the girl and strode away in a swirl of lab coat and glossy hair.

The girl grinned nervously at everybody. "Um, I'll just put this on the front steps, and you can find your names, I guess."

A girl with slumping posture and stringy black hair looked sideways and murmured, "I guess if we can get into Claybourne, we can find our rooms." That made everybody laugh, but also made them all determined not to seem helpless or needy, so they shuffled forward, found their name and room number, then walked cautiously up the front steps.

Lydia's room was on the second floor, facing the main building. It was small, with only a desk, a chair, a bed, and a dresser. The floor and ceiling were painted light blue, except for the spot under the chair, which was scratched down to pale wood. There was a small, oval rag rug by the bed, and a blue floral curtain to hide the tiny closet. It felt like a room you might stay in at somebody's vacation home by the sea, pretty but impersonal.

Lydia tried to imagine sitting at the desk, looking out the window, and doing something amazing; writing poetry maybe or inventing a machine that could suck the greenhouse gases out of the atmosphere. Probably Sorcha could do that. Marin probably wrote ten novels before breakfast every day. Matthew had done it—well, not ten novels, but the writing part. When Lydia had read the stories he'd written his first year at Claybourne, she couldn't have said what made her like them, couldn't have said even that she *liked* them. It was as if his words lifted her out of herself and put her into the minds of the people in the stories. They sang to her as if they knew her secret language. They shone light into cracks Lydia thought she'd forgotten.

They made her scared.

The stories weren't scary, but Matt was. How could he write those things? How could her oldest friend turn out to be a person who could write like that?

Lydia put her backpack on the desk and sat on the plastic mattress of her low bed. Loneliness rose like a cold, sucking tide around her knees.

Last year at her regular high school, when she was a freshman, there had been a few weeks when everybody was trying to find out where they fit in. It was as if all the freshmen had been dropped into some kind of sorting machine and those weeks had been spent falling. Occasionally you landed in a group—Soccer Players or Good Kids or Ponytails—and if you didn't fit well, the machine bounced you out again, until everybody had settled into the right spots.

Lydia had bounced lightly around the academic crowds—the kids who'd already done college visits and whose parents checked their homework each night (too anxious), the kids who were tan from vigorous and expensive outdoor activities (too self-righteous)—and finally landed with the kids who put together the school literary magazine twice a year. The falling time, when she hadn't been with any group, had been uncomfortable. Lydia didn't know if she had felt invisible or terribly obvious.

But this was worse. What if she couldn't keep up? On an island there was nowhere to hide. Suddenly her loneliness turned acidic, and the walls of the pretty little room echoed back every doubt Lydia had had for the past nine months. She stood abruptly and fled along the hallway with her chin tucked. She skipped down the front steps of the porch, past the flock of girls on the swings, and launched herself farther into the campus.

Lydia walked past another white clapboard dorm and guessed it was the upperclassman girls' dorm. Already there was evidence of elite talent floating out of a window in the form of violin music. Lydia was both fascinated and repelled. Did she really belong in the same school as somebody who could make music that was the auditory equivalent of a waterfall? How long would it be before they found out she was only a good student and not any kind of genius?

Beyond the dorm was a greenhouse and some other buildings Lydia couldn't identify, though she remembered that the school map in the brochure had shown several studios and labs. The paved path turned around the back of the main building and led toward a lovely brick building with a wide stone staircase. Lydia sensed immediately that this was the library.

Even before her eyes adjusted to the dim light inside, the smell of books confirmed the identity of the building. A smile tugged at one corner of Lydia's mouth as the sacred hush enveloped her like a familiar hug. The front desk was empty, but Lydia didn't get the sense that she was forbidden here, so she walked forward on the thick burgundy carpet. The wooden paneling of the walls and shelves glowed a warm butterscotch color, and there was a reverent stillness to the air. Lydia saw an actual card catalog in a beautifully inlaid wooden cabinet. She approached it as you would a work of art and slid out one of the drawers. A long, tidy row of index cards was nestled perfectly in the drawer.

A small scuffling noise made Lydia turn. She found a thin, bleached woman smiling kindly at her from a few feet away. Her hair was white and wispy, pulled into a bun, and her skin was papery looking. Lydia guessed that the woman had made the scuffling noise on purpose so as not to startle her. It was something Emily would have done at her library, and Lydia wondered if they taught the technique at library school.

"Do you know how it works?" said the woman, indicating the card catalog.

Lydia nodded. "I do. I've just never seen one before."

The woman smiled. "They have a certain charm, I think, that makes up for any inefficiency."

Lydia smiled shyly. "My mom's a librarian. She wishes she could have kept the old card catalog, because it made her feel . . . like each thing had its place."

The woman nodded. "My thoughts exactly."

They both let the words and the sentiment be absorbed into the silence for a second, and then the woman moved quietly behind the desk. "I am Mary Ann Alton. I am the librarian here."

"I'm Lydia Boswell," said Lydia, moving forward to offer her hand.

"Well, I don't need to lecture you about library rules, I expect. Go and explore, if you like. I'll be around."

A thought struck Lydia. "I read that you have a really good collection of biographies?"

"We do," said Ms. Alton. She was being modest. The Claybourne collection of biographies rivaled any other in the United States.

"Do you have any books about former students? I mean, Claybourne alumni?"

Ms. Alton tilted her head to one side, frowning. Lydia thought at first that she'd asked something tiresome or brown-nosy, but then Ms. Alton motioned her to follow and headed up some wide wooden stairs.

"We do have several about Claybourne alumni, but as many are still alive, we are still waiting for definitive biographies to be written."

Lydia followed Ms. Alton into a room that was marked by a small bronze plaque:

THE CHOW BIOGRAPHY COLLECTION
GIFT OF JUN LEE CHOW, '96

The room was lined with bookcases that reached up to the ceiling. There was a beautiful wood and bronze ladder on wheels that helped you reach the tops of the bookcases. The whole room was centered around a cluster of dark leather chairs that sat facing a window. There was a bronze bust of somebody that

Lydia guessed was Jun Lee Chow sitting on a pedestal in the center of the window. The whole library, and this room in particular, was drenched in a heady coating of privilege. It was a far cry from the metal shelves and folding chairs of Emily's library at home.

Ms. Alton showed Lydia a second card catalog for biographies, and Lydia left the library an hour later with five books. She would have taken more, but Ms. Alton gave Lydia the impression that she didn't approve of biographies that were written about a person who wasn't dead yet. Lydia felt a certain fondness for Ms. Alton's slightly stuffy code of ethics. She sensed that whatever else might happen at Claybourne, the library would be a safe haven.

Chapter 4

Galvanized by her discovery of the library, Lydia went back to her room to face her unpacking. Somebody had brought her giant duffel bag and two boxes and left them outside her room. Lydia dragged it all inside and stood looking at her room for a minute.

A lifetime of watching horror movies had made Lydia nervous of closets. She peered under the curtain that acted as the closet door to reassure herself that no one was standing in there, and then whipped the blue fabric aside. The closet was empty, just a strange play of shadows from the window. Lydia released a breath. She climbed onto her chair and unhooked the curtain from the rod, letting it drop to the floor. Now there was nowhere for anything to hide in her room.

She spent an hour putting away clothes, hanging up her uniforms, and making her bed. At around six o'clock she looked out the window and saw students walking toward the main building in groups. She realized she was starving.

Lydia went out to the porch and waited for somebody else to come out. After a minute the girl with the lank black hair walked through the door and slumped up against a porch pillar.

"Hey, are you headed over to dinner?" said Lydia. She spoke more loudly than she had intended and couldn't figure out how to hold her hands as she waited for an answer.

"Yeah, you want to come?" The girl reminded Lydia of a wet watercolor painting that had been allowed to drip to the bottom of the page; her shoulders were stooped, her arms were limp, and her hair was thin and lifeless, but she seemed self-contained, unintimidated.

"I'm Lydia."

"Naomi. I'm just waiting for Pilar."

Right as she said that, the sturdy girl came out and smiled at Lydia and Naomi.

"Hey! Are you going over too?"

Lydia nodded and introduced herself, relieved when they didn't ask her what she would declare for. Then they walked across the lawn to the stone steps that led up to the cafeteria, all desperately relieved not to be entering the cafeteria by themselves.

Inside was an echoing wooden room with long wooden tables and tall windows placed high up on the walls. It was exactly how Lydia imagined a British boarding school cafeteria would look. She realized that this was not a cafeteria, but a *dining hall*. The floor was polished wood, the chairs were wood, and there were actual chandeliers high up in the ceiling.

The three girls followed a scuffed path on the floor into the back to pick up their food. The kitchen was a striking contrast of modernity and stainless steel, with little homey touches like a wreath of dried flowers on the wall, and shells and dried starfish on a display shelf. The food looked good, like real food. It wasn't cheapened by the large quantity, the way the food in Lydia's other school had been.

The three girls found a table along one wall and made several shy attempts at conversation. They were saved when two boys—one with a round face and Asian features, and one with dark brown hair and sleepy brown eyes—came and sat with them.

"Did you guys hear about the boat pranks?" said the Asian-looking boy, grinning, his eyes twinkling with mischief. He lunged across Lydia for a napkin, popped a green bean into his mouth, and then tilted his head toward the other boy. "This is Gus. I'm Ben. We came over on the last boat, and somebody had taken all the candy out of the vending machine and replaced it with pieces of wood"—he shoved in three more green beans—"and fortunes."

"I got 'Beware the men's room,'" said Gus.

"Yeah, I'll be dead by the next full moon." Ben raised his eyebrows like this was the funniest news he'd ever heard. "It was definitely the best boat prank."

"I think I know who did it," said Lydia. She pointed with a bread roll to the table where Seth and Sorcha were sitting. Seth was wagging his finger at another kid, and they were all laughing.

"Were there other boat pranks?" asked Pilar.

"Yeah. The kids on the eight o'clock boat did a catapult. Kind of lame, and they got in trouble for ruining some brooms. Ten o'clock made a firecracker out of nondairy creamer." Ben shook his head in wonder.

"I saw some kids doing something with soda bottles on our boat," said Gus, "but I don't think it worked out."

"So, is that, like, a thing? Boat pranks?" asked Naomi. She was sitting with her chin about two inches from her plate, spooning five grains of rice almondine at a time into her mouth.

"Yeah, but only on the first day. You don't do it every time." Ben leaned back in his chair and wiped his hands. "I can't wait to do one."

Naomi looked sideways at the other students at the table. "Do you guys know what you are going to declare for? I mean what you'll study or whatever?"

"Nah," said Ben. "You don't declare until after orientation, right?"

"I think math probably," said Gus.

"Marine biology maybe?" said Pilar.

"Art," said Naomi. She sounded certain.

Everybody looked at Lydia. She shrugged.

"I'm pretty much good at everything," said Ben with a laugh. "But I wouldn't really call myself a genius. Not yet, anyway."

Lydia thought it was odd. Here she was at a school for geniuses, and only Naomi seemed certain of her own genius. Everybody said that they'd know after orientation. So what was so special about orientation?

Lydia skimmed through two biographies before bed. Both people had had lonely childhoods, had first shown their potential at Claybourne, had rocketed to success or fame (solar-powered irrigation, diplomat), and had changed the face of their respective arenas. The irrigation guy was still alive, as far as Lydia knew, saving one developing nation after another, but the diplomat was a suicide.

Lydia glanced at her closed door and then retrieved her two special lists from the bottom drawer of her desk.

The first list was a spreadsheet that had information about every Claybourne alum who had committed suicide.

Alison Breely, painter, aged 31, shot herself April 14, 2009

Tanaka Xi, composer, aged 24, hanged himself in his apartment closet December 4, 1998

Wilson Abernathy, mathematician, aged 19, hanged himself in parents' barn March 14, 2015

There were twenty-one names on the list.

The last one was Matthew's.

Chapter 5

Lydia had been in the library when it happened.

If Abilene and Matthew's house had been Lydia's second home, then the library where Emily worked was her third home. She and Matt had spent a significant portion of their childhood reading in the children's room, then later, watching anything spooky they could find on the library's old television. Finally, they'd graduated to helping Emily put plastic covers on the new books, shelving, and even cataloging.

It was late fall of Lydia's freshman year of high school, Matt's second year at Claybourne. Matt's Thanksgiving break was longer than the one at the public school Lydia attended, so she knew he was home, but she hadn't seen him yet.

Lydia was shelving books in the young adult section, starting with *The Wolves of Willoughby Chase*, one of her favorites, when the word ** *river* ** popped into her head.

She would have said that she'd heard ** *river* **, but no one was around to speak it and that wasn't quite accurate anyway. She saw the word ** *river* ** written in Matt's handwriting and then saw the muddy bank of the river at the same time. Just as in a dream when you know something is true without knowing how you know, Lydia felt terrified urgency in the word. If someone had spoken it to her aloud, it would have been in a panicky shout.

Lydia put *The Wolves of Willoughby Chase* back on the cart. She walked past the table of chess players without smiling and then leaped down the stairs. By the time she punched through the front door of the library, her heart was thudding and tingles of fear were sizzling along her limbs. She jogged down the steps of the library and turned left on the sidewalk. She knew exactly where to go. She didn't question why.

The river was modest and wound through the town almost without being noticed until you got to a small park. In the park there were tall, gracious trees, a winding cement path, and a few monuments and plaques on rocks. The grass had always seemed dirty there to Lydia, always filled with chewed gum and scraps of plastic or paper.

Now the grass was brown and muddy. It had been raining for days, and Lydia's shoes skidded and slipped as she jogged across the park. She crossed the path that went along the river and pulled up short. The river was high from a week of rain, and she saw that it had risen all the way up to one of the cement picnic tables and was sucking hungrily at the bench. The water was thick, brown, and speckled with debris.

Lydia paused, panting. This was the farthest she had run since two summers back, when she and Matt had decided to improve themselves. It seemed like a very long time ago.

She looked around, then turned resolutely to the right, downstream. The muddy bank she'd pictured in her head was just around the bend of the river where it narrowed into a tunnel under a bridge. It would be very deep there now, Lydia knew, since it was the part of the river that was always deepest: Even in the summer there was a cool, iced-tea-colored pool where the fish always hid out.

Lydia walked quickly downstream, trying not to slip and breaking into a run every few yards when her lungs permitted. She rounded a cluster of bare, woody shrubs that usually reached out over the river bend but were now submerged and trembling with the rush of the current. She could hear the roar of water increase as the river surged toward the tunnel, could feel the vibration of the roar in her chest and in the ground.

Great, smooth curls of water peeled off the cement walls on either side of the tunnel, disappearing into a thundering darkness beneath the bridge. Lydia studied the surface of the water, scanned up the river, and peered into the dark tunnel. There was nothing. She began to feel puzzled. Why had she been so sure?

Something flickered in the corner of her vision. It was a notebook. The cover had blown open, and the pages were turning jerkily in the wind. Lydia gave one last look at the river and walked up the bank to the big rock, on top of which rested the notebook.

Dread rose in Lydia's limbs, so heavy that it was a struggle to lift her fingers to the pages. It appeared empty of writing. Lydia touched the pages gently, then picked up the notebook and flipped over to the cover. Nothing was written there, either. Lydia opened the book to the first page. In Matt's writing were the words

I am not me.

There was nothing else.

Matthew's body washed up against a bridge support a few miles downstream, where it was spotted by a jogger and reported just twenty minutes after Lydia got back to the library. A sheriff showed up at Abilene's office, and somebody called Emily, and then they were all shivering in a naked grayish-green room waiting to understand. Abilene identified Matt's sneaker and jacket. She was not asked to identify his face.

Somebody handed Lydia a mug of warmish tea. The mug said WORLD'S BEST MOM on the side.

They waited.

The sheriff came in and asked everybody to sit. They huddled together on a low couch.

The sheriff explained about the stones in Matt's pockets. How they'd weighted him down.

Abilene shattered.

Lydia wandered out of the terrible room, where pieces of Abilene's pain were zinging about like shrapnel, and followed a hall out toward the front door. She heard a man talking in a low voice.

"Kid must have changed his mind at the last minute. His hands were all torn up like he was trying to hang on to something."

In the face of Abilene's grief, Lydia's own grief was negligible, barely even noticeable. Abilene's grief buried her like a mountain. It surrounded her like an odor, warped the air around her, so that you could hardly bear to look at her. Lydia's grief felt more like anger or disbelief. She felt like she had been stabbed, not fatally, for no reason. It was as if the laws of gravity had been reversed for a few seconds, and now she no longer trusted her feet to hit the ground every time.

Emily was Abilene's best friend. She was flattened and exhausted from trying to help Abilene carry that mountain around, and so Lydia grieved quietly in her room or in stolen moments on the bus to school. She started wearing sunglasses everywhere so that her red-rimmed eyes wouldn't alarm anybody. Her new friends at school hadn't known Matthew. They hadn't known anyone who'd died. One guy actually told her that she was lucky because pain brought out the best art in people.

So maybe it was the secretiveness she felt that made her hesitate to type Matthew's name into the search engine on her laptop. The police had called it a suicide, but . . .

Kid must have changed his mind at the last minute.

She couldn't bring herself to type "Matthew Hafford suicide," so she typed "Claybourne student suicide" instead and got the second shock of her life.

Twenty-one people.

They were every age and were every kind of expert. They had nothing in common that Lydia could tell except Claybourne.

It took her four weeks to figure out what else they had in common, and it happened by accident.

Lydia was getting discouraged and feeling a little restless and angry. Emily had sent her to a shrink, who was nice enough but wore giant white sneakers that made her completely unrelatable. Lydia told her that she felt sad, and that was true. But what she really felt was angry. Sometimes she was so mad that she didn't even miss Matthew anymore, and then she felt guilty. At the beginning of each session the lady asked Lydia if she had thoughts of harming herself. Having to convince somebody that she wasn't suicidal was like try to breathe normally after being told to breathe normally. It felt impossible. Lydia had to spend each session trying to answer questions the way she would have before Matthew died.

After one of these sessions Lydia came home and went up to her room. She was too dispirited to do any more research, so she tabbed idly over to Facebook.

People born during a full moon are great kissers.

People born during a quarter moon waxing have good luck.

Click <u>here</u> to find out what moon you were born on!

Lydia clicked. She typed in her birth date. New moon. "Beautiful eyes," read Lydia. She wondered what the other moon phases would predict, so she typed in Matthew's birth date. He was a new moon too. Lydia felt a stab of sadness that they'd never known that when he was alive. She typed in her mom's birthday. Gibbous moon waning meant her mom had a sweet tooth.

Lydia cast around for other birthdays. Her spreadsheet of Claybourne suicides was still open, so she tabbed over. Would the moon chart predict geniuses?

She typed in the birth date of Alison Breely, the painter. Also a new moon. "Beautiful eyes" again. Lydia felt impatient. What about Justin Gosevner, a twenty-three-year-old Claybourne alum who had "advanced the field of prosthetics by decades in just two years"?

New moon.

Lydia went very still. She tabbed back to her list and found another birthday.

New moon.

Another.

New moon.

Another?

Every birth date on her suicide list was during a new moon. She knew only six birthdays of Claybourne alumni, but still.

Half an hour's research found the birthdays of four other Claybourne suicides, and all four were born on a new moon. For the next three days Lydia continued her research. As far as she was able to determine, every student who'd attended Claybourne had been born on a new moon.

That was how Lydia decided that she had a shot at getting into Claybourne.

And she was right.

Lydia smoothed the second list from her folder onto her desk between the two biographies. It was a printout with the date of every new moon stretching back fifty years. She checked the politician and the irrigation guy. Both had been born on a new moon. It no longer surprised Lydia, but it certainly didn't make any more sense than it had when she first noticed it.

Lydia looked out the window of her dorm room in time to see a boy walk across the main green with a large telescope tucked under his arm. His shadow, cast from the porch light, lurched and scrambled after him like a clumsy servant. Lydia felt the urge to call out, to warn him he was being followed. All she had in common with the boy was that they'd both been born on a new moon. Her hope that she might be brilliant like the rest of them seemed both selfish and laughable.

I'm here for Matthew, Lydia told herself firmly. She looked at the biography of the politician. *And all the others.*

Chapter 6

Lydia sat up in bed, bleary eyed and nervous. Today was her first full day.

Do I feel suicidal?

Nope. Just terrified.

Lydia stared blankly into her closet at a row of identical uniforms. They swung uneasily on their hangers as if someone had just passed a hand over them, but it was probably a breeze from the window. Lydia swallowed and glanced outside. The maple tree branches were waving their surrender to autumn. Lydia decided on a long-sleeved shirt (dove-gray button-down) and a skirt (pleated, knee-length crimson). Both had the stiff, scratchy feel of clothing that was meant to last a long time. Or perhaps it had been designed to keep students too uncomfortable to doze off in class. Lydia pulled her hair into a ponytail, tucked a notebook and some pens into her backpack, checked her eyes for crust, and stepped into the hallway just as Cora, a.k.a. Selfie Girl, stepped out of the room next to hers.

"Oh, hey, neighbor," said Cora. Evidentially, Cora had dressed the way she thought a genius would dress. Certainly, she had done much more to personalize her style within the restrictions of the uniform. She had on thick-rimmed glasses that exactly matched the light green of her eyes, and her hair was piled up in a messy bun. Lydia thought she could detect some expert hairstyling in the artfully arranged corkscrew tendrils that fell to either side of Cora's perfect face. Again Lydia quelled a feeling that was half envy and half disdain. Cora had her old-fashioned camera with her and the cumbersome selfie stick as well.

"You going to breakfast? Then all-school meeting, right?" asked Cora.

"Yeah," said Lydia.

"All right," said Cora.

Lydia fell in awkwardly next to Cora. Something about her extreme perfection made Lydia want to walk behind her, maybe throwing flower petals, but she forced herself not to genuflect every time Cora wafted a slender arm in her direction.

As they walked over to the dining hall, Lydia revised her opinion of Cora slightly. It wasn't that Cora was stupid, it was just that she was the single most self-absorbed person Lydia had ever met. She spoke knowledgeably about promoting your YouTube channel the whole way across the dewy lawn and well into the line for breakfast. Lydia listened with half an ear and told herself to be alert to opportunities to find out more about orientation.

She and Cora left breakfast together a little early to give themselves time to find the auditorium. They went down a hall that led to the back of the building, and Lydia noticed that the first door on the right had a plaque that said:

DR. HENRY GADDIFY
HEADMASTER

Her heart jumped. If somebody was doing something that was causing students and alumni to commit suicide, the most obvious suspect was Dr. Gaddify. Maybe there was a flaw in the Claybourne Method he had developed for teaching students. Maybe he made students promise something terrible in exchange for teaching them to be geniuses.

There was a single narrow window in the door of his office, and Lydia could see that nobody was inside.

"Are you sure we're going the right way?" she asked Cora. She groped for a reason to study the office. "We can ask in here."

Lydia tried the door. It was locked. She peered in the window and saw that on the opposite side of the room was a window to the outside, slightly open. The headmaster's desk was under the window, and there was an open notebook right on top of the desk. On one corner of the desk was a tray of instruments that Lydia would have associated with primitive dentistry. Was that a clue?

"What are you doing?" whispered Cora. "That's, like, the headmaster's office."

"Oh." Lydia shrugged innocently. "I think we should turn back."

She and Cora turned to go back to the dining hall, but Lydia's thoughts were churning. What were all those wicked-looking tools for? Certainly not something associated with education. Torture devices, right out in the open, or something innocent?

Cora was nattering on about how being mixed race was "really trending" right now.

The two girls spotted a group of older students walking down a hallway that paralleled the front of the main building and started to follow them.

Suddenly Lydia stopped. The outside window in Dr. Gaddify's office had been slightly open. She might be able to sneak in.

She paused, and while she wrestled with whether or not to investigate, a girl in front of her leaned toward her friend and said loudly: "Yeah, well, that was Mandelbrot with his concept of theoretical fractional dimensions." That's not the kind of phrase you can hear in casual conversation without wondering about your own intelligence and general purpose in life.

I may not be a genius, Lydia thought, *but I didn't come here for that.*

"I'll be right back, okay?" she said to Cora. "I'm just have to run back to the dorm."

"Wait," said Cora. "Will you drop this off in your room?" She held up her camera and the selfie stick.

Lydia frowned, reluctant to be associated in any way with a selfie stick, but Cora was already handing the items over.

"The camera's really valuable, okay? And that's, like, my invention."

"I'll lock it my room," Lydia promised, and stuffed the camera and stick in her backpack.

Lydia dodged through the stream of students leaving the cafeteria, trying not to biff too many people with the stupid selfie stick, and then threaded her way through the dining hall and out to the front lawn. A few stragglers were jogging in the opposite direction, but nobody stopped her. Instead of going toward the dorm, Lydia turned and walked back along the side of the main building to where the window into Dr. Gaddify's office was. The dining hall windows were set high in the wall, so nobody could see her, and the kitchen had only high, small windows, and then there was the office window, still slightly open.

There was some kind of prickly evergreen bush right below the window, and two large lilac shrubs on either side. Lydia looked in both directions, saw no one, and ducked behind one of the lilacs. Her heart was pounding so loudly that she could feel it pulsing in her ears.

The office window was higher off the ground than Lydia had thought it would be, and the evergreen bush was going to be no help at all. For one, it was incredibly pokey, and secondly, its branches were springy rather than strong. She stepped on one experimentally. It simply bent all the way to the ground and then boinged back into place with a shower of needles.

Lydia could fit between the bush and the foundation beneath the window, but only some sort of superhuman feat would allow her to pull herself up inside. During their self-improvement phase three summers ago, Lydia had suggested that she and Matthew learn all the lyrics to every song Bob Dylan had ever written. Matthew had proposed that they "get buff." In the end, listening to *Blood on the Tracks* a dozen times had been a lot more appealing than jogging, and then they'd given up on the whole thing. Lydia had argued that there was really no need to ever do a pull-up in real life. Every once in a while, though, Matthew would suddenly drop to the floor and do a few push-ups "just in case."

Here, finally, was a real-life example of when being able to do a pull-up might be useful. *Okay, Matthew*, thought Lydia, *you were right*. Using her backpack to shield herself from the worst of the bush needles, she worked her way to under the window. The sill was just over the top of her head. Lydia strained her ears to detect movement inside the room, but there was nothing. Moving quietly, she stretched her hands overhead to the sill and gave an awkward sort of hop.

For one second she kept her eyes above the level of the windowsill and was able to peek inside. There was the desk, some filing cabinets, some impressive bookshelves, and a hearty collection of framed diplomas. Lydia's fingers slipped and she crashed to the ground beneath the bush. The selfie stick jabbed her hard in the kidneys and she hissed with pain.

"Stupid selfie stick," she whispered. "Stupid, stupid—" Lydia stopped, frowning, with a sudden thought.

She scrambled out of the bush, checked again to see if anyone was around, and then huddled back into the lilac. She got the selfie stick and Cora's camera out of the backpack, then fitted the camera onto the end of the stick. It took a minute to figure out the mechanism to take a photo, and Lydia had to admit it was pretty clever.

Lydia adjusted the focus so that something close would be clear and gently worked the camera inside the window to face the papers on the desk. Maybe, just maybe, they were worth reading. Panting as if she'd just sprinted around the whole island, she took several photos of the desk and then turned the camera to try and get a picture of the tray of instruments. The whole operation took only four minutes, but by the time Lydia crawled back out of the bush, she was covered in itchy scratches and out of breath.

With relief, Lydia crashed out of the lilacs and stumbled right into the path of a woman in a gray nurse's uniform.

The woman had skin the same color as Abilene's, but the resemblance ended there. This woman's eyeballs popped from their sockets as if all the skin on her face were being pulled back by a fierce wind. This look was not improved by her hairstyle, which was done in severe cornrows.

For a long second the woman looked at Lydia and Lydia looked at the woman.

"I—I . . . lost a—" Lydia stammered.

"You don't belong here," said the woman. Her voice was curiously whispery, not at all what you would expect, and it was a strange choice of words. For a moment Lydia thought she might be referring to Claybourne. Lydia didn't belong at Claybourne.

"You belong in the auditorium. What are you doing in the bushes?" The woman's broad nostrils flared.

"I just lost my lens cap," said Lydia, holding up the camera. The lie sounded tinny in Lydia's ears, but she wasn't able to look away from the woman's eyes. "It rolled right in the bushes."

The woman's eyes pulsed over the headmaster's window and then over Lydia's scratches. It felt like being groped. "You better come with me," she said.

Lydia's heart was thudding with nerves. She stuffed the camera into her backpack and stepped up onto the sidewalk. The woman started walking toward the front entrance of the main building. Lydia could hear the *zip, zip, zip* of the woman's nylon-encased thighs rubbing together.

"What is your name?" whispered the woman.

"Lydia. Lydia Boswell."

"I am Nurse Proctor," she said without looking at Lydia.

Lydia trotted after Nurse Proctor, feeling a bruise form where the camera was slamming into her back. Nurse Proctor's body was divided in half at the waist by a thick red belt. The top half of her body was normal size, maybe even narrow in the shoulders. The bottom half was twice as big, and every seam of the gray skirt was stretched. The colors of the uniform were slightly off. The gray had tan in it, so that it looked like it had been dyed in dirty dishwater, and the red was too orange to match the crimson of the school colors. Lydia had the thought that maybe Nurse Proctor didn't really work at the school.

Nurse Proctor stopped outside of some double doors and turned to face Lydia.

"There are not a lot of rules here," she said in her harsh whisper. "But there are many *expectations*. One of those expectations is that you are where you are meant to be." The great, bulging eyes probed Lydia again.

Lydia nodded.

Nurse Proctor turned and opened one of the doors. "You are meant to be in here." She stood aside to let Lydia pass through the door.

"Thank you," whispered Lydia. As she scurried inside, she noticed something else odd about Nurse Proctor. She had a bandage wrapped around her palm, and there was a bright blotch of blood seeping through.

Chapter 7

When Lydia slipped into the back of the auditorium, the rest of the student body was singing what Lydia guessed was the school song. She slunk into the back row and sat down before she realized that she was just one chair away from Dr. Kennedy. Dr. Kennedy swiveled in her seat and looked at Lydia with narrowed eyes. Lydia couldn't tell if she was in trouble or if Dr. Kennedy always looked at students like she had just been asked to wipe their nose. Dr. Kennedy turned forward and stiffly handed Lydia a clothbound book, open to the page with the school song.

Hymn to Claybourne

From clay we are born, to clay we return.
Let life and inspiration inside of us burn.
Our gifts we will share with the world we improve,
Our wealth we will share with the school that we love.
We open our hearts to spirit of greatness,
We open our minds to genius that's latent.
We are but vessels, our souls will be free.
We pledge ourselves to Claybourne Academy.

Lydia was too out of breath to do any more than mouth the words. She looked around. Had Nurse Proctor followed her in? The nurse was nowhere in sight. Lydia couldn't tell if she'd been caught or not. What exactly had Nurse Proctor seen? Lydia felt a hysterical giggle tumble from her lips. Didn't anybody else find the lyrics sort of silly? Lydia glanced down the line of teachers in the back row. They were as solemn as the statues on Easter Island. Lydia took a calming breath and faced forward, folding her hands like an innocent girl.

There was a man onstage, sitting in a large wooden chair off to one side, and a young woman playing the piano that was on the other side of the stage. When she finished, the man stood, gestured to her and bowed briefly, then walked over to the podium in the center of the stage.

Lydia squinted to get a better look. He was medium height and had a full head of salt-and-pepper hair. He moved easily, and though he wasn't a large man, his presence completely filled the entire auditorium.

"Well done, well done, and wel*come*, everybody. Welcome, new students and faculty. Welcome back, old friends and colleagues." The man beamed around the room and did a half bow. Everybody applauded and whistled.

The man patted the air to quiet the room. "Thank you. As many of you know, I am Dr. Gaddify." Several whistles pierced the air. "I love you, Dr. G.!" shouted someone to Lydia's right.

Dr. Gaddify shaded his eyes from the spotlights and pointed toward the shouter. "Ah! Thank you, Mr. Redford. The feeling is mutual. Especially since you did *not* blow a hole in the bottom of the ferry. For a second time."

All of the returning students roared with laughter, and Lydia felt herself smile despite her suspicions.

"Thank you, everybody, for showing restraint with your boat pranks this year. Somebody made off with quite a haul of candy bars. . . ." More laughter. "But I understand from Captain Whelk that you were otherwise fairly well behaved."

Dr. Gaddify quelled another round of cheering, then detached the microphone from the podium and began to pace around the stage.

"Now, every year I must beg you not to break the rules we have regarding technology. I know that *someone* will attempt to build a router from the ground up. In fact, I would be almost disappointed if somebody did not get caught with at least a homemade radio, but I beg you, please, save us the time and resist the urge to prove your intelligence in such a predictable way. Our school has sent several students to the halls of government agencies we are not even sure exist, and I am telling you this so that you know that we have some very good tech interrupters. We ask you again not to break or attempt to break that particular rule. I think we can all agree that the results we get from creating this very special environment are more than worth having fewer twits or tweets, or whatever they are, in the world." Dr. Gaddify smiled graciously at his audience and then straightened his shoulders and went over a few more rules about uniforms, boundaries, swimming, and writing letters home.

"I must apologize to our new students," he said. "We are about to test you to within an inch of your life. We intend to tease out every last *molecule* of potential you have so that it has the opportunity to bloom. Everyone here can attest that you will be exhausted. You may feel as if you don't even remember your own name. This is normal." Lydia heard some dry chuckles and groans. "I must ask you to be patient and to trust the process."

Lydia narrowed her eyes at the man onstage. Just what was this mysterious process? Why did she feel so eager to begin when she knew she shouldn't trust anyone here?

"Now, my office would be bombarded with questions if I did not take the time to reassure everybody that, yes, there will be truffles." The auditorium filled with the loudest cheers yet. "My famous homemade truffles, which I will use to bribe you returning students to be *on time* for your start-of-year check-in with me. I expect you all to acquaint yourselves with the schedule that is outside my office door and to show up promptly. There are seventy-four of you and one of me. So show up on time or no truffle! New students, I welcome the opportunity to introduce you to this long Claybourne tradition when we begin your orientation in two days' time. In the meantime, I believe you have a meeting with Dr. Kennedy after this. You may remain here when we are finished. Again, I am so pleased you could join us, and welcome to all!"

Lydia couldn't help but join in the clapping and cheering when the headmaster left the stage and walked down the aisle toward the door. Around her, everybody stood and gathered their things. Lydia hoped to make a getaway during the commotion, but Dr. Kennedy pinned here with a glare.

"Where were you? Why were you late?"

"I'm really sorry, Dr. Kennedy. Did I miss anything important?"

Dr. Kennedy narrowed her eyes and raked her gaze over Lydia.

"Sorry," said Lydia. "I got lost."

She immediately wished she hadn't said she'd gotten lost. Dr. Kennedy's expression changed from reproach to pity that was mostly disgust. She walked down the aisle and didn't look at Lydia again.

Dr. Kennedy divided the new students into four groups, and true to Dr. Gaddify's warning, they were tested all day. In groups of six or seven the new students shuffled from classroom to classroom, filling out quizzes on paper, but also being tested. Lydia's eyesight, color acuity, and pattern recognition were evaluated. Her hearing and range were measured. Her puzzle-solving ability, her memory, her capacity to accurately mimic language she'd never encountered before, were all tested. This last test seemed to be the only thing at which she was in any way exceptional.

The teacher who tested Lydia on languages was Mr. Harcourt, a reedy-looking black man wearing a crimson tie with little Harvard *H*s on it. He smiled at her encouragingly.

"Are you any good at math?" he asked. He had very long, spatulate fingers, which he used to flip through the folder holding all of her tests.

"I'm okay, I guess," said Lydia.

"Have you taken any languages besides English?"

"Just one year of French."

"Well, I think you might just have a knack for language."

"Really?"

"Time will tell. We'll see what happens—"

"After orientation. I know," Lydia interrupted.

Mr. Harcourt nodded at her, smiling, and then opened the door to show that she should leave. Ben came in and gave her a thumbs-up sign before sitting down in the seat Lydia had just vacated.

In the afternoon Lydia walked back to the dorm with Naomi, feeling so tired that her vision kept playing tricks on her. Shadows capered in the periphery of her sight. Naomi, on the other hand, seemed an inch taller.

"They think I'm tetrachromatic!" she said.

"You're what?"

"You know how your eye has rods and cones? Rods for bright and dark; cones for color?"

This was vaguely familiar to Lydia, so she nodded.

"Well, most people have three kinds of cones, but they think a few of us have four. Tetra—'four'; chromatic—'color.' Get it?"

"Whoa. What does that mean?"

"It means . . . it shows . . . well, it just means that I really *do* see more colors in every color than normal people. Like this grass. What color is it to you?"

Lydia snorted. "Uh, green."

"To me, there is a lot of green, but every green is a little different, and there is a lot of yellow and ocher, and purple and sienna and indigo. . . ." Naomi sighed happily.

"Naomi, you just named about half the colors in the rainbow," said Lydia.

"I know." Naomi smiled. "That's how I see."

As they reached the dorm, Cora motioned to Lydia from a porch swing.

"Hey, listen, Charlie Rhinebeck is going to show me the darkroom, so can I get my camera from you?"

Lydia paused for a second. "Sure, I'll just go get it from my room."

The camera was still in her backpack on her back, but Lydia needed a minute to think of the lie that would explain the photos she'd taken *and* get them developed so she could have them.

Lydia was not that good at lying. Both Emily and Abilene had a sixth sense for sniffing out even a half-truth or an omission, so lying had never really done Lydia or Matthew any good.

In her room, Lydia thought a minute, then grabbed the camera. She leaned the selfie stick up against Cora's door and then walked down to the common room.

"Hey, Cora. I think I might have taken some pictures by accident when I was putting the camera in my backpack."

Cora shrugged and Lydia plowed on.

"But, uh, they told me today that I have pretty good eyesight? So I thought maybe I could come to the darkroom with you. Learn the ropes." Lydia winced inwardly. *Learn the ropes? Really?*

Cora shrugged again. "I don't care if Charlie doesn't care. Let's go."

Cora took four more pictures, mostly close-ups of curled leaves, to finish off the roll before they got to a small brick building with a plaque that said:

BENTON ART BUILDING

GIFT OF SARAH BENTON, '99

Outside the door was a tall, broad-shouldered kid with a shaggy haircut and a hint of facial hair. Lydia blushed as she realized that not only was Charlie extremely good looking, but he had clearly set his sights on Cora and now Lydia was only in the way.

Charlie shrugged when Cora introduced Lydia, then he showed them inside the building, down some stairs, and into a series of darkrooms. Charlie and Cora chatted about f-stops and double exposures and other terms that Lydia had to assume were about photography. Charlie asked Lydia a couple of questions about "her work," but when it became clear she'd never moved beyond the autofocus of her mom's digital camera, he ignored her completely and bent all his charm toward Cora.

Developing the film didn't take very long, but then they had to stick the film in a special drying machine. Charlie flicked a switch that started a low hum, and offered to show them the rest of the art building.

Lydia didn't know much about art, but even she could see that the paintings and sculptures done by the students had some quality that drew your eye and ignited some emotion. Charlie paused in an alcove with a tall, sinuous statue that was part woman, part swan.

"Gordon Griggs did that here when he was a junior," he said. "It's not the original, because that's worth millions, but this is the only copy and it could probably pay for a nice house on the Cape."

After that they went back to the basement and made a contact sheet, which was a page that had miniature versions of the photos she and Cora had taken.

Charlie frowned, looking at the contact page with a magnifying lens. "Not great focus on these," he said, running a finger along the ones Lydia had taken of the headmaster's office.

"I know," said Lydia quickly. "I just thought I could practice the developing part on those."

"Sure," said Charlie, holding the door to the darkroom open with a gentlemanly flourish for Cora's benefit.

Developing photos was hypnotic. The images on the paper appeared in the solution as if coming out of a mist, and Lydia found the strong smells to be pleasant in a perverse sort of way, just like gasoline smelled good or a moldy basement. She'd taken eight pictures, and she developed each one by herself after Charlie and Cora showed her how. Neither of the other two even pretended to be interested in her photos, which was a relief. Lydia thought that if you wanted to do spy work, having somebody as beautiful as Cora around was a good way to become invisible.

Lydia hung up the 8 x 10 prints she'd made on a small clothesline under a red light. She fanned them with her notebook to try and hurry the drying process and studied them at the same time. The four of the desk had managed to capture some handwritten pages, a coffee cup, a stack of mail and a lethal-looking letter opener. An expensive pen lay atop the written pages, but otherwise you could read the page pretty easily. It was a list of names in two columns.

She'd gotten two shots of the tray of instruments, and when she saw what they were, she felt a flush of embarrassment.

A candy thermometer, a chocolate crusher, a filling injector.

Not torture. Chocolate. For making truffles.

Lydia sighed.

Lydia thanked Charlie and Cora, who seemed surprised she was still there, and headed back to her room. The only photo that really had anything interesting in it was the one that showed the piece of paper with two columns of names written out like this:

Angus McCracken	Joshua Lawrence Chamberlain
Bethany Ming	Fanny Mendelssohn Hensel
Sophia Nowel	Norma Merrick Sklarek
Corbin Palisin	Linus Pauling
Benjamin Loi	John Templeton
Calliope Smith	Agnes Arber
Trenton Stuart	Edwin Land
Frances Trombly	Julia Child

If somebody had offered Lydia a trade—her pinkie toe for an hour on the Internet—Lydia would have said yes.

The only name she recognized was Julia Child. She was the French-cooking lady with the gluey voice. Mendelssohn was the name of a classical music person, but Lydia was pretty sure that that was a man and that the first name was not Fanny.

Lydia wasn't certain how the names were organized, either. Was it one list or two separate lists? Did the names on the same line have anything to do with each other? Were these even real people?

After a minute Lydia realized that the names on the left side of the page were in alphabetical order by last name. She thought that this probably meant the names on the left side of the page had something in common with one another. They were a group that had been sorted by alphabet. Lydia copied down the names onto a sheet of notebook paper, since it seemed risky to be carrying around evidence of espionage. She resolved to go to the library after dinner.

In the dining hall Lydia sat at a table with Ben, Gus, Pilar, and Naomi.

"I feel like my brain has been X-rayed," said Pilar.

"An X-ray is probably another thing that's banned here, otherwise I'd agree," said Ben. He picked up a stewed mushroom. "This is my brain right now."

"Actual size?" asked Gus innocently. Gus ducked as the mushroom came winging over the table.

"What are they testing for, anyway?" said Pilar. "We got in, right? They wouldn't have accepted us if we weren't smart, so why test us now?"

"How *did* we get in?" said Gus, frowning at his chicken à la king. "I don't think I could pass first grade right now."

Lydia looked around the table, wondering if anyone would mention birthdays or moon cycles. Nobody did. Was she the only one who had figured it out? The question was, what did a new moon birthday have to do with potential for genius? Maybe the new list in her backpack would have a clue.

When dinner was over, Lydia was so tired that all her limbs seemed heavier than normal. All she wanted to do was sleep, but as she lay back in her bed with all her clothes on, the names on the list seemed to call to her from the pocket of her backpack. Lydia heaved herself into a sitting position with a sigh and walked heavily down the hall, almost stomping down the stairs, and back to the library.

Ms. Alton was at the front desk, so Lydia mustered a smile and then found the reference section. With a grunt, she pulled out a stack of encyclopedias, *Mc* to *U*. One after another she crossed off the names on the left side of the page without finding even a hint of an identity. Her brain did feel like a stewed mushroom. After she'd spent five minutes looking for "Frances Trombly" in the *St–Ta* encyclopedia, she gave up and packed away her list.

"Find what you were looking for?" called Ms. Alton as Lydia passed the front desk.

"No," admitted Lydia. "I'd kill for Google right now."

Ms. Alton shook her finger at Lydia. "Don't say that in front of the books!"

Lydia grinned. "Sorry."

"Come back tomorrow and I'll see if I can help," said Ms. Alton.

"Thanks," said Lydia.

"Good night."

Back at the dorm, Lydia found a stack of empty suitcases and one giant trunk blocking the hallway to her room.

"Sorry!" said Cora, dragging another suitcase into the hall. "I'm bringing these to storage."

Lydia bent tiredly to lift a lime-green-and-pink suitcase out of the way. A matching pink-and-green luggage tag got caught on the buckle of another suitcase, so Lydia had to work it free.

"Frances Trombly!" Lydia was so surprised that she wasn't even aware that she had read the luggage tag out loud.

Cora turned and grimaced at her. "Nobody calls me that," she said, jutting out her chin.

"You're Frances Trombly?" asked Lydia.

Cora rolled her lovely green eyes. "It's a family name, okay?"

"No, I was just—"

"Are you gonna help me with this? Pretty please?" Cora clasped her hands under her chin and batted her eyelashes. "I took you to the darkroom."

"Yeah, sure." Lydia put her backpack down and grabbed a suitcase. "Hey, Cora, do you know anybody's last name?"

"Uh, not really. I think Gus's is, like, MacGregor or something Scottish. Naomi, what's your last name?" shouted Cora as they passed Naomi's open dorm room door.

"Arnold," called Naomi.

Lydia thought maybe there was a Scottish name on the list, but definitely no Arnold.

She and Cora dragged the suitcases down into the basement and stacked them up against one wall, then went back up to the first floor.

"Thanks," said Cora. She waited to go upstairs with Lydia, but Lydia shooed her away.

"I just want to check something."

Lydia looked around the common room for Dr. Kennedy's list of new students' room assignments and finally found it pinned to a bulletin board in the front hall.

Bethany Ming, Sophia Nowel, and Calliope Smith were all new students. Lydia felt both excited and slightly deflated. Of course a headmaster would have a list of new students. Fanny, Norma, Agnes, and Julia weren't there, which seemed to confirm that the paper actually held two lists. Maybe the right side was returning students. Maybe they were all going to get mentors or something. It didn't seem as if there was anything nefarious about the paper after all.

Chapter 8

That night Lydia had the dream. The components of the dream were always the same, but the setting varied. Always, she was doing something with Matthew: hanging on the jungle gym bars from elementary school, walking along Railroad Street at home, sitting on a tree branch. Always, everything seemed ordinary except that there was an undercurrent of anger. Anger was like a flammable gas waiting for a spark. It was like a bank of black clouds, a rumble Lydia could feel in her chest.

This night she and Matthew were on the Claybourne ferry. Both of them were balanced on the steel railing that went around the deck of the boat. They were sitting side by side, watching the seismic unfurling of water below. Lydia could feel the tension in her muscles as they worked to keep her body balanced. She could sense the anger in the roar of the ferry engine. Matthew didn't seem to notice or be at all concerned. He was chatting away, but his words were lost in the noise.

Lydia knew what was coming. Her muscles jerked and clenched, but she couldn't move to prevent it. Matthew turned to look as her, like he always did. He lifted one eyebrow, and then he leaned forward and fell off the railing.

Sometimes he let go of the monkey bars or stepped off the sidewalk or jumped off the tree limb. Always, Lydia felt a moment of horror and then the anger. The anger ignited the air around her and burned up all the oxygen. Lydia hated Matthew so much that her muscles trembled with it. How could he? How could he just let go?

Lydia woke, panting, and threw off her blankets. She sat up and put her feet on the cool wooden floor. Now came the guilt. She sat with her head in her hands for a minute and then stood up to press her face against the window.

Outside, leaves skittered across the lawn. There were two lights on in the dorm on the opposite side of the green, and the flagpole was clanking in the wind. One of the lights went off, and then a second later another light bloomed in the doorway. There was a brief chiaroscuro—a disproportioned figure silhouetted in the orange light across the green, and the negative of that, a light figure against the blackness of the building.

Lydia glanced at her clock. The red, squarish numbers read 3:27. Nurse Proctor was out late. Lydia watched the bowling-pin-shaped blob of gray move across the green. Perhaps this meant that Nurse Proctor lived on the island. The idea caused Lydia to shiver.

The next day the anger from the dream hovered over Lydia's skin like mist on a pond. She endured another round of testing, but she was certain she hadn't done well. She saw conspiracy everywhere. Orientation loomed with equal measures of promise and doom.

Lydia wasn't sure what the returning students were doing, since she knew they weren't being tested, but when she saw Seth coming out of the headmaster's office, he acted like he didn't recognize her and so she didn't try to ask. Lydia scanned the start-of-year check-in list for returning students to meet with the headmaster. She didn't find any of her names from the right side of the list, but yesterday's had already been taken down, so she couldn't be sure that they hadn't just been on the other page.

Lydia spent the afternoon with Naomi, helping her decorate her room. Naomi had a half dozen paintings and elaborate doodles that she'd done and she needed help hanging them straight.

"These are amazing," Lydia told her, and it was true. Lydia held up a piece of notebook paper that looked like an elaborate textile design. On the wall over Naomi's bed was a painting of a woman crouched over a fire in a desert. The flat horizon divided the painting into two; the top third was sunset colors, and the bottom was cool desert purples and blues. The seemingly solid blocks of color were actually intricate patterns, the colors so alive that the painting seemed to pulse when Lydia looked at it.

Naomi shrugged away the praise. Since her shoulders were normally already around her ears, a shrug was more about bringing her shoulders together in front. "Take one if you want. I'm going to have hundreds," she said. "Kennedy told me that once I declare, I can spend at least five *daylight* hours in the studio every day." Naomi's face, usually sort of sullen, lifted in a way that made her seem both pretty and very young. She obviously loved to paint.

When the last frame was hung to Naomi's exacting standards, Lydia stretched and flicked open the shade. Outside, the sunlight was golden and warm. The leaves winked and glittered, showing that there was a light breeze.

"Do you wanna explore the island a little?" asked Lydia. "Get outside?"

"Yeah," said Naomi. "Let's see if anyone else wants to come."

Five minutes later Pilar, Cora, Naomi, and Lydia were strolling down toward the beach where the ferry had arrived. About halfway between the main lawn and the shore, the path hit a crossroads. Straight ahead would lead to the ferry. The paths to the right and the left seemed likely to circumnavigate the island. The girls decided to take the path to the left. It was wide enough for two of the island's golf carts to pass each other, but looked less trafficked than the one that went to the ferry. This path curved back toward campus but stayed closer to the shore. If the main building was the center of an oval target, then this path was the third ring out.

The girls chattered as they walked beneath the pine trees, the sweet smell of needles mixing with the tang of warm sand and ocean. After a few minutes they came out to an open area that was dotted with cottages.

"Oh," said Cora, "how sweet! This must be where the faculty live."

A dozen cottages looked like blocks spilled from a bag. Each one was identical in structure, but painted in an array of colors and oriented slightly differently so that each maintained a unique character. Some had flower boxes, one had a mountain bike leaning against a short section of picket fence, a few had trees. It looked like summer camp for grown-ups.

"I wish we lived here instead of in the dorms," said Pilar.

"Look over there," said Naomi. She pointed down a short path on the ocean side where there was a gazebo overlooking the water.

"No fair!" said Cora. "Why do the teachers get all the cute places?"

The girls kept walking, comparing notes on the testing they'd undergone and speculating about how they'd declare.

Now the path went up over rough, rocky bands in the ground. The trees here were short and twisted by the wind. The girls scrambled up onto a bald, windblown rock face as big as a tennis court, hunching forward against the wind. For a few minutes they couldn't find where the trail continued after it left the naked rock, but then Naomi spotted a break in the trees.

This trail was even smaller and less trafficked than the last one. Lydia was in front, and she walked into dozens of spiderwebs that had been built between the scrubby trees on either side. The wind was picking up on this side of the island, accelerating from a playful breeze to a creature that tore the sound from your lips as you spoke. Lydia bent her body forward against the wind and hurried down the uneven rocky path. After five minutes of breathless scuttling, they were back in the tall pines.

"Whew! I thought we were going to be blown away," said Pilar.

Cora was threading her fingers through her curls, trying to rake them back into place. "I hope we don't have to go back that way," she complained.

"I bet this path goes all the way around the island," said Lydia. "Let's keep going."

"There's a clearing just up there," said Naomi.

Up ahead was a meadow. Lydia could tell it was windy by the bands of silvered grass that swept toward them. Just visible on the far side of the meadow was the upper story of a building. This house was covered in gray cedar shingles and cowered beneath the protection of a lone tree. Nobody cooed or said they wished they could live in there. The trail led toward it, yet nobody was inclined to head in that direction.

"Let's go back," said Naomi.

"I am not climbing over that rocky, windy spot again," said Cora, patting her hair.

"It'll be windy out there, too," said Pilar, pointing to the meadow and a chaotic flock of leaves that scattered from the tree by the house.

"Let's just keep close to the woods. We'll run into the trail on the other side of this meadow if it keeps going around. If not, we can just cut back through the woods," said Lydia.

"If you say so," said Pilar doubtfully.

The undergrowth beneath the pines trees was not thick, but it would be challenging to walk through because many of the lower branches of the huge trees had died back and fallen to the forest floor. There was a band of scrubby shrubbery inside the edge of the forest where light from the meadow had encouraged growth.

"We'll walk in the grass," said Lydia. "It will be a little windier, but a lot easier."

The girls weren't talking anymore because a sense of unease had slithered its way into their midst. Taking high steps through the grass, Lydia led the way along the edge of the meadow, inscribing a large arc around the house. As they dropped down over a hump in the meadow, the wind died further and the unease began to dissipate.

"What's that?" asked Naomi, who, as usual, had spotted something before the others.

There was another lone tree, small and gnarled. An apple tree, Lydia thought. An old iron fence leaned higgledy-piggledy in a crooked square around the tree, and inside the fence was a handful of small gray tombstones.

"A graveyard?" said Pilar.

The girls approached the graveyard cautiously, as if one of the corpses buried there might rear up and chase after them.

"I am freaking out!" declared Cora.

"This is pretty freakin' spooky," said Pilar.

"It's fine, guys," Naomi said. "It's just an old graveyard."

"Not that old," said Lydia, reading one of the stones. "That one was buried here thirty years ago."

"God, people, let's get out of here," said Cora.

Pilar crossed herself and mumbled something in Spanish that sounded religious.

"Boo!" Naomi shouted.

Everybody screamed and giggled nervously. Before, unease had quieted them; now their hearts were jumping and eyes darting.

"Come on." Lydia started toward the trees. "There's the path back." She took two big leaps through the tall grass, then looked over her shoulder with a grin. She turned and began running up the path.

"Wait!" screamed Pilar.

Cora and Naomi cackled and whooped, then they were all running through the pine forest. After thirty seconds Lydia stopped sprinting and hunched over, gasping, her hands on her knees. She smiled as Cora came careening around a tree and skittered to a halt. Cora smiled too, panting. Pilar and Naomi came into view. Pilar was patting her chest and grinning. Naomi collapsed dramatically onto the ground.

"I . . . can't . . . breathe," she moaned.

"Cora," gasped Pilar. "I've never seen anyone run so fast."

"Well," said Cora, straightening up and looking down her nose. "You don't have to run faster than a ghost, you just have to run faster than your companions."

It made them all laugh, and they kept laughing all the way back to campus.

After dinner Lydia was too tired to go back to the library. She'd already figured out half the list, and besides, tomorrow was orientation. After tomorrow Lydia would supposedly be a genius, so why not wait until then to keep searching?

Chapter 9

Lydia woke with a start. The word ** *truffle* ** was like an echo she wasn't sure she'd heard aloud. It was, in fact, just like when she'd heard/seen the word ** *river* **, and like then, there was an emotional residue to the word. Revulsion.

Lydia did the check that was becoming routine to her days at Claybourne.

Do I feel suicidal?

No.

But suddenly I'm freaked out about truffles.

Lydia walked over to breakfast with Naomi, Pilar, and Cora. They were all anxious about orientation and so got there before most other students. Dr. Kennedy was sitting by herself near the door.

"You're all here early," she said, holding a burned piece of toast halfway to her mouth.

"It's orientation," said Pilar.

"Right. After only two days of testing." Kennedy looked disapproving. "Last year it took two *weeks*."

Lydia wasn't sure if she should be proud or worried that their testing had taken only two days. "Is it always different?" she asked deferentially.

Kennedy carefully placed the toast on her plate and looked up. "I've been here since last year. Dr. Gaddify only offers two-year contracts."

The other girls went up to the line, but Lydia paused a moment. "Do all the teachers have two-year contracts?"

Kennedy sighed to let Lydia know that she was running out of patience. "We're mostly researchers—in the hard subjects, that is. The arts are taught by actual artists. A steady paycheck for two years is nice for *them*."

"But why so short?" persisted Lydia.

"It's a good way to train as many people in the Claybourne Method as possible. Dr. Gaddify says that with the right teaching, the human race has the potential to do anything." Kennedy's hot glare softened a fraction. She was a true believer. "He thinks that the only reason the method isn't as effective in other places is because people aren't willing to forgo their Internet. It's a shame."

"Oh," said Lydia. She wanted to ask more, but the way Kennedy was looking at her indicated that if she didn't leave, then Dr. Kennedy couldn't eat her toast, and if Dr. Kennedy couldn't eat her toast, she couldn't get back to her laboratory, and if she couldn't do that, then she couldn't save the world and that would be bad.

"Have a great day," said Lydia. She all but ran into the kitchen.

Lydia's insides jumped with nerves, but she forced down half a bagel and some tea. She knew from experience that if she didn't eat, she got grumpy. Everyone picked at their food and then it was time. Feeling like a sheep in a feed lot, Lydia bumped along in a crowd of new students to the auditorium.

Nurse Proctor was standing in the hall that led to the auditorium. It reminded Lydia that she wanted to ask one of the boys if anyone had been sick the other night. She studied Nurse Proctor's profile as long as she dared. It was hard to tell what she was thinking because her protuberant eyes gave every expression a wash of shock, but Lydia thought that Nurse Proctor seemed to be evaluating every student, as if one of them might be carrying a terrible disease. Lydia dropped her eyes as she neared the nurse, then felt the prickle of the nurse's gaze on the side of her face.

There was a line to go into the auditorium, and Lydia saw that Dr. Gaddify was standing just inside the door, grinning like a flight attendant and handing out napkins with a single truffle on each one.

Dread smothered Lydia like a thick fog. Her classmates were cheerfully nibbling or gulping their truffles.

"As promised!" called Dr. Gaddify. "My famous, homemade, fresh-rolled chocolate truffles!"

Ben was standing off to one side with a smeared napkin and a smudge of chocolate on his upper lip. "Okay, now I get it! I thought the seniors were just teasing us or something, but this really is amazing!"

Dr. Gaddify boomed, "Nourish the body and the mind!"

Lydia was three people back in line.

Dr. Gaddify handed Pilar a truffle and watched her try it with a look of anticipatory delight on his face.

"Good?" he asked.

"Great!" said Pilar.

It was too late to turn around and run back to the dorm. Should she drop her truffle? Slip it into her backpack? Lydia wasn't even sure she *shouldn't* eat it. It was just a dream, right? Or part of one? But then, it was so like ** *river* **, and that hadn't been a dream. Dr. Gaddify handed her a napkin with a truffle on it and smiled at her. "Welcome to Claybourne!"

Lydia took the truffle and turned to walk away.

"Ah, now let me see you try a nibble," called Dr. Gaddify jovially.

Lydia froze then turned mechanically back to Dr. Gaddify. He looked as eager and expectant as a golden retriever that had just dropped a drool-covered ball at her feet. In a panic, Lydia popped the whole thing in her mouth. She tucked it quickly into her cheek with her tongue and gave Dr. Gaddify a thumbs-up. He held her gaze a minute, then turned to give a truffle to a tall boy behind Lydia.

The chocolate was delicious. Smooth, creamy ribbons of flavor were spreading from Lydia's cheek over the back of her tongue and down her throat. All around her, her classmates were smiling and emitting little sounds of contentment. Lydia pushed through them and hurried down toward the front of the auditorium. She pretended to wipe her mouth with the napkin and spit as much of the truffle as she could into the napkin. Now she had a wad of sticky brown paper in her hand that was leaking chocolate. She let her backpack slip off her shoulder into one of the rows of seats. As she bent down to retrieve the backpack, she gave the wad of napkin and truffle an underhand toss along the row.

Her cheeks and neck burning, Lydia refused to look back and check if anyone had seen her throw the napkin. She made her way down to the second row and took a seat. A moment later Naomi climbed over her legs and sat down.

"Did you throw up or something?" she asked. "Your eyes are all watery."

"No." Lydia pounded her own chest. "Went down the wrong pipe. Did everybody see?"

"Nah," said Naomi, her eyebrows raised in sympathy.

Lydia coughed and wiped the corners of her mouth. "I thought I was going to spit the whole thing onto the floor."

Naomi laughed. "Good, though, huh? I never had a real homemade truffle before."

"Me neither," said Lydia.

Now the house lights dimmed and the lights came up onstage. The students hurried to the front of the auditorium, and Dr. Gaddify closed the doors, then walked down a side aisle. As he took the stage steps two at a time, the students quieted and looked up at him.

Dr. Gaddify squinted into the light, shading his eyes, and then shrugged. "All right," he said, "can everybody hear me?" Various sounds of assent came from the students. He walked to the edge of the stage and sat down, dangling his legs over the side. "Can you all see me if I sit right here?" Again everybody assented.

Dr. Gaddify smiled into the group of students, catching everybody's eye in turn. "Let's begin with the school hymn," he said. "Page fourteen in the hymnal on the back of the seat in front of you."

Rather tunelessly, the new students, who had heard the song only once, made it through the hymn.

"From clay we are born, to clay we return.
Let life and inspiration inside of us burn.
Our gifts we will share with the world we'll improve,
Our wealth we will share with the school that we love.
We open our hearts to spirit of greatness,
We open our minds to genius that's latent.
We are but vessels, our souls will be free.
We pledge ourselves to Claybourne Academy."

"Again," said Dr. Gaddify with hypnotic calm. Lydia looked at Naomi to see if she thought that was strange too, but Naomi was gazing forward, her expression slack. Lydia froze. As subtly as possible she turned her head to the other side. Pilar stared fixedly at the stage, the words of the hymn coming robotically from her mouth. Lydia's skin pricked with fear.

The backs of the heads in front of Lydia were still and facing resolutely forward. Lydia didn't dare look behind her, but she had the impression that nobody else thought this was at all strange.

Lydia looked up at Dr. Gaddify. He was studying them, completely unsurprised. When his gaze came in her direction, Lydia dropped her eyes quickly to the hymnal.

Fear made Lydia feel as though a thousand spiders were crawling over the skin of her back. Why wasn't anyone else alarmed? Without moving her head, she looked at Naomi again. She was drugged, Lydia realized. They all were. Everybody had eaten a truffle except for Dr. Gaddify.

And except for her.

Chapter 10

"Okay," intoned Dr. Gaddify. His manner had gone from cheerful delight to deadly calm. "Everybody, please look up here."

There was the slightest sound of movement around Lydia. She did not dare stick out by disobeying, so she looked up too. Dr. Gaddify's gaze, when it passed over her, was as keen as a knife. Lydia tried to deaden her expression, tried not to let the confusion show on her face.

"You will obey my voice," commanded Dr. Gaddify. "Stand up."

Lydia stood, as around her almost everybody shuffled to his or her feet. A girl in front of her and to the left remained seated. She was squirming in her seat, shaking her head from side to side. Dr. Gaddify slid off the stage and knelt before her. He snapped his fingers in front of her face and began to murmur. He was hypnotizing her, Lydia thought. After a minute Lydia heard him say again, "You will obey my voice. Now stand up." The girl rose quickly. Dr. Gaddify passed to someone behind Lydia. She didn't want to risk turning her head to see.

Lydia wondered. Was *this* the Claybourne Method—hypnotism? Did Dr. Gaddify make them all *believe* that they were geniuses? Should she tell Dr. Gaddify that it wasn't working on her? *But he drugged them,* reminded the voice of caution. *He drugged them without telling them.* Maybe hypnotism worked better that way, reasoned Lydia. *The whole thing is too secretive to be innocent, and whatever it is has caused twenty-one people to commit suicide.*

Her mind buzzing, Lydia stood still for ten more minutes while Dr. Gaddify went around to those students who needed extra coaxing. The whole room echoed with quiet. There were only little shuffling noises and the drone of Dr. Gaddify's voice.

Dr. Gaddify came to the front of the room again. "Sit down," he called, and Lydia was glad to do so. Her limbs were itchy with the need to fidget, but she didn't want to move more than the students around her. Seats creaked everywhere as the students all sat. "Close your eyes and wait until I come get you," said Dr. Gaddify.

Lydia closed her eyes reluctantly. Having to imagine what was happening around her multiplied the fear. She heard a door open and then footsteps on the stage.

"We're ready for you," said Dr. Gaddify quietly.

Lydia heard some papers rustling, and then the footsteps retreated. Dr. Gaddify read off nine names and said, "Open your eyes, stand up, and follow me. The rest of you wait here."

Lydia's heartbeat accelerated as she heard people around her getting to their feet and walking up the steps to the stage. Was it safe to take a peek? Lydia slowly lifted her chin and then let her eyelids drift open a fraction so that she could see a flickering, shadowy version of the stage through her eyelashes. Four of her classmates were shuffling steadily forward out of sight behind the curtain. Cautiously, Lydia tried to turn her head to see if the person Dr. Gaddify had spoken to was still there. There were only students. Eventually the room became quiet again, and Lydia could hear footsteps fading upward. Upward? Were there stairs backstage?

Lydia sat with her eyes closed and her heart pounding. She tried so hard to listen that her ears actually wiggled on the sides of her head. All she could hear was the steady breathing of Naomi and Pilar on either side of her. Lydia opened her eyes and looked up cautiously. Around her, the remaining seventeen students sat as if frozen there or paused in a movie. All of the faces Lydia could see were as still and blank as masks.

Lydia touched Naomi's arm and gave her a gentle poke. Naomi swayed away from the poke but otherwise didn't move. Lydia snapped next to Naomi's ear. Her cheek twitched, but she betrayed no emotion or sensation. Lydia looked around the auditorium for a clue to what was happening, but there was none to be found. Panic buzzed in her ears with increasing volume.

Lydia stood. No one was here to stop her from walking out the door. She'd say she went to the bathroom and got lost. But what about Pilar and Naomi and the rest of them? She jiggled Naomi's shoulder. No response. Lydia decided to go for help. Surely, someone else would also think it was strange that Dr. Gaddify had drugged all the new students. Mr. Harcourt would help, or the captain of the ferry maybe.

Adrenaline surged as Lydia decided on a plan. Now that she was moving, it seemed urgent. *Get out! Get out! Get out!* She was lifting her backpack, about to clamber into the aisle when she was swept by a wave of sheer terror. The emotion was so strong that it felt physical, as if she'd just been drenched in icy water. It liquefied Lydia's joints and made her drop back into her seat. Cold sweat broke out all over Lydia's neck and forehead. Her heart stuttered and caught like a drunken moth. Lydia saw her classmates sway back in their chairs and wobble, then bob back forward like saplings in a gale.

Now Lydia's brain was filled with white static. She clawed her way to her feet to flee, but she was clumsy with terror. She tripped over Pilar, which was like stumbling over a corpse, since Pilar didn't move or react to Lydia's full weight on her legs other than to start to tip slowly forward and to one side. Horrified, Lydia propped her friend back up in the seat.

"Pilar," she whispered. "Wake up! Naomi!" Lydia pinched Pilar's arm. "Come on!"

The sound of footsteps walking down a staircase made Lydia jerk around to face the stage. She was too far from the auditorium doors to escape before Dr. Gaddify came out. Lydia made a split-second decision. She dropped back into the seat on Pilar's other side and shut her eyes, willing her breath to slow. All of her anxiety and suspicion flooded her lungs and made it hard to breathe, but one thought floated like a life raft.

Matthew.

Whatever had happened to Matthew, Lydia had to know. She would fake being hypnotized and just follow along. If this was the big secret, then Lydia would be able to find out.

Dr. Gaddify sounded slightly out of breath. He read out another list of names.

"Naomi Arnold, Lydia Boswell, Ben Loi . . ."

Lydia opened her eyes and swallowed her fear. She stood and followed Ben up the stairs and behind the curtain of the stage. Dr. Gaddify dropped a brown sack over Ben's head and then guided him through a small door to a stairway going up. After placing Ben's hand on the railing, he intoned something in his ear. Lydia kept her eyes blank and staring as Dr. Gaddify turned and dropped a brown sack over Lydia's head. She swayed with momentary terror, and Dr. Gaddify caught her shoulders, then gently guided her forward.

"Go up the stairs and wait," he said in a low voice in her ear. Lydia was strangely reassured. He sounded excited and confident.

Lydia could see out of the bottom of the sack, and so she didn't trip when she got to the stairs. She heard Naomi's steady footsteps behind her. The stairs curved in a tight spiral up and up and up, and then Lydia sensed that she was in an open room with daylight coming in. She stepped to the side next to Ben and tilted her head to see what she could of the floor. It was a pale wood floor with dark reddish-black patterns drawn on the surface. The patterns might not have been patterns at all, but maybe symbols that looked religious or something. Lydia sensed space at her side as Ben was led away. After thirty seconds a pair of gentle hands took Lydia's elbow and led her forward into the room. More symbols flashed by the gap at the bottom of Lydia's hood, candles too, with wax spattered on the floor, and then Lydia passed a pair of feet she recognized as Ben's. He was lying faceup inside a pattern of symbols. Lydia was led to a corner next to Ben and then helped to lie down on her back. The gentle and efficient hands pulled Lydia's arms out to forty-five-degree angles and then positioned her legs in a slight V shape. The hands came back to Lydia's wrist and probed along the inside. Lydia realized that whoever it was was taking her pulse.

"Hmm." It was a female "hmm," and it sounded as if Lydia's pulse was not optimal. A pair of legs in white pants and white moccasins stepped over Lydia's body and walked away. Lydia willed her pulse to slow. She tried holding her breath, but that only made her heart pound harder. The legs came back, and then Lydia felt the hands pushing up her sleeve, a sharp jab, pressure, and then a tissue held briefly against the meat of Lydia's shoulder. She'd been given a shot.

Matthew or no, this was too much. She tried to sit up, but the hands held her firmly and expertly.

"Shhh, shhh, shhh," said the woman's voice. "Lie still." The words were pitched high, like to a baby, and the meaning seemed to take a long time to distill from the words. *Lie still*, Lydia thought groggily. She was lying still. But she should be paying attention. Where was everybody?

** *I am here.* **

Lydia relaxed. Matthew was here.

Chapter II

Lydia was seated in the front row of the auditorium, which was strange, because she had been in the second row next to Pilar and Naomi. Why the front row? Was she in trouble because she'd thrown away her truffle? She opened her eyes wider and looked up. There was Dr. Gaddify, smiling, kneeling in front of her with her hands clasped in his. She made an effort to pull her hands away from his thin, dry ones, but he held her firmly.

"Nancy, wake, are you there?"

Was her name Nancy? Dr. Gaddify seemed to think so, so she nodded. She just wanted him to go away. "Good." Lydia's eyelids dropped closed again and she felt Dr. Gaddify move away.

Lydia's skull seemed to be a washing machine, and her brain, tiny gray lump that it was, was sloshing around inside. *Nancy, wake. ** I am here. ** Orientation.*

Orientation. Her mind seized on the word, grasping it like a buoy in a storm. *We're here being oriented. Strange word. "Set in the right direction," but why the Orient? What came first, the East or the Orient?* And then her mind was off again, tumbling about. She let it tumble. Looked in wonder at her hands. Thought of spitting out the truffle. Giggled.

Ben was next to her now, and Naomi was on the other side. Dr. Gaddify was kneeling in front of Ben. "John Templeton, are you there?" Dr. Gaddify's voice was warped and distant. It was comfortable to be here in this seat surrounded by her new friends, but something was itching on her upper arm. *Ouch.* It was sore. The itch seemed to travel to her brain. She had forgotten something. Homework? No. A truffle. It wasn't funny. She'd been afraid, but—

"Everybody, please look up at me." Dr. Gaddify was back up on the stage. Lydia moved her head to look at him with an effort. She did her best to listen as he said a lot of stuff about memories, but it was too hard to concentrate. Her mind drifted again.

Suddenly Dr. Gaddify clapped twice. Evidentially, the long lecture was over. Lydia concentrated with all her effort.

"You are all extremely tired. You will go back to the dorm and take a nap. When you wake, you will remember the lecture I have given you about realizing your potential. You will remember the exercises we did to build the connections between the synapses of your brain. If your friends seem different to you, *do not be alarmed.* If you seem different to yourself, do not be alarmed. You will remember nothing else from today. Now go."

Lydia stood and wobbled, but standing seemed to help her brain settle more firmly into place. What a strange thing for Dr. G. to say. She didn't trust him. What was it about spiraling stairs that she couldn't remember? What brain exercises? What lecture? On one count he was exactly right; Lydia was extremely tired. Perhaps she would remember more after her nap.

Chapter 12

Lydia woke up with the feeling that the washing machine in her skull had been replaced by ball bearings. Her brain now slid from side to side whenever she moved her head. She sat up and waited for her mind to settle.

She'd been drugged.

She rubbed her arm and inspected the tiny pinprick in the center of a sore spot. Instead of being angry, she felt grateful for the proof of what she remembered, because the rest of it was so strange. Had she been hypnotized? The fact that she could remember Dr. Gaddify telling them *not* to remember suggested that she hadn't been. She remembered the wave of terror and Ben lying faceup on the floor. What about her classmates? Were they okay?

She hurried down the hall of the dorm, steadying herself against the wall a few times, and then walked carefully down the stairs. She heard a thunderclap of laughter coming from the common room, followed by a gale of giggles.

Cora was sitting on the low coffee table in the center of the room holding up an 8 x 10 photo of herself. It was one of the ones she'd taken on the ferry, and her expression was pensive and pouty.

"This one is called *Shh, I Think I Hear My Other Brain Cell*," said Cora, her eyes dancing with humor. Another thunderclap of laughter from her audience. "Ooh look, *My Farts Smell Like Roses*!" She held up a photo of herself that was a profile with her eyes half closed and her nose in the air. It looked like it belonged in a perfume ad, but when Cora gave it a title like that . . .

Lydia's mouth quirked up into an uncertain grin.

"Oh! Lydia! Thank goodness you're awake! We're starved! Do you want to see if they'll let us have a roll or a bun or a bowlful of gruel?" Cora seemed delighted to see Lydia, and Lydia couldn't help it; she was delighted to see Cora, too. How could she not be? Cora was like a beam of caramel-colored sunshine, her eyes sparkled with warmth and humor, and when she looked at Lydia, Lydia felt like they'd just shared a private joke.

"Come on, Naomi, old bean, help me up!"

Lydia hadn't recognized Naomi from behind because she was sitting with ramrod-straight posture. Her hair was pulled back, exposing a long and elegant neck that seemed naked without Naomi's shoulders on either side.

Is this what Dr. G. meant about not being alarmed at changes in our classmates? Lydia wasn't alarmed; she was charmed. *Who knew that Cora had such a wonderful sense of humor? How poised Naomi looked.*

The crowd of girls eddied around Cora as they made their way out to the front steps and across the lawn to the main building. Laughing and giddy, Pilar attempted a cartwheel. The girl named Sophia walked on her hands for a few yards. Naomi did a clumsy somersault. Cora grinned at Lydia and said, "Hold my sweater," then did a long gymnastics pass right up to the steps of the main building. Everybody whistled and clapped.

"God, don't you just feel so alive?" Cora beamed around her. "I didn't even remember I could do that!"

"How could you forget something like that?" asked Lydia, half teasing.

"I know what you mean," said Pilar. "Orientation did something to me. I'm, like, watching my own memories."

"Yes!" gushed Sophia. "That's exactly it!"

Lydia looked at her classmates, trying to stop her bewilderment from showing on her face. They seemed so happy. Lydia felt bedraggled and slow next to them. Not remembering you could do a handspring seemed ominous, but all of the other changes she noted in her classmates were definitely positive. What did they mean about watching their own memories? Lydia searched her mind for a memory, but it was still reeling.

Inside the door of the cafeteria, Mr. Harcourt and another teacher, Dr. Weatherby, were sitting at a table with boxes and lists. They called each girl over and gave her a bracelet with at least one key attached to it. The bracelets were actually kind of cool: wide, colorful embroidered bands with soft leather on the inside, against the wrist. The keys were small enough that they were almost like charms dangling off the bracelet.

"Wear these every second, okay, ladies?" said Mr. Harcourt, handing a bracelet to Naomi. "These are the keys to your dorm rooms and your studios or labs, whatever you might need."

Dr. Weatherby smoothed his shirt over his paunch. "Since you young people keep odd hours, the keys should prevent you from rousting your poor professors out of bed at two o'clock in the morning when inspiration strikes."

"A studio key?" gasped Naomi. "What studio? *My* studio?"

"Should be a room number on your key," said Dr. Weatherby. "If it is a studio, it will be in the art building."

Naomi stared at him, awestruck. She turned for the door, changed her mind, went to the bread table and stuffed her pockets with rolls, then sprinted out the door. At least Naomi was acting the way Lydia thought she should. Except for the posture.

Lydia was surprised to see Gus and Seth sitting together, involved in a debate.

"No, no, no." Seth was frowning. He had deep-set blue eyes and when he frowned they almost disappeared into the dark crescents of his eyelashes. "A person with extraordinary gifts has no business presenting himself as cannon fodder. It would be a waste of talent."

"I'm telling you, the people in charge shouldn't ask the men beneath them to do anything they are not willing to do themselves." Gus had an earnest look on his face, his square chin set and stubborn.

"Lydia!" Seth motioned Lydia to sit down next to him.

She paused a moment. So, suddenly he remembered her name again?

"Lydia, help me talk some sense into this boob."

"A *boob*? You're calling Gus a *boob*?" Lydia laughed and gave in. "What?"

"Say you're in charge of an army," said Seth. He flapped his eyelashes, trying to ingratiate himself.

"Okay," said Lydia, rolling her eyes.

"Now, you are already at war, so there is an urgent need to place your soldiers where they will be most effective. *I say*, test the new recruits and advance the intelligent ones immediately. Don't waste the brainpower scrubbing toilets!"

"And *I say* that the truly talented will show themselves after an initial training," said Gus. "Just because a person is smart doesn't mean that he will make a good commander."

"Did I hear the words 'scrubbing toilets'? This should be good." Cora sat down and smiled around at everyone at the table.

The debate raged all through dinner. Lydia noticed that Seth seemed like he was winning because he was a better speaker and he seemed absolutely certain that he was right. Whenever he spoke, he addressed each person at the table, leveling a twinkle-eyed gaze at them all one by one. But she was secretly rooting for Gus because he presented a convincing moral argument that made his basset hound brown eyes nearly swim with heartfelt passion. Cora was the moderator and inserted a joke whenever the debate got too heated.

"Gentlemen, gentlemen," said Cora. She got instant silence by holding up one elegant finger. "What does Lydia have to say?" She nodded graciously at Lydia, and Lydia felt herself warm to Cora's attention.

"It seems to me that a compromise is in order," said Lydia. "Let everybody start training together, but accelerate the training of those who show promise. A leader will not know exactly what his or her troops are capable of if he hasn't done it himself. Plus, a lot of smart people aren't that good at tests, so you could miss a lot of potential that way."

Seth and Cora clapped. Gus nodded, seeming embarrassed that he hadn't thought of it himself.

Lydia noticed that Pilar was particularly quiet during dinner. When Pilar got up to give her tray to the dishwasher, Lydia followed her.

"Are you okay, Pilar?" asked Lydia.

"Yeah. I just . . ." Pilar looked pained. "I just figured out that my dad cheated on my mom." She swiped her hair out of her face and stared at the ceiling. "I've had all the clues, all the memories, but I just put it all together, just now. I've been so mad at my mom since they divorced, but . . . I . . . ."

Lydia patted Pilar's arm awkwardly. "Sorry, Pilar. That—that sucks."

"Yeah." Pilar huffed out a sigh. "I'm going to write my mom a letter."

Back at the table everybody was examining their bracelets.

"My key says 'AUD,'" said Cora.

"Auditorium, probably," Seth informed her.

Cora shrugged.

"Hey, can we go there?" asked Lydia. "I lost something today and it might be in there." She wanted to see about the stairs backstage. Maybe if she could get to that room with the symbols on the floor, she'd understand more about what had happened.

Cora tilted her head and smiled at Lydia. "Why not? Maybe there will be a clue as to why I have a key."

Cora took Lydia's elbow as they walked down the hall together, and Lydia couldn't say that it was uncomfortable. She had heard about charisma, the force of personality that made everybody like and trust a person, but she'd never before experienced it as strongly as with Cora. She glanced at Cora's profile. God, she was beautiful, but it didn't make Lydia feel jealous anymore, it just seemed right.

The auditorium was empty and dark. Just the smell of it made Lydia's heart accelerate. She had to force herself to follow Cora inside. Cora found a light switch, and the house lights came up.

"Okay, I'm just going to check backstage," said Lydia.

She hurried nervously past the spot where she'd tossed the truffle. She imagined she could smell it, sweet and a little rotten.

As she passed the front row of seats, a ripple of the terror she'd felt that morning splashed around her ankles. Cautiously now, she mounted the stage and stepped around the curtain to where the door had been.

There was nothing there but a wall, painted black and crisscrossed with old electrical tape. The facing wall had some ropes and pulleys for the curtains, but the only door backstage led downstairs, and that couldn't be right. Lydia crossed the stage and checked the other side.

Nothing.

"What are you looking for?" called Cora.

"Uh, my notebook," Lydia lied, with her back to Cora.

"Find it?"

"Nope. But thanks for letting me check."

Back in her room, Lydia pulled out the notebook she had never lost and wrote down everything she remembered. The school song, twice, the hypnotism, that wave of terror. Were the spiral stairs real? What about the room with the symbols? She wrote down *Nancy* and wished she could remember the name that Dr. Gaddify had used in front of Ben. Everything that came after the shot was either missing or fuzzy. She was pretty sure he had used a full name, not just a first name, which was frustrating. No use in trying to guess which Nancy he was talking about. The sun went down and Lydia flipped on her desk lamp, still thinking.

She studied her bracelet. It made her uneasy for some reason, as if it were a snake coiled around her wrist rather than some leather and thread. She worked it over her hand and stuffed it in a drawer. She'd find out what the label on her key, LANG, meant in the morning.

She lay in bed, looking out the window and trying to order her thoughts. There was another thing too. Why had testing taken only two days this year but two weeks last year?

There was a branch from a maple tree outside her window outlined in copper from the porch light below. She could see stars from where she lay. This far out in the ocean, away from the ambient lights of a town, there were so many stars that it seemed like she was on a different planet.

No moon tonight, thought Lydia, and then she remembered. Tonight was a new moon.

Chapter 13

Do I feel like committing suicide?
No.

It was morning time again.

Lydia sat up in bed and looked around her room. The small painting that Naomi had given her was propped on top of her dresser. Her notebook was on the wooden desk at the window. Alone in her room, Lydia could admit that her feelings about orientation were decidedly mixed. She was fairly certain that whatever Dr. Gaddify had intended to do hadn't worked on her. She hadn't been hypnotized. She remembered. The confusing part was how she felt about it. Her classmates seemed illuminated by orientation, buoyant and elated, but her gut told her that something about it was wrong. Was she glad she hadn't been hypnotized? Yes. Was she glad she wasn't a genius? Not really. At least, she didn't think she was a genius. Now she had to keep anyone else from realizing that she wasn't.

At Claybourne each student had Regulars in the morning and Specials in the afternoon. You might have lab time or studio time, but Specials meant working with your declared major. Regulars were the basic subjects: math, history, English, and science. The students attended classes with their grade regardless of their talent. This meant that Lydia was in a math class with Seth, Jay, Sorcha, Marin, and Kit, and some others who were all sophomores. Algebra II was taught by Mr. Veblen and four students who were far beyond any sort of math that Lydia had ever heard of. Lydia was paired up with Kit, the freckled boy with long bangs that Seth had introduced to her as "physics."

Mr. Veblen handed out a work sheet with problems on it. Kit held it at arm's length for a few seconds, slapped it on his desk, and scribbled for about a minute, then handed his in. He turned to face Lydia, squinting at her as if she were a problem set of imaginary numbers.

Kit had long, dark bangs that flopped over his right eye and made him tilt his head severely to the right, peering up from behind them.

"You know how to do linear equations?"

"Nope." Lydia felt a little defiant, so she stared at Kit while he grimaced at her.

"Okay. Well, I can teach you."

"Okay."

In the next forty-five minutes Lydia learned how to not be insulted by Kit's teaching method. She also learned how to do every problem on the work sheet. She supposed she'd get used to the feeling that Kit was trying to put the understanding of variables and axes directly into her brain by staring at the side of her face while she worked out a problem. She was satisfied at the end of class not to be the last non–math kid to finish, and also to realize that in forty-five minutes she'd learned as much as she would have in a week at her old high school.

Seth had not fared as well. He was paired up with a tiny girl who had the blackest skin Lydia had ever seen. She kept pointing to the page and saying, "No, no, no! Don't you see?"

Obviously Seth didn't see, so eventually Sorcha took pity on him and explained. Seth sighed when the bell rang.

"I guess I'll finish this tonight," he said, stuffing the paper in his bag. "Homework already."

The next class was English with Ms. Windham, whose whole purpose in life seemed to be to flog a piece of writing until she had wrung every last bit of meaning from it. She reminded Lydia of a Mafia henchman trying to find out who'd betrayed the boss by ripping off the poem's toenails.

Biology was similar to math because certain students did most of the teaching. Then, Dr. Weatherby taught history by handing out textbooks and telling the students to read the first three chapters. Lydia took notes until she realized that she was the only one doing so. She closed her notebook guiltily and tried to read as fast as Marin, who may have been only looking at the pictures, she flipped the pages so fast.

The lunch bell brought Lydia as much relief as if it had signaled the end of a boxing match rather than just the first morning of classes. She stumbled down the hall feeling like she'd been pummeled, knowing only that she wanted food.

Seth, who hadn't been in Lydia's history class, was standing like a jetty against the tide of students streaming into the dining hall.

"Lydia!"

"Can't talk. Must eat," said Lydia.

Seth held up a stack of sandwiches. "I've got apples and cookies in my bag. I want to show you something."

Lydia eyed him suspiciously, then dropped her backpack in a pile outside the dining hall and snatched a sandwich off the top of the stack. She liked Seth in spite of his inconsistent friendliness. She wanted to trust him.

"Good girl," said Seth, as if he were talking to a spooked horse.

Lydia used her free hand to punch him.

"Hey! Sandwiches!"

Seth led Lydia down the front steps of the main building, across the lawn, and along the path past the boys' dorms into a pine woods. Lydia stuffed the last bite of peanut butter and jelly into her mouth and said: "If 'ish 'om ina 'abing?"

"What?"

Lydia swallowed and pounded her chest, grabbing another sandwich. "Is this some kind of hazing thing? You take me down here and push me off a cliff or something?"

"You ask that? Even as you're stuffing down another one of my delicious sandwiches?" Seth put on a wounded face but didn't bother to dim the twinkle in his eyes.

Lydia pointed a crust at Seth. "I know that there is a stack of these sandwiches sitting on a table in the dining hall. Don't pretend you made them."

"Ah, but I chose them for their perfect ratio of peanut butter to jelly and the fact that not one has a jelly leak. No one else has such discerning taste in PB and J."

Lydia smirked. "All right, so where are we going?"

"You'll see."

Their footfalls were almost completely muffled by a thick layer of pine needles over a sliding layer of sand. The path headed steadily down, and then suddenly they were standing on an enormous expanse of gray granite.

There was the ocean. The bright, briny gust of wind and the huge, sparkling plain of water still stunned Lydia every time she encountered them. She shaded her eyes with her hand and scanned the view.

"Nice, huh?" Seth nudged Lydia with his shoulder.

She didn't say anything; she just let the sun warm her face and the wind cool her skin. Neither element was winning and she was just the right temperature.

Seth walked up to the edge of the rock and peered down, then backed up a bit and sat.

"Come on," he said, patting the rock next to him.

Lydia walked over to the edge and looked down. They were about twenty feet above the water in a rocky little cove.

"High tide?" asked Lydia, noticing a line of barnacles that appeared in between waves.

Seth nodded, his mouth full.

"Does anyone swim here?"

"Nah. For one, it's freezing, but also this is the wavy side of the island. That's east, so there's a pretty good current. People who want to swim go on the side that faces the mainland." Seth chewed. "On a windy day you can get soaking wet just sitting where we are. Sometimes the wind comes all the way across the Atlantic with nothing to stop it."

Lydia stepped back and sat on the gritty rock next to Seth.

"Thanks for bringing me here," she said. "This is cool."

"I think I owe you some sort of apology," said Seth. "I abandoned you on the ferry, and I should have said something when Marin—"

"Don't worry about that," said Lydia. She thought a second. "But why didn't you say anything to me when you were coming out of Dr. Gaddify's office?"

Seth frowned and looked puzzled.

"I was right there, and you walked by me as if you didn't even see me."

Seth shook his head. "I'm sorry. Sorry if I did that, but I honestly don't remember."

"Don't you think it's weird, all the stuff people don't remember here?" Lydia blurted out.

Seth looked at her, surprised. "Like what?"

"I don't know." Lydia looked out to sea. "Do you remember how Cora was taking all those pictures of herself on the ferry? How totally vain she was before orientation?"

Seth shrugged. "Yeah, I remember."

"You don't think it's weird that after orientation she is suddenly sooo cool? She's amazingly funny and kind—"

"I guess I can see that there is a difference, but it's not alarming."

"Not alarming!" Lydia broke off. She wasn't sure if she should tell Seth about the hypnotizing. "Well, there's Naomi, too. She used to walk like a buzzard, and now she's got great posture."

"But that's not a bad thing."

"No? What about you? How did you change after your orientation?"

Seth squinted at her. For the first time he seemed to be serious. His eyelashes were extraordinarily long, and Lydia felt the absurd urge to put mascara on them.

Seth turned, and Lydia saw his jaw jut.

"I started to paint a little," he said musingly. "Nothing amazing, but I'd never done that before. I guess . . . ." Seth frowned at the sea. "I guess I remember feeling like somebody had taken everything in my head and reorganized it. My grandmother used to watch this home improvement show where they go to a really, really messy house, or maybe just a messy room, and the people come and reorganize everything. You know, put it away so there's a spot for everything and throw out the garbage and just make it so you can see where everything goes. That's what it was like in my head. After that, everything seemed obvious. Patterns, connections, logic; it all was right there. It was like it had always been there, but just not in the right spot." Seth paused, chewing. "Before I came here . . . I was . . . sad. I guess. Well, depressed, honestly. I had medication. Now I'm not." Seth nodded and then looked at Lydia again.

"So what's your specialty, then?" asked Lydia.

"Strategy."

"Like what?"

"I got you to come have lunch with me, didn't I?"

Lydia grinned. "Yeah, but I'd do anything for a peanut butter and jelly sandwich."

"Duly noted," said Seth, tapping the side of his head. "Now come on, you've got your first Special."

Lydia was not particularly thrilled to see that Mr. Harcourt was the teacher scribbling on the whiteboard when she walked into a classroom on the second floor for her first afternoon of Specials. Nor was she feeling very optimistic about a lecture that included the word "phonemes." So she was very relieved indeed to see Gus sitting in one of three chairs at a small table.

"Ah, Lydia," said Mr. Harcourt. "We're ready to begin, then."

Lydia sat nervously on the edge of her wooden chair. "Just us?" she asked.

"Yes." Mr. Harcourt checked his paper. "Lydia Boswell and Angus McCracken?"

"Gus," said Gus, scrubbing at one of his ears, which had suddenly gone red.

"Okay, Gus, Lydia, you two are here to learn as many languages as I can cram into your heads. So we will begin by exposing you to nearly all the phonemes in spoken language, excepting some of the clicking languages and of course the more unusual diphthongs. . . ."

Gus was squinting at Mr. Harcourt as if he had already begun speaking another language. Lydia found this immensely comforting.

After two hours of listening to the difference between the *k* in "kit" and the *k* in "skill" (the *k* in "kit" had a small breath called an aspiration), Lydia felt as if her head had been stuffed with soft wool. She at least was able to reproduce almost all of the phonemes they had heard to Mr. Harcourt's standards. Gus, however, couldn't make the trill at the back of his throat for a French *r* sound without sounding as if her were trying to expel a hair ball.

"Well, this is a good start," said Mr. Harcourt. "I can't tell you how excited I am to put my theories into practice. I believe that when we have finished here, you will be able to pick up most languages in a matter of months. You are still young enough that we can train your ear and shape your palate to almost every sound. You'll sound like native speakers in any language you choose!"

"So this is what we are? We've declared for language?" asked Lydia. She could not keep the dread entirely out of her voice.

Mr. Harcourt frowned. "Well, not just languages. I believe you both have a special reading list: strategy, negotiation, military history, and analytics." Mr. Harcourt stopped reading from his list and looked up. "I'd say you're being groomed as international business strategists or diplomats." He frowned again. "Or spies." Mr. Harcourt stacked his papers into a neat pile. "Now, I understand that you both have some background in French? Tonight's assignment it to spend an hour in the language lab. It's on the third floor, room three twenty, and you should

99

have a key. I'd like you to complete the first two lessons for Beginning French. I expect that you will not find it to be difficult. If you struggle, please let me know. Dr. Gaddify says he can reorient you if necessary. Oh, and here are these." Mr. Harcourt pulled two thick packets of paper out of his pile. "These are the orientation exercises. You should keep these in your room and do them at your leisure. The exercises are designed to improve your cognitive abilities."

Something about the way Mr. Harcourt handed her the packet made Lydia study his expression carefully. His bottom lip was nearly twice as thick as his top lip, which normally gave him a pouty expression, but now he looked decidedly resentful.

"Is it part of the Claybourne Method?" asked Lydia, trying to tease out where the resentment was coming from.

"So we are told," said Mr. Harcourt shortly. He stood and ushered them out of the room, but Lydia wasn't done yet.

"Does it work on adults?" she asked.

"I wouldn't know," replied Mr. Harcourt, holding the door open as stiffly as an English butler.

Lydia couldn't help but think he was lying. Maybe it worked on adults, but it certainly hadn't worked for him.

Chapter 14

Gus waited for Lydia at the end of the hall. "You want to go to the language lab?" Gus was taller than Lydia, and his earnest brown eyes gave him a slightly forlorn appeal. Lydia stopped to tie back her hair, and Gus picked up her backpack in a gentlemanly way that seemed so habitual that Lydia couldn't take offense even though both Emily and Abilene had drilled her in proper feminist behavior.

"I do want to go to the language lab, but not right now," said Lydia. "My brain is about to pop and it looks like a beautiful day outside. You want to meet there after dinner?"

Gus had a sweet dimple in his cheek when he smiled. "Sure. I want to see what I can find out about our reading list too. Do you want to hit the library afterward?"

"Okay," said Lydia. She thought of the other names on her list. "I've got some stuff I want to look up too."

Gus and Lydia walked in comfortable silence past a classroom where three students were studying a projected image of a building. Another classroom had a strange assortment of furniture and four students writing furiously under the gimlet eye of Ms. Windham. They went downstairs and out onto the main lawn into a splendid, breezy afternoon.

"Hey, Gus," said Lydia, looking over at the boys dorm. "Was somebody in your dorm really sick the other night? I saw Nurse Proctor coming out of the dorm at, like, three in the morning."

Gus frowned. "You know, I wonder . . . I wonder if she was trying to help the kid who was crying. Somebody on the first floor was just *wailing*. I didn't ask why."

"Poor kid," said Lydia.

Gus nodded, then handed Lydia her backpack and gave her a sweet little bow before heading off toward his dorm at a gentle lope.

Lydia allowed herself a moment to shake off the stress of the day, turning her face up to the blue sky and watching some fasting-moving clouds tumble by.

Back at the dorm Lydia found Cora sitting on a porch swing with one leg tucked beneath her and the other kicking off the porch railing, setting the swing into a jerky motion.

"Hey, Cora," said Lydia cautiously. Cora's face looked more like that of the self-centered girl from the boat than the girl who'd artfully steered an entire conversation last night.

Cora gave Lydia a small smile and patted the swing. "Come cheer me up," she said.

Lydia dropped her backpack and climbed onto the seat. "What's going on?"

"Just a bit glum, I guess," said Cora.

Lydia's throat closed with alarm. *Not suicidal already.* "How glum? Or I mean, glum how?" she babbled anxiously.

"Oh, it's not that bad." Cora patted Lydia's arm and laughed. "I am just a little disappointed. You see, I thought I was coming here to be a *genius*, and instead they tell me that I am to study *acting*."

"Acting?"

"I know," Cora moaned, and put her face in her hands. "It's *too* mortifying."

Lydia's relief that Cora didn't appear to be suicidal was blocking her ability to reassure her friend.

"You're horrified too!" said Cora. "I knew it!"

"No! No, no, no." Lydia laughed. "I'm not at all horrified. I guess I'm surprised too. I mean you're, like, beautiful, but I thought—"

"You thought we're here to *improve the world* not just"—Cora made a disgusted face—"act."

Lydia wished that she didn't have the woolly-brain feeling left over from phonemes, so that she could help Cora feel better, but Cora didn't seem bothered. She held up a script.

"I'm supposed to learn this. *Romeo and Julia.*"

"*Romeo and* Juliet?" Lydia frowned.

"Yes! See? I really am too stupid to be here."

"No! It's not you! It's just I don't really like that play. I think it's stupid that Romeo and Juliet are so young. Nobody should kill themselves when they're, like, fourteen."

"Well, it's punishment for the families, right?"

"Exactly." Lydia said it with vehemence, which sent Cora's eyebrows into her hair. "Besides, Cora, lots of actors are really smart. The girl who was Hermione went to an Ivy League school, I think."

"Yeah, but she played somebody really smart. I'm just supposed to be a simpering teenager in love."

"You don't have to play her that way. *Romeo and Juliet* is usually all dramatic, right?"

Cora waited with her eyebrows raised for Lydia to make her point.

"Well, make it funny. Use your brain"—Lydia tapped gently on Cora's forehead—"to make people see the play how you want them to see it. Make Juliet a rebel or a feminist or, I don't know." Lydia flopped her hands into her lap. "Make her you. We'll all love her."

Cora's eyes traced over Lydia's face. They were a darker green today with flecks of gold. Cora's loveliness made Lydia's heart ache. No wonder they wanted her on a stage.

"*Romeo and Julia*, the comedy, huh?"

"Sure," said Lydia. "Only, I am pretty sure you still have to call yourself Juliet."

"Dang! I am never going to get that right."

"Could be worse, though. Look at Pilar."

Pilar was walking across the lawn carrying an armload of long sticks, a notebook, and an assortment of other things. Her face and uniform were almost completely blackened by something that made her look like a coal miner from the nineteenth century.

"Pilar!" called Cora, standing up. "What in the world?"

Pilar grinned, her teeth white and comic against the smudges on her face. She strode quickly across the last yards of lawn and smiled up at them from the bottom of the porch steps.

"Did something explode?" asked Lydia.

"No, I made a fire." Pilar dropped her collection of sticks, which turned out to be propellers or wings of some kind. "We get to rediscover the principles of flight, so I was using smoke to see how air moves over a wing."

"That explains why you're covered in soot, but not why you're so happy about it," said Cora with a grin.

"I think I get it. Flight, I mean."

Cora gave Lydia an exasperated look laced with humor. Lydia threw up her hands. "Don't look at me! The only thing I did well today was roll my *r*'s." Lydia turned to Pilar. "Cora's upset because she doesn't feel genius enough. She's supposed to act out Shakespeare."

"Never mind," laughed Cora. "Pilar's making me feel quite content to *not* be a genius."

"Hey!" said Pilar. "Methinks I hear an insult from yon porch."

"'She speaks, yet she says nothing,'" said Cora, a single eyebrow raised like a bow.

"See?" laughed Lydia. "Now you can insult people in Shakespearean."

"I will become a genius of insults!" cried Cora. "Come on, let's help this poor peasant get cleaned up."

Chapter 15

The debate at dinner that night could have been called "Who Has the Worst Special?" Nobody felt sorry for Cora, especially when she told them that an indie film heartthrob was coming to perform the balcony scene with her in two weeks as part of a student showcase. Pilar offered a singed eyebrow as proof of hardship but confessed immediately to loving her Special. Naomi showed up only long enough to inhale a mound of mashed potatoes, stuff some cookies into her pockets, and race back to the studio. Finally, Lydia and Gus won by reciting the list of phonemes and diphthongs that Mr. Harcourt was making them practice. Lydia did a wicked impression of Mr. Harcourt describing his theory for learning languages, but sat down blushing when she saw Mr. Harcourt come in the door with Dr. Weatherby.

The language lab was about as much fun as Lydia had guessed it would be, which was not fun at all. She and Gus were not the only ones there. The girl with all the instruments on the ferry was muttering something Germanic under her breath, and two seniors wearing headphones spoke beautiful Italian sentences, one a couple of seconds behind the other.

Lydia was surprised to feel a slender blade of competition with Gus. She had told herself that she was at Claybourne not to be a genius, just to figure out what had happened to Matthew, but clearly some part of her was still trying. It made the time go quickly and put a little thrill into getting things right first. She definitely had a better ear than Gus did, but for the written parts he didn't even have to look up verb conjugations.

"How do you know this already?" asked Lydia, erasing yet another verb ending.

Gus just smiled at her. "You're much better at the listening than I am," he said with infuriating modesty. "Are you ready to go to the library?"

"Let's go. I can finish later."

"I don't mind waiting for you to finish."

"No, this is getting embarrassing."

Outside, Gus and Lydia savored the cool dusk air and stopped a minute to listen to piano music that was coming from one of the studio buildings. Whoever it was could play a complex series of notes faster than Lydia could wiggle her fingers randomly. He or she charged into the piece of music, then stopped for some reason Lydia couldn't detect, then started again with the same vigor. After listening to the same part three times, Lydia and Gus moved slowly on to the library.

The music reminded Lydia how very un-genius she was. Even though she'd made it through the first day without anyone finding out that orientation hadn't worked on her, she could all too easily imagine that another bout of testing would reveal her inadequacy, or that compared with Gus in language she would fall farther and farther behind. What would happen to her when they found out? Would she be expelled? Or worse?

Lydia slumped into the library and collapsed at a table. Gus went off to the card catalog, and when his back was turned, she let her forehead rest against the cool wood of the table. Lydia turned her head to the side and made her backpack into a pillow, but before she closed her eyes again, she caught sight of the shelf of encyclopedias.

Lydia sat up and looked around before cautiously pulling out her copy of the list of names she'd gotten from Dr. Gaddify.

Angus McCracken	Joshua Lawrence Chamberlain
Bethany Ming	Fanny Mendelssohn Hensel
Sophia Nowel	Norma Merrick Sklarek
Corbin Palisin	Linus Pauling
Benjamin Loi	John Templeton
Calliope Smith	Agnes Arber
Trenton Stuart	Edwin Land
Frances Trombly	Julia Child

Angus McCracken was standing a few yards away, peering into a long drawer of cards—she knew that now. So who was Joshua Chamberlain? She grabbed an encyclopedia and heaved it onto the table.

Joshua Lawrence Chamberlain was a college professor from Maine who'd volunteered to fight for the Union in the Civil War. From his picture Lydia could see that he was a handsome man, if you liked enormous mustaches. He believed strongly in the Union cause and rose through the ranks until he was a brigadier general. He earned a Medal of Honor for his role in the assault at Little Round Top, survived the rest of the war, and went on to become governor of Maine and president of Bowdoin College.

Lydia chewed on the end of her pencil and watched Gus scribble a number on a piece of paper and then wander off into the stacks. Did this Union soldier have anything to do with Gus?

The next name was Fanny Mendelssohn Hensel, sister to the famous classical composer and a composer in her own right. Her brother may have gotten credit for pieces she wrote.

Norma Sklarek, the first licensed African American female architect, was also the first African American woman to establish and manage an architectural firm.

Linus Pauling was a chemist and the only person ever to receive two unshared Nobel Prizes.

John Templeton started the Templeton Growth Fund and became a billionaire in the 1950s. He donated hundreds of thousands of dollars to research that supported the connection between science and Christianity.

Agnes Arber was a renowned British botanist.

Dr. Edwin Land had improved almost every aspect of photography with a series of inventions. The first he accomplished as a Harvard student.

Julia Child was indeed the famous television cook who'd brought French cooking to the Unites States after World War II.

In just twenty minutes Lydia had discovered everybody on the list. On the left were future geniuses, on the right were past geniuses, but how were they connected?

Chapter 16

Lydia had to admit that asking herself if she wanted to commit suicide every morning was not the best way to start the day. She also had to admit that the exercise was fairly pointless because she had no plan for what to do if one day the answer was yes. Presumably, if she felt like killing herself, she wasn't going to do anything to save herself.

Lydia pulled a box out from under her bed and began to paw through the contents. She hadn't yet found spots in her room for everything she'd brought, and the box held the sorts of things that weren't exactly useful, but that Lydia didn't want to be without. She took out a scented candle she wasn't allowed to light, a small green pin in the shape of a tortoise that had been her grandmother's, some embroidery thread she'd meant to turn into a bracelet, and a dried flower from her homecoming date last year. At the bottom of the box was a postcard from New Orleans. Matt and Abilene had gone down to see Abilene's family one summer, and Matt had bought the postcard. It had a picture of Madame Revenue's Voodoo Palace in the French Quarter. Matt had written on the back.

Matt's handwriting was childish and erratic, and there was
no postmark because he'd never mailed it, just handed it to her
sheepishly when they got home.

Lydia sniffed it, imagining she could smell the stink of a
city that was filthy and spooky and mystical, hoping there was
still some trace of Matt there that she could absorb. She taped the
postcard to the wall next to Naomi's painting on the dresser.
Maybe she couldn't stop herself from committing suicide, but
she could remind herself of a good reason not to.

At breakfast there was a scrum of students clustered
around the bulletin board at the front of the dining hall. Lydia
took advantage of the short line and got some scrambled eggs
and bacon, then toasted a bagel in peace. She was just
assembling her breakfast sandwich when Seth slid into the seat
next to her and took one of her slices of bacon.

"Hey!"

Seth smiled wickedly at her, but there was tension in his
eyes.

"Thanks!" he said loudly, and then he leaned forward to
stand. As he got to his feet, his mouth passed Lydia's ear.
"Pretend total indifference to the war," he whispered, and then
he went away, humming, to join the line. Lydia was still sitting
there with the ketchup poised over her bagel when Gus sat down
next to her.

"What did Seth want?" Gus was looking around the room as he asked, as if expecting an imminent attack. Lydia took advantage of his inattention to school her expression out of the puzzlement Seth had left there. "He stole a piece of my bacon."

Gus leaned forward to grab a piece himself.

"No way, Jose!" said Lydia.

"Come on, language buddy," said Gus. He leaned in and whispered, "I know he's recruiting you." Then he left too.

"What the heck is going on?" asked Lydia when Cora and Pilar sat down.

"Bourne War!" said Cora. Her eyes twinkled and she scooted forward in her chair with a little shimmy.

"Bourne War?"

"It's like capture the flag—" said Pilar.

"But better," said Cora. "Charlie Rhinebeck was telling me about it."

"Oooooh, Chaaaarlieee," Pilar teased.

Cora gave Pilar a withering look. "Each class gets a flag and there's a general and they have twelve hours to hide the flag and then you have to find the other flags and there's assassins—"

"And spies." Gus was back with Ben. "Don't forget, Lydia is a sophomore, ladies."

"What are you talking about?" squawked Lydia. "Could somebody please explain—"

"General McCracken here knows your wily ways," scolded Ben, shaking his finger at Lydia. "Now shoo!"

"I was here first," said Lydia. "You go somewhere else." Lydia was about to beg somebody to explain when she remembered Seth's whispered instructions. *Pretend total indifference to the war.* "Go! Do war stuff somewhere else. Git!"

Gus and Ben narrowed their eyes at Lydia and took their bagels to the next table over.

"Tell us more about *Charlie*," said Lydia to Cora.

Cora intentionally misunderstood Lydia's prompt. "Well, he said that Dr. Gaddify assigns a general for each class. We've got Gus, and you've got Seth. The juniors have Ellie Martin. That's her with the pixie cut." Cora indicated a small, dark-haired girl who was kneeling on a chair surrounded by excited juniors. "I think the senior general is Thomas Wain. That must be him." A very tall black boy stood like a tree trunk rooted among a herd of smaller excited students. He was frowning in a way that suggested he rarely smiled, tilting his head to a girl who cupped his ear and whispered something. He smiled then, but it was a smile of triumph, not merriment.

Lydia shrugged. She was torn between following Seth's mysterious instructions and learning all she could about Bourne War. Luckily, Naomi plopped down next to her at that moment.

"What's going on?" she asked. Naomi had multicolored crescents of paint under her fingernails and a big daub of aquamarine on her forehead.

Cora started with the basics again and then went on. Lydia got her notebook and pretended to finish up her French verbs.

"So they hide the flag, but it has to be visible for at least five feet in two directions. Up and down count."

"So you can't just bury it or something?" asked Pilar.

"Right, and it's got to visible for five feet at all times, not just low tide or something like that. There are about a million rules."

"What did you say about assassins?"

"Well, that's the other part. We all get these little Velcro dots, and if you put your dot on someone, then they're dead."

"So someone can just dot me anytime?" asked Pilar, alarmed. She looked around for an approaching murderer.

"No, you have to be alone. If you're with another freshman, you're safe."

"A sophomore doesn't count?" asked Pilar, looking at Lydia.

"Nope," said Cora.

Naomi raised an eyebrow. "I'll be dead in no time. I'm always alone in my studio."

Cora frowned. "Yeah, I think that the main building is a safety zone, but studios and labs, I don't know. You want me to come with you?"

Naomi grinned. "It's all right. I'm too busy for this stuff."

"Me too," said Lydia. "Good luck, everybody."

During Regulars, Lydia maintained her stoic indifference to Bourne War with great difficulty. In spite of having to bite her tongue on a hundred questions, she learned that the first task was for each class to develop a code and then use that code to publicly announce meetings on the bulletin board in the dining hall. The cipher for the code was distributed secretly by the general, but if a person was "killed" carrying the code cipher, then he or she was honor-bound to hand it over to the assassin. If the code was cracked by another class and three members showed up to the meeting spot before the meeting began, then the class that had called the meeting had to sacrifice a secret. Secrets had to do with the location of the flag.

Lydia guessed that Seth had assigned code making and breaking to Kit and Malia, the tiny black girl who'd been unable to teach him math. Sorcha spent a good part of math class trying to convince Seth that she could develop a metal detector to locate the other classes' flags by finding the metal grommets.

Stories of past Bourne Wars were traded like rapidly inflating currency among the students: A story about a code based on musical notes that never got cracked. The class who'd protected their flag with booby traps that ended up amputating two fingers. The general who went three days without sleeping and had to be hospitalized. The more gruesome the sacrifice, the more respect and awe there was painted on the faces of the students.

During Specials, Gus pounced on Harcourt, begging for the reading that discussed military history and strategy. After class he had an escort of three freshmen to get him safely back to the dorm. Lydia hadn't really thought of how to get back to the dorm safely, so feeling more than a little ridiculous, she waited on the front steps of the main building until the coast was clear and then sprinted over the lawn to the dorm.

She was panting and embarrassed when she got to the front steps, and so wasn't thrilled to see Marin on a porch swing.

Marin raised her eyebrows in half a sneer. "Lydia, right?"

Since they had two classes together and had met on the ferry, this hardly seemed like an honest question. Lydia did not feel as though it deserved an answer, so she raised her eyebrows right back at Marin and waited.

"This is from Seth." Marin looked around and then roughly handed Lydia a piece of paper. She rolled her eyes, gathered up her things, and went inside.

The piece of paper said *Sho 942.23*. It took Lydia only a minute to figure out it was a call number for a library book. Lydia hesitated. She wasn't supposed to go anywhere alone if she didn't want to be assassinated, but she didn't really know any sophomores very well. Finally she took a deep breath and went to Sorcha's room.

"Sorcha?" Lydia knocked lightly.

"Yeah? Come in if you're a sophomore," called Sorcha.

Lydia pushed the door open and slipped inside. "Hey," she said, embarrassed.

Sorcha put down a pad of graph paper and a compass on her desk and looked curiously at Lydia. Sorcha paused, and even though she was plain looking, she did the thing that beautiful girls do, giving people a second to look at her before going on. "Hey yourself," she said.

"Umm, Seth said I am supposed to be indifferent to the war, but now he gave me a clue or something," said Lydia. She was a bit unnerved. "I think I need to go to the library."

"Ahh, you've got a mission!" Sorcha shoved back from her desk and stood up. "The library? You can't go alone. Come on!"

"Won't it look funny, though, if you and I are hanging out all of a sudden? I'm supposed to act like I don't care about the war. . . ." Lydia felt even more embarrassed to point out that Sorcha was not exactly her friend, but this seemed to delight Sorcha even further.

"You're right." Sorcha sat on her bed and stuffed her feet into her sneakers. "You go first, and I'll follow, like, five feet behind. People will just think I'm using you for cover."

It was an awkward walk to the library, made slightly comical by Sorcha's attempt to act as if she'd just decided on the spot to go into the library. Acting was *not* her forte, and she seemed more like a mime than an indecisive student. Lydia was concealing a grin by the time they got inside.

Lydia found the book quickly and pulled it off the shelf. It was called *Spy Craft in the Twentieth Century*. Lydia wondered just what she was supposed to do with it, when she noticed a small paper inside the front cover. It was heart shaped and said: *Be Mine?*

Lydia's heart hammered and she blushed. Seth's wicked grin and sparkling eyes popped into her head with a lurch that made her feel as though her stomach had made a bid for freedom out her toes. Seth was—*wait a minute.*

Lydia's stomach shot back into position with an even more brutal force. Seth wasn't asking her out. He was asking her to be his spy.

For a moment Lydia was so embarrassed by her own thought process that she felt certain everybody in the library had followed each emotional swing and was snickering at her. On the heels of embarrassment came a swirl of disappointment, a wisp of relief, and then a slight twist of anger. She couldn't help but suspect that Seth was messing with her.

Lydia scanned the card catalog for the perfect book. *YES! The Power of Positive Thinking.* She wrote down the call number and left the piece of paper on the corner of the card catalog. She caught Sorcha's eye and then stared pointedly at the paper. Lydia waited by the door, retying her shoes while Sorcha retrieved the paper. She looked at it and then turned a puzzled expression to Lydia.

"For Seth," Lydia mouthed. It would have been a perfect spy moment if Sorcha hadn't given her a broad smile and a big thumbs-up.

Chapter 17

At dinner Ben announced that he had already been assassinated by a junior.

"He got me right as we were walking out of the main building after our economics Special. I thought he was giving me a friendly pat on the back because I *nailed* it in our discussion, but no, I'm a goner, not even one day in." Ben didn't seem as heartbroken as Lydia would have thought, and soon she found out why. He had organized a complex betting table with odds and everything. Students were betting on which class would win, which class would be the first to lose its flag, who'd have the most kills, and which general would be the first to win a battle.

Battles were logic puzzles presented onstage by Dr. Gaddify at a special assembly. If a general won, then the class got resources. The general could bring members of the class back to life, or he or she might be excused from announcing the meeting time in public, or the general could ask for a secret.

Naomi and Bethany Ming were dead already as well. Naomi had been killed by a senior outside her studio, and Bethany Ming, who had declared for music, had been killed leaving her piano. Neither seemed too bothered, and none of them had received the code cipher yet, so there was no great loss.

Gus came in, flanked by four freshman boys. He had a folder tucked under his arm, and the expression of alertness on his face was at odds with his usual sleepy brown eyes. He smiled with half his mouth at Lydia and then looked at her dining companions.

"You're eating with a sophomore spy? *Et tu*, Ben?"

Ben shrugged and looked sheepish. "I'm dead. We're all dead except for Lydia, so don't get your panties in a bunch. Take a look at the odds I gave you." Ben slid aside the book that was covering his betting docket and wiggled his eyebrows, then covered it up again.

Gus went and sat at another table, which quickly filled in with eager freshmen. The table looked like a flower that had closed up for the night with all the students' heads so close together in the center.

Bethany and Naomi were talking rapturously of having their own studios, and Ben was trying to explain the betting odds to Lydia, when Dr. Gaddify came into the dining hall and walked up to the front, where the bulletin board was. He raised his hands over his head for quiet, and after some scraping chairs and shushing noises he got it.

Dr. Gaddify smiled around the dining hall. "I understand that there has already been bloodshed," he said. "And if the rumors have been reported correctly, the usual urban legends of past exploits are in hot circulation?" There was a small flare of laughter, but the tension in the air smothered it very quickly.

"Now, I will go over a few rules and reminders," said Dr. Gaddify. "Over the years we have collected quite a few rules, because you are forever coming up with new things that need to be forbidden." Again a thin vibration of laugher came from the crowd. "A copy of the full rule book has been given to each general. You will also find one in the library and here by the

119

bulletin board. Generally, the rules forbid anything that would cause damage to school property or damage to the health of your classmates and teachers. Let me rephrase that; damage to any living thing is forbidden. I am particularly fond of the shade trees on the main lawn and the forsythia by the library.

"I will remind the bloodthirsty that the main building and a person's own studio, lab, and room are safe zones. After some very messy and unmentionable accidents, we have had to make bathrooms safe zones as well. You are, however, free to murder one another in the corridors of your dorms."

Dr. Gaddify smiled while delivering these reminders but then became serious. "Generals, you may come with me. The rest of you may join us when you hear the bell."

It was quiet while the four generals picked their way through the tables to Dr. Gaddify, but as soon as the door closed behind them, the noise in the dining hall swelled.

"What's happening now?" asked Naomi.

"Victory bell," said Ben. "There's, like, a ritual and stuff."

After five minutes of wild speculation about the ritual, Lydia heard the bell. It was not the brassy trill that marked the end of classes, but a real bell that sent out a sound so thick it felt as if a membrane were passing over you with each *bong*.

As one, the student body rose and filed out the front door to the green. There, in between two oak trees, were Dr. Gaddify and the four generals. Dr. Gaddify stood next to stone plinths that were as tall as he was. The bell was hanging between the stones, and he struck it one last time before turning to watch the students coming out of the dining hall. Dr. Gaddify and each of the generals were wearing hooded crimson capes, and the generals all carried silver swords. Lydia felt uneasy. The whole setup looked cultish. As the last vibration of the bell bounced away through the trees, Dr. Gaddify held up his arms.

"We gather now to declare war!"

The cheer that went up was wild and deafening.

"The long tradition of Bourne War is a way to measure intellect and craft. A way to pit your formidable talents against one another so that we may declare a victor in the end!"

Everybody cheered and screamed again. Lydia clapped but also studied the fierce looks on her classmates' faces.

"Generals, I assume you have each assigned your spy by now. Bourne War depends on a strict code of honor that should be upheld. If you are assassinated while in possession of the cipher, you are on your honor to give it to your assassin. Spies, especially, we rely on you to be fair. No one knows who you are, but you must betray a secret if you are assassinated. It is the price for earning a secret for every three kills you make in a single class. Let us now swear to be honorable."

Dr. Gaddify held up his hand. In a ragged sort of unison the students intoned: "We swear."

Dr. Gaddify sealed the swearing with the bell.

"As you know, it is my solemn duty to keep and distribute secrets. Generals, by eight o'clock tomorrow morning, I expect five clues to the whereabouts of your flag. You should also have placed your flag by that time. After you place your flag, you may not touch it again. Now I will bestow the flags."

An excited rumble filled the air as Dr. Gaddify reached into a leather satchel. "For the freshmen!" The freshman class cheered, maybe a beat too late. Gus stepped forward and knelt in front of Dr. Gaddify. "Do you, Angus McCracken, swear to protect this flag to the best of your ability and to uphold the honor of Bourne War?"

"I swear it," said Gus. Dr. Gaddify handed him a green flag that was a long strip of material with a brass grommet on one end. The freshmen cheered again, more convincingly this time.

Seth stepped forward, knelt, and swore. The sophomores were much louder than the freshmen had been. Seth's flag was yellow.

The juniors got a blue flag and the seniors a red one. The generals all turned and held the flags over their heads to great cheering. After a minute Dr. Gaddify signaled for quiet.

"Now, when I strike this bell, go back into the dining hall. You will find the announcements of the first meetings on the bulletin board. Play fair and good luck!"

Again the bell cast a bubble of sound over the crowd. When it broke, a tide of students surged up against the dining hall doors and burst inside. Lydia hung back—after all, she didn't know the cipher—but then Sorcha caught her eye. With all the subtly she had displayed in the library, Sorcha twitched her head up at the bulletin board and mouthed the word, "Go." Lydia frowned at her to show that she was being really obvious, but Sorcha took it as confusion. She pointed to her own heart and smiled encouragingly.

Lydia moved through the scrum toward the board, more to stop Sorcha from giving her away than because she knew what she was doing. Lydia wondered why she couldn't just ask Sorcha where the meeting was, but had the sense it was a point of pride to figure it out. She tried to look casual as she studied the bulletin. The notice for sophomores was a square piece of paper with a checkerboard grid of tiny squares drawn on it. Each square had a letter or number, but it seemed as though there were no order or sense to the letters and numbers.

People around her were scribbling on pieces of paper or mumbling to themselves. Lydia scanned the crowd and saw at least three people with looks of dawning comprehension. Sorcha had tapped her heart. Seth had drawn her a heart. Were they related? Was the heart the cipher?

If you drew a heart onto the grid of Seth's paper, starting from the notch in the middle and going right, the first few squares spelled out: G-J-R-E-2-F. That made no sense, so Lydia started one square lower. P-I-E-R-7-0-0.

Lydia couldn't stop herself from looking around in triumph. The meeting was at the pier at 7:00. Maybe she *was* a genius! She studied the letters that came after if you continued around the heart. After a few wrong turns she got B-R-I-N-G-B-A-T-H-I-N-G-S-U-I-T.

Again Lydia looked around. Freshmen were gasping and sprinting out the side doors in twos and threes. Lydia looked at Gus's notice. It was a very simple code, just the number of the letter in the alphabet. It said:

12-1-14-7-21-1-7-5   12-1-2   14-15-23

With only a little bit of puzzling Lydia figured out that it said "language lab now." It was a clever strategy because it hadn't needed a cipher, and by having the meeting immediately, Gus was betting that his freshmen would look at their own poster before three members of any other class looked at it and solved the puzzle. Lydia admired Gus, for she saw that he had left three freshmen behind to try and work out the other codes. She had to admire Seth as well. His clues had been very clever and had required some decisive action on his part.

The junior announcement was just a yellow circle in the upper right-hand quadrant of the paper. Clearly, the cipher was essential to understanding. The senior announcement was equally unsolvable: a series of wavy and straight lines. Lydia noticed that Cora was hovering over the freshman math student who was tackling the senior announcement, her expression carefully blank. After a few seconds he turned and smiled up at her. Cora gave him an oppressive frown and then they left together, walking very quickly toward the language lab.

Lydia narrowed her eyes at Cora's back and returned to her table. It was six thirty. Most of the dining hall had cleared out, but there seemed to be a fair number of folks sitting around with expressions that were either alert or unconvincingly casual. Two sophomores followed Ellie Martin and her cohort without bothering to be subtle about it. Seth had somehow disappeared without Lydia noticing. Tom, the senior general, sat curling the red senior flag around his finger and looking very impressive.

Lydia said good-bye to Ben, Naomi, and Bethany, then cleared her tray and went with Sorcha back to the dorm. They separated in the stairway, and Sorcha told Lydia that she'd come get her at 6:50. In her room, Lydia quickly put on her bathing suit under her clothes. She was pacing nervously, and suddenly screamed when Sorcha's grinning face appeared outside her window, two stories above the ground.

"Sorcha!"

"Let me in!"

"What are you doing? You're going to fall!"

"I came to get you. Marin's room is one floor up, and she let me set up this block and tackle line to get here. Open the window farther, will you?"

Sorcha was hanging from a very complicated series of ropes and pulleys that was attached somewhere overhead and out of sight. Lydia opened the window all the way and pulled Sorcha in over her desk.

"There," said Sorcha, slightly out of breath. "You ready?"

Lydia just shook her head at Sorcha. "You nearly gave me a heart attack, you know."

"You might want a towel," said Sorcha, ignoring this jibe.

"Won't that give it away?" asked Lydia.

"Ahh. Good point." Sorcha guiltily pulled a towel out of the back of her pants. "I'll just leave this here, if that's all right? I'll be escorting you back to your room after the meeting anyway."

"You'll go back out the window?"

"Yep, Marin's my neighbor, so it's safest."

"Going out the window is safest?" Lydia snorted.

Sorcha and Lydia walked down the front steps and out into the purpling light of dusk. The chill in the air made Lydia pray that she wouldn't have to use her bathing suit. She didn't mind being a spy, but she wasn't sure she cared enough about Bourne War to jump into the freezing-cold ocean at dusk.

Sorcha was singing under her breath, and it made Lydia realize that she was happy here. She hadn't even thought of Matthew since this morning. If she wasn't careful, she could get very comfortable at Claybourne.

The path spilled out onto a gravelly beach where small waves hissed through pebbles as they sank back from the shore. To the left was the ferry dock, which was about eight feet over the water and a hundred feet long. To the right, making a cove, was a smaller dock, which hosted the school's fleet of modest boats: four rowboats and four small sailboats. Seth was sitting at the oars in one of the rowboats. Jay, Kit, and a girl Lydia didn't know each had another of the rowboats, and they were all bobbing on the dark water about thirty feet from the rocky shore. The sailboats were moored to the swimming buoy, empty but out of reach. A person would have to swim out to get them in order to sail. Lydia saw that Seth had arranged this so that none of the other classes could get near the meeting spot, and again her estimation of Seth rose.

Seth saw Lydia and Sorcha and waved. "I'll meet you at the dock!" he called. He rowed with more passion than skill, so he hit the dock hard, bounced away, and made a grab for the pier that almost upset the boat.

"Come on, come on!" he said, holding his hand up to Lydia so that she could step into the boat. His grip was very warm in the cooling evening air.

"Step into my office," said Seth. He pulled Lydia close and whispered, "Package under your seat." Then he steered her to a spot on the right side of the boat.

Two older boys had followed Lydia and Sorcha down the path.

"Can we have a ride too?" one asked. His hands were folded over his chest, and he looked both annoyed and impressed.

"Sorry, Wallis, exclusive passage this evening. Beautiful ladies only."

"Doesn't matter," said Wallis. "You stink at rowing, Finn."

Seth smiled innocently and then sent a gout of water up onto the dock with his oar. "You're right, Wallis, I need to work on my stroke."

Wallis and the other boy cussed while Seth rowed away.

Masking her movement by pretending to look over the edge of the boat, Lydia reached under the wooden bench to feel along the damp and gritty bottom until her hands felt a small plastic bag. She tucked the bag into the instep of her sneaker and straightened up. Seth winked at her and started humming happily.

In twos and threes, more sophomores came down to the pier and were invited into the rowboats. At 7:10 Seth directed them all out to the swimming buoy. They pointed the bows toward the buoy, making a small daisy of boats. Lydia grabbed the gunwale of the boat on her right, Sorcha grabbed the boat on the left, and so it went around the circle of boats, so that about eighteen students were out on the slick black water, their faces bobbing up and down like the reflections of moons.

Seth stood up in the bow of the rowboat and looked around him. "All right, sophomores," he said, "I would give you a rousing speech, but sound carries over water and I can see at least four people hiding in the woods up there. So let me just say that we are going to win this year."

Even though Seth had said this in a very matter-of-fact voice, a surge of energy went through the boats and everybody cheered. Seth grinned at them all, but Lydia could see that there was steel in his gaze. A Seth Finn who wasn't joking around was a rather impressive person, and Lydia was glad of the dim light. She could feel her cheeks redden as she thought again of that second in the library when she'd thought that Seth was asking her out.

"Okay, a quick word about the ciphers." Seth lowered his voice. "Kit?"

Kit coughed into his fist and looked around at his classmates through his tilted bangs. "As I am sure you know, there are certain letters in the alphabet that are the same shape whether upper- or lowercase. Each cipher will contain a word with *one* of those letters. That will be the shape of our message on our grid of letters and numbers. Each cipher will also have two numbers, which will tell you where to start. The first number will be the number of squares over, the second will be how many squares down. Subtract four from the first number and seven from the second number and then start there. Got it?"

From the way Kit was peering up through his tilted bangs, Lydia could tell this had been his idea. Seth reached over two boats to give Kit a high five. "Kit's going to put a lot of false trails in the grid, so make sure you start at the right spot."

Seth glanced up at the sky. "I have a handful of assassination Velcro dots here," he said, handing around a bag of nickel-size black Velcro patches. People who hadn't gotten any yet took some and passed it around. When it had gone the circuit and everybody had made jokes about needing twice as many as anyone else, Seth looked at the sky again.

"I think it is dark enough," he said. "Jay, Robin, can you get the sailboats back to the pier?" They nodded solemnly. Another boy climbed out of their boat into Kit's boat. "Okay, follow me, everybody," said Seth, loosening the mooring rope from the swimming buoy and sitting back behind the oars.

"Wait, Seth," said Lydia. "I think that Cora got the cipher for the senior announcement. It seemed like the freshmen figured out what it said." Lydia was nervous because it was just a hunch, but Seth paused midstroke. "Jay!" he called. "Hold up." Seth wildly pivoted his rowboat and bashed into the side of Jay's boat. After they got themselves sorted, Seth leaned into Jay's boat and whispered, "You and Robin do what you have to do here quickly, then get back up to the dorm. If you see a group of three freshmen going out, get another person and follow them. They've already had their meeting, so either they're going to plant their flag or they might be going to the senior meeting. Sorcha, Lydia, is Marin still alive?"

"I think so," said Sorcha.

"Good. Get her and do the same thing. Follow any group of freshmen who look like they know where they're going." Seth told the others to stay still for a minute, then turned the boat toward shore and deposited Lydia and Sorcha in the shallow water. He grabbed Lydia's arm. "Go get me a secret," he whispered. Hot blood shot through Lydia's body, all the way to her toes, which were already turning icy in the cold water.

"Where are you going?" she asked.

Seth considered, then relented. "I am going to make a very heroic and very cold diversion," he said in a low voice. "Wish us luck."

He turned the boat away from shore and rocketed toward the ferry pier with a few good pulls on the oars. "Come on!" he called to the two other rowboats.

The boats were nothing more than ghostly blobs on the water at this point, and Lydia watched them round the corner of the cove to the left. Above her in the woods she heard people moving about, following the rowboats. The diversion seemed to be effective, but what were they being diverted from? Lydia wondered who was placing the flag if Seth's group was just a diversion.

Sorcha and Lydia walked back to the dorm in the dark, the electric feeling of having a secret tight between them. The whole campus seemed to be tingling with importance. They found an empty porch swing, kicked off their wet shoes (Lydia was careful to keep the tiny bag hidden and safe), then waited on the porch, slapping mosquitoes, to see if any freshmen were going somewhere. Around ten o'clock, having donated pints of blood to the insects, they gave up and went inside. Lydia and Sorcha escorted each other to the bathroom, giggling, and then Lydia helped Sorcha climb back out her window. When Sorcha had made it safely to the third floor, Lydia pulled her head inside her room and settled down on her bed to inspect the small bag.

The bag was the size of a folded dollar bill and contained about twenty Velcro dots like the ones they had gotten for assassinations from Seth. Instead of being black, however, these were yellow. With the dots was a piece of paper that Seth had written on, but it was completely soaked and illegible. Lydia guessed that since she was a spy and spies could earn secrets by killing people, the spy dots had to be distinguishable from other dots. If she was clever, she could assassinate people without revealing her identity as a spy or even that she cared about Bourne War at all. She decided to tell Sorcha that she was the spy. Maybe Sorcha would let herself be framed for the assassinations Lydia did. Feeling thoroughly bloodthirsty, Lydia went to sleep.

Lydia hadn't been asleep long when she woke to the sound of sobbing. She couldn't tell where it was coming from, but it wasn't directly next door. She sat up in bed and listened, wondering if she should try to find the person and help her. Straining her ears, she was able to discern the words: "I don't want to die. I don't want to die. I don't want to die." Then the sobbing stopped abruptly.

Lydia's heart was pounding. She willed her ears to hear more. Where had the voice come from? Was the person okay? She sat, hardly daring to breathe, for three more minutes. Hearing nothing, she slid back under her covers and listened some more. *Maybe she's worried about Bourne War,* thought Lydia. *Or maybe something is trying to kill her.*

Chapter 18

Lydia managed to kill three freshman girls before breakfast by wandering sleepily down the hall outside the bathroom and bumping into her victims. After she stuck her yellow dots onto their shoulders, she sent Sorcha into the bathroom to point out that they had been killed. Sorcha's lack of acting skill was actually a benefit in this case, because it made it seem like Sorcha was trying to pretend that she hadn't done it. By 8 a.m. everybody thought Sorcha was the sophomore spy.

It was Saturday, which meant, Lydia realized, that people would be wearing their normal clothes to breakfast instead of their uniforms. She would not have admitted it to any adult, but wearing a uniform was actually kind of nice, since it meant you never had to think too hard about clothes in the morning. It was pouring rain, so Lydia wore jeans, tall boots, and a dark green sweatshirt that had a hood. She didn't admit even to herself that she was wearing her favorite jeans in the hopes of looking good when Seth got the news she'd earned a secret.

Sorcha wasn't going to come in the window with the weather like it was, so Lydia stood on her bed and knocked on the ceiling with her history book, which was the signal to Marin to get Sorcha and come get Lydia so that they could all go to breakfast together. Marin was an unwilling participant in all this "mock-martial nonsense," but Sorcha simply wouldn't take no for an answer, so Marin was a part of it whether she wanted to be or not.

Breakfast this morning included brunch-type items like fresh fruit and pastries, but the real feast was the gossip. Apparently, Lydia's hunch had been right. Kit, Jay, and another sophomore boy had followed three freshman boys to a studio room, which turned out to be the meeting place for the seniors. Tom was livid and Charlie Rhinebeck was in disgrace. Cora confessed that she had assassinated him yesterday after Specials and gotten the cipher from him. Then she grinned.

"He didn't mind *too* much," she said, waggling her eyebrows.

Five sophomores had been seen swimming around in the dark on the south side of the island, and according to Ben, some juniors had been out at first light in the pouring rain to look for the sophomore flag out on the rocks in the water.

"Gus doesn't believe that Seth would be so obvious," said Ben. "Also, the juniors took all the boats, so even if the freshmen wanted to look, they'll have to wait."

Lydia hadn't been sure how Seth would find out that she'd earned a secret, but apparently the three freshmen she'd killed had reported themselves to Dr. Gaddify, and he'd left a clue to the location of the freshman flag with Seth just minutes before Lydia had gotten to breakfast. Sorcha abandoned Lydia to go find out what the clue was, so Lydia was stuck walking back to the dorm with Marin.

Marin flatly refused to escort Lydia to her room, so Lydia sprinted down the hall, feeling foolish and resigning herself to a lonely day in her room. She wrote a letter to her mom and started one to Abilene, but she didn't know what to say. Should she tell Abilene about the hypnotism and the truffle? She wished she could ask Abilene if she had noticed anything different about Matthew when he came home from Claybourne. Lydia remembered how weird he was that one movie night. Now she wondered if it had to do with being hypnotized.

After a while Lydia gave up on the letter to Abilene. If she said anything suspicious, Emily would find out and hop right in the car to come get Lydia.

She considered the possibility that Dr. Gaddify didn't know he was causing people to commit suicide. He was so likable that it was hard to remember he was a suspect. She had to find out whom he had been speaking to on the stage at orientation.

Lydia scratched a bug bite on her ankle, folded up her letter, and looked out the window. Most of her view was filled by the main building, but if she went all the way to the right side of her window, she could see the main lawn and the underclass boys' dorm on the other side. There was a flagpole in the center of the lawn, and the flag was flopping wetly, making a repetitive clanging noise against the metal pole. A group of very wet juniors splashed across the lawn, so completely soaked that Lydia wasn't sure if they'd gone swimming or just been out in the rain since dawn. They slogged their way to the dining hall, looking discouraged, so Lydia guessed they hadn't found anything.

A knock on her door made Lydia start. "Come in?"

Cora peeked around the doorframe. "Truce?"

"Yeah. Come in."

"You won't kill me?"

"No. You either. Truce, right? What's up?" asked Lydia.

Cora smiled and slipped in the door. She had a mound of something covered by a paper napkin balanced on top of a script.

"I need somebody to help me with my lines, and I brought these to bribe you with." Cora lifted up the napkin to expose some sandwiches and cookies. "If we're brave, we can also go down to the kitchen to make tea." Cora pulled a handful of tea bags out of her back pocket and dropped them on Lydia's desk. "Will you help?"

"Sure," said Lydia. "You didn't have to bribe me, but this is definitely safer than going back to the dining hall."

"Bourne War is going to turn me into a hermit," laughed Cora. "I'm too nervous to even use the bathroom without Naomi, but she's in her studio. I heard that some of the guys have started peeing into soda bottles so that they don't have to risk it."

"I guess we could just hang our butts out the window," said Lydia.

"The rain is like a bidet," said Cora seriously.

Cora and Lydia spent the next few hours going over Cora's lines for the balcony scene. Just when Lydia was beginning to feel like she knew Romeo's lines by heart, Naomi knocked and came in.

"I thought I heard you guys laughing in here." Naomi closed the door behind her. "Oh, food!"

"Wait!" said Cora. "You're dead already, so will you bring us three mugs of hot water for tea?"

Naomi narrowed her eyes. "Save me some cookies."

"Deal," said Cora.

It was a very cozy afternoon. Cora was a great mimic, and pretty quickly she could run through the list of phonemes better than Lydia could. For a while they tested Naomi's eyes for seeing color. She could even tell the difference between four strands of Cora's hair.

Around four everyone felt a bit restless. Naomi looked out the window and frowned. "Whoever made that American flag didn't do a very good job keeping the red dye consistent," she said. She was showing off a little, Lydia thought. "But the rain has stopped. You guys wanna go outside?" Lydia went into Cora's room and pounded on the ceiling, since Sorcha was right above.

Sorcha came and found Lydia "conspiring with the enemy." But they all went out and slid around on the main lawn, skittering after a Frisbee and getting thoroughly soaked in the grass.

At dinnertime Sorcha hung back a little and handed Lydia a small piece of paper. It said, *HOT 6, 13*. Lydia figured out that the message would be shaped like an *O* and that it would start on the second square over, sixth square down.

After dinner the four generals put four new announcements on the board. Lydia quickly solved the puzzle and learned that the sophomores had a meeting in the library at 6:45.

At the library Seth informed them that they had seventeen sophomores left and that the senior flag was in the northwest quadrant of the island. The freshman secret, earned by Lydia, said that their flag was mobile and most visible between the hours of 8:00 a.m. and 4:00 p.m. Last of all, he informed them that there was a school-wide ban on assassinations from 7:30 to 10:00 tonight so that anyone who wanted to go see an X-Men movie in the auditorium was free to go.

"I, personally, am going to use the time to shower unmolested," said Seth. "I hope the rest of you use the time to scour the island for a patch of red, blue, or green. The red flag especially. I want to get the seniors."

Lydia walked back to the dorm with Sorcha, alert to any splotches of color in the gray, cloudy campus. There was green everywhere, all of it sparkling and glossy with rain. The only red or blue she saw was on the American flag, which now hung limp in the still air. Lydia looked at it a long time. *Whoever made that American flag didn't do a very good job keeping the red dye consistent,* Naomi had said.

What if . . . ? Lydia peered up at the flag in the dusky light. It was too hard to tell from here.

"Sorcha, we have to get Seth," said Lydia.

Sorcha and Lydia waited on the front porch of the underclassman boys' dorm while Ben went up to get Seth. Seth came down wearing only a pair of jeans and carrying a towel. Lydia didn't know where to look when she spoke to him. The smooth trenches of muscle that led into his pants were, frankly, distracting. She whispered her suspicions to him, aware of the heat that rose off his shoulder when she tilted her head near. Seth's whole body tensed when she told him, then he grabbed both her arms and shook her.

"Lydia . . ." She thought for a moment he was going to kiss her. "I wish you could be a part of this, but I need you to stay undercover. You two get out of here. Go back to your dorm, but watch the flag!"

Sorcha and Lydia jogged back to the dorm and up to Sorcha's room, where they had a great view of the front lawn and the flagpole. The lawn was deserted, but Lydia could see two sophomore boys sitting on the front steps of their porch across the lawn. There was a shout, and then a tide of boys swarmed the flagpole. In seconds the flag was down, and Seth had detached the red senior flag from the bottom stripe of the American flag, where it had been almost perfectly camouflaged. Shouting and cheering, they carried the flag into the dining hall, drawing a crowd behind them.

All in all, it had been a very good day.

Chapter 19

Sunday morning, Dr. Kennedy came to collect the letters home and inform the girls that the sophomore class was widely considered to be winning Bourne War. Having captured the senior flag, they also got all the senior secrets. They learned that the freshman flag was mobile but was not moved by students or teachers. The junior flag was attached to a building. Lydia had been instructed to kill juniors to get a junior secret, but by Wednesday she was getting a little frustrated. She had killed eight people, but two turned out to be seniors and five of the rest had already been killed. She had gotten a cipher off the last one, a teenage boy who'd managed to grow a full beard. She'd spotted him walking alone down to the pier with a leather-bound notebook under his arm. He had bowed to her and handed over the cipher without a word, then resumed his walk. Her spy status was no longer a secret, and even Naomi refused to talk about Bourne War when Lydia was around.

Oddly, Gus seemed to relax around Lydia once he knew she was the sophomore spy. He was doing very well too. He negotiated with Seth to share secrets about the juniors, in hopes of eliminating their mutual enemy. Lydia wondered if he had made the same deal with Ellie, the junior general, about sophomores, because she suspected that Seth had.

Cora was the freshman spy, and as Ben had predicted with his odds, she was leading the game for the number of kills. She seemed to have a gift for making people forget that they were in peril, and was forgiven immediately by everyone she assassinated. Lydia hoped for Pilar's sake that the war would be over soon, because Cora had talked Pilar into sleeping in her room and walking her to the bathroom and the main building every morning.

Cora's dedication to her craft earned the freshmen another secret, which Gus honorably shared with Seth. The junior flag was most easily seen from above.

Dr. Gaddify reminded everyone that only members of a class who were still "living" could contribute technology to the class's efforts. Sorcha said that both the seniors and the juniors had invented drones that could take photos from above, but the seniors were out, and the juniors had used illegal tech. She became determined to invent and build something that would be useful for aerial spying, but her dedication proved fatal in terms of the game and nearly in terms of her real life. She stepped right off the end of the ferry dock while she was looking up at her prototype. The junior girl who saved her, by throwing her a rope and then towing her in to shore, brought Sorcha up to the dorm, made sure she didn't have hypothermia, and then said: "Um. Well, since you're okay, um, you're dead." Then she stuck a Velcro dot onto Sorcha's shivering shoulder.

So it was Pilar who, working in secret, built a very large but light airplane that could fly only in straight lines. She rigged a very rudimentary camera to the plane's propeller, so that with every hundred rotations of the propeller the camera would automatically take a picture. Tragically, after only a half dozen passes over the main part of the campus, Dr. Gaddify came running out to tell her that an airplane she couldn't steer was too risky for the campus windows. She was allowed to fly it over the woods, though.

It took the freshmen two and a half days, but by the next Tuesday they had retrieved the junior flag.

Chapter 20

Meanwhile, classes happened. In Regulars, Lydia learned so quickly that she wondered if she might be a genius after all. If she really thought about it, though, the big difference between Claybourne and her old school was that the teaching style was clean, somehow, without any time spent on laborious instructions or telling people to behave. Learning at her old school had been wine, watered down by classroom management and taking attendance. Learning at Claybourne was straight liquor and came with the attendant headaches.

Being a good spy for Bourne War had made Lydia a lousy spy for Matthew. She had checked out the door that led downstairs from backstage but found only stale-smelling dressing rooms and a locked boiler room. By Wednesday she had begun to feel guilty every time she looked at the postcard from New Orleans, so she swore that she would spend time after Specials looking for the mysterious staircase.

When their language class was over, Lydia waved good-bye to Gus and his escort and went back to the auditorium. When she found that the door was unlocked, her heart skipped with excitement, but then she heard Cora: "Swear not by the moon." And she let the door fall closed again.

She found a janitor's closet and a locked door that said BOX OFFICE. How far had they gone that day of orientation? Had they left the auditorium? Lydia didn't think they had, but it was hard to trust a memory that had at least one gaping hole. Feeling defeated, Lydia considered sprinting for the library but decided it was too risky. She wandered by Dr. Gaddify's office, not entirely convinced she would be brave enough to snoop inside if the door was open and he was gone, but as she slumped by the door, she heard voices inside and felt relieved.

Lydia woke the next morning and for the first time in a few days thought not of Bourne War, but of Matthew and how to find the mysterious room.

At lunch Lydia found Naomi and Cora and sat down at their table with a flop. They were obviously in a complaining mood too.

"I can't explain," Naomi was saying as she stabbed a pork chop with unwarranted venom. "It's like sometimes I am thinking about one painting and then suddenly I realize I am doing something totally different. I have this idea in my head, but on canvas—"

"Sounds like every time I do art," said Lydia. "I think it's going to be a beautiful horse, but it ends up looking like a giraffe-dog."

Cora groaned with sympathy. "Whittle asked if I had any 'concepts' for the set, so I drew this castle thing that looked like something that belongs on the refrigerator door." Cora's eyes fell on Naomi and beamed at her. "Hey! Would you want to draw something? I mean, design it and stuff? It basically just has to be a wall, for Romeo and Juliet, but it's got to be okay for the other performances too. It would be so great if you did something with the big shells you've been painting. You could make it into a work of *art*. I know you could."

Naomi frowned. "How big are you talking?"

"It's about eight feet high? No, twelve. It's supposed to be a wall leading to a balcony, you know, but I think you could make it better than that." Cora turned and smiled coyly at Lydia. "And *you* can be my stage manager."

"What?"

"Stage manager. You just hand me props and stuff. Make sure my wig's on straight."

"I've never—"

"It's not rocket surgery. You'll be great."

"You're just trying to assassinate me, Cora Trombly!" said Lydia, but her mind was racing. She would never get a better chance to search the auditorium than this.

Cora threw her head back and cackled. "Okay. Truce for anything related to the show."

"And walking to or from the show."

Cora held out her hand. "Truce."

"Spy's honor?"

"Spy's honor."

At the end of lunch Dr. Gaddify announced a battle between Seth and Gus. It would be held in the cafeteria because there was a bunch of lumber for the set on the stage in the auditorium. There was a second school-wide truce from 3:00 until 4:30 or until the battle was finished, whatever was later.

Gus got excused from Specials early that day. When Lydia made her way down to the cafeteria, he was already there, standing in front of the bulletin board with a very determined look on his face. His dark brown eyes were inwardly focused, like an athlete about to perform a very difficult feat. Seth was there too, joking but twitchy. When he wasn't smiling, he clenched his jaw in a way that made a dimple appear along his jawline, and Lydia could tell he was nervous.

The students made an informal fan of chairs around the two generals. The feeling in the room was relaxed but excited, and most students exhibited that special kind of giddiness that comes from relief at not having to participate in what you're about to watch. Lydia slid into a chair next to Cora and Naomi toward the back.

"It's nice to be able to hang out with you two again," she said.

"Well, we'll see plenty of each other now that you're my stage manager and set designer," said Cora.

"True," agreed Naomi, "but I'm still rooting for Gus."

Gus did look very appealing at the moment. Lydia couldn't help but admire how his hands hung confidently at his sides. They were powerful hands, and Gus's stillness was oddly stirring compared with Seth's electric movements. Lydia was rooting for Seth out of class loyalty, but she wouldn't mind if Gus won either.

Dr. Gaddify walked jauntily into the cafeteria, bringing with him the usual charge of energy. He was a match for Cora in this way. He drew the eye even when more exciting things were happening.

He got to the front of the room and stood with Gus and Seth. He spoke to both of them, and even before he called for silence, the room went still.

"Okay, welcome, everybody. I trust you all got here safely? No more causalities?"

Seth said something Lydia couldn't hear, but it made the front of the room laugh and Dr. Gaddify shake his head.

"This is one of my favorite parts of Bourne War. A spectacle of wit, a real and appreciable battle between two very bright men. History wants to know: In this confrontation of famous intellects, who will prevail?" Dr. Gaddify made it sound as if Seth and Gus were already well-known leaders instead of two high-school-aged boys, but it made the tension in the room pull tighter.

"So today's challenge is a battle of logic. I will ask each general a logic question, classic questions, which may be familiar to many of you. If one misses the question, the other shall have a chance to answer correctly. If he does so, he is the winner. If not, we go on to the next question. Gentlemen?"

Seth stepped forward and held out his hand to Gus, who nodded and shook Seth's hand with a firmness that was visible even to Lydia in the back of the room.

"Then, we begin."

The entire room sat up straighter and focused on the three men.

"Seth, we'll start with you." Dr. Gaddify cleared his throat. "A traveler comes to a fork in the road. Twin brothers stand at the fork, and the traveler knows that one brother always tells the truth and the other always lies. One path leads to certain death, the other to great riches. The traveler, wishing to avoid certain death and attain great riches, may ask *one* brother *one* question. What should he ask?"

Seth bobbed his head with relief. "Sir, he should ask, 'Which way would your brother say lies certain death?'"

Seth had answered so quickly that Lydia guessed he had heard the problem before. Lydia worked it out in her head. Both brothers would point to the riches, because one would lie about what his brother would say and the other would truthfully point out that his brother would lie.

"Very good," said Dr. Gaddify. "Mr. McCracken. A farmer has a sack of grain, a rooster, and a fox. He must get them all across a river, but his boat can hold only himself and one other. How does he get across the river most efficiently without risking the rooster eating the grain, or the fox eating the rooster?"

Gus looked intently at Dr. Gaddify, then after a moment he straightened and turned to face the students. He answered the question slowly and perfectly.

"First, he brings the rooster over. Then he goes back and gets the fox. He leaves the fox on the far shore and takes the rooster back with him. Then he swaps the rooster for the grain, brings the grain over and leaves it with the fox, then finally retrieves the rooster."

When he had finished, Dr. Gaddify slapped him on the back and turned to Seth. This time he held up a large piece of paper that had a sketch on it. On the left was a person who was facing right, staring straight at a wall. That person wore a black hat. On the other side of the wall were three more people, all facing left. The one closest to the wall also wore a black hat. The two behind him wore white hats.

"Now," said Dr. Gaddify. "The people pictured here know that there are two black hats and two white hats. They do not know what color hat they are wearing. They cannot turn their head, or look over or through the wall. They are told to say so as soon as they have figured out what color hat they are wearing. Which one will figure it out first?"

Seth turned his back to the crowd to study the sketch. After a full minute of shifting silence he started humming, loud and tuneless, more like bees buzzing or a small motor. Another minute dragged by, and finally he shook his head. "I have narrowed it down to two, and I could guess, but I assume you want an explanation as well?"

"Yes, we will need to know your logic," said Dr. Gaddify, smiling.

Seth nodded and turned to look at the sketch again. After only a few seconds he scrubbed his head and smiled ruefully. "I yield to Mr. McCracken."

A hint of a smile played in the corner of Gus's mouth. He gave a nod to Seth that was almost like a bow.

"Just as in the Sherlock Holmes story 'Silver Blaze,' where it was the *absence* of barking that revealed the clue, here too it is the absence of sound that will give one person an advantage."

Lydia saw now where Gus was going, but at that second his easy confidence wavered. Lydia heard a noise at the back of the dining hall and saw Gus's eyes widen, just slightly. Seth's eyes flickered to the back of the dining hall, and Lydia twisted in her seat to see what they had both noticed. She saw the door swing closed again but didn't see who had gone through. The moment was over. Gus recovered himself and continued.

"The guy in the back, all the way to the right, can see two hats in front of him. One is black and the other is white, so he knows that he is wearing either a black or white hat, but cannot say for certain. Since he doesn't call out, the two guys in front of him can deduce that they are wearing different-colored hats. If they had on the same color hat, then the guy in the back would know what color his hat is."

Dr. Gaddify was smiling, and Seth bridged his hands in front of his forehead, hiding his eyes. He'd just figured it out too.

Gus went on, smiling a smile that lit up his whole face. "The guy in the middle can see that the guy in front of him is wearing a black hat. Therefore, he can be sure that he's wearing a white hat." Dr. Gaddify bowed his head with a small smile. "Gus McCracken, you are correct and you are the winner of this battle."

Gus nodded the half bow again, still grinning. "We'll take a sophomore secret, then, please."

The dining hall flooded with cheers, and half the freshmen were hopping up and down and hugging. Seth and Gus shook hands, and then Seth pulled Gus into a manly hug with a lot of backslapping. Dr. Gaddify shook Seth's hand, gripped Gus's shoulder, and steered him out of the dining hall toward his office, a small detail of freshmen surging after them.

Lydia couldn't be sure, but it seemed to her that Gus looked a little worried as well as proud, and Seth was more triumphant than he should have been. She watched him quickly work his way through the crowd and then over to her.

"Good job," said Lydia.

Seth grabbed her arm. "Thanks." He bent and whispered to her, the smell of his deodorant making her blush. "I think I know where the freshman flag is."

Lydia startled and then looked around.

"Act like you're comforting me."

"What?"

"Pat my shoulder or something."

Lydia tentatively patted Seth's shoulder. He rolled his eyes. "You look like you're brushing dandruff off my shirt. You can do better than that."

Blushing even hotter, Lydia hugged Seth and patted the back of his shirt. He hugged her back, and Lydia could feel the solid bulk of his chest and arms. "The janitor," whispered Seth. "Did you see Gus's face when he walked in?"

"I heard a noise and saw Gus's face, but I didn't know it was the janitor."

"It was. The flag is most visible between eight and four. It's mobile but not moved by students or teachers. We've been looking in the water, but I saw his face when the janitor walked in and—it's almost four. Let's go. Lead me out. I just suffered a humiliating defeat."

Seth was doing a very poor job of acting like he was humiliated, but Lydia supposed that was in character. She hooked her elbow through his arm and led him out through the back of the dining hall.

"Okay." Seth grinned down at her, giving up all pretense of disappointment. "I don't suppose you know where the custodial closet is?"

"Actually, General, I do."

"Good spy."

She led Seth just past the auditorium, hurrying ahead of the crowd, which she could hear was leaving the dining hall. They caught the janitor just as he was pushing his cart into the closet.

He was a middle-aged man with a thick head of sandy hair and a well-established beer gut. He raised his eyebrows at Seth and Lydia as they approached, and then crossed his arms over his chest.

"Yeah?" he asked aggressively.

"Hello," said Seth, as if the man had just greeted him with a friendly salutation. "Do you mind if I take a look at your cart there?"

The man looked at Seth sideways, frowning, and then stepped back with a shrug. The flag was tied to the mop head, in among the strands of the mop and looking much worse for wear. Lydia wouldn't have wanted to touch it, actually, but Seth untied it and held it over his head with an ear-shattering whoop.

He shook hands with the janitor and then grabbed Lydia's hand and dragged her back toward the dining hall, grinning all the way.

"She was right, you know!" he shouted.

"Who?" Lydia was slightly out of breath from jogging.

"Nurse Proctor. She said I should make you my spy."

Before Lydia could digest that, she and Seth caught up with Gus and his contingent right outside the dining hall.

"No!" cried Gus, spotting the flag.

Seth stopped grinning and bowed his head to Gus.

For a second Gus looked heartbroken; all the lines of his long face drooped downward, so that he truly looked like a lovable basset hound. Then he stepped forward with his hand out.

"It was on the swim buoy, wasn't it?"

"Yup!" said Seth, laughing. "Jay and Robin put it there during our first meeting."

"Really?" said Lydia.

"Pretty slick," said Gus. "At least now I don't have to swim out and get it. Well done, man."

"You too, Gus. Great battle. It's been an honor."

Seth and Gus gave each other a nerdy sort of salute, and then a group of sophomores swallowed Seth and dragged him to the cafeteria. Lydia stayed behind with Gus.

"Really good job," she said. "That was just bad luck that the janitor came in right then."

Gus's sleepy eyes crinkled into a smile. "It's all right. I'm actually relieved that it's over. We can go to the library together now."

Lydia laughed. "Well, that will be fun." She had meant it to sound sarcastic, but she found that she was looking forward to it. She got the feeling that Gus understood. For a second it was almost like having Matthew back.

"You better go celebrate," said Gus.

"Yeah," said Lydia without enthusiasm. What Seth had told her about Nurse Proctor was bugging her. Had Nurse Proctor seen her taking pictures in the headmaster's office? If so, why hadn't she turned her in?

Chapter 21

Friday felt like the day after Christmas, sort of deflated but still fun. The sophomores had won a trip to the mainland next weekend and would be treated to a pizza party for lunch. Gus, Pilar, and Cora were everyone's favorite targets for commiseration, and they enjoyed a sort of martyr's status that meant everybody wanted to hug them and talk about how close they'd been to winning. Gus started taking back stairways and running around behind buildings to avoid this. Cora didn't have time to adjust to her new role as martyr because Nikhil Patel, the actor who would play Romeo, was arriving and he expected her to be "off book."

"It means I have to have my lines memorized, which I have for, like, a week now," said Cora. She was playing it very cool about doing a scene with a famous actor.

"You're not even a little nervous?" asked Pilar. "My mom would, like, sacrifice a goat to hang out with Nikhil Patel."

Nikhil Patel's acting career had been launched by a small indie film about a young man whose twin sister died when they were two. His sister's spirit accompanies him through his everyday life until he finds love and reconciles himself to his part in her death. Patel had depthless, liquid brown eyes, chiseled cheekbones, and a succulent bottom lip, all of which he used to express soul-deep anguish that was irresistible to about ten million female moviegoers.

Since then he had turned down two franchise movies and been panned in three off-Broadway plays. He'd recently played the role of the spoiled bully in a remake of an eighties movie, which was also a flop. Finally, he'd made some very uninformed political comments during a charity concert that sent his status down the proverbial toilet.

From what she was able to glean from Mr. Whittle, Cora suspected that playing Romeo at a famous high school was the best part that Nikhil Patel could get right now. This opinion was confirmed when Nikhil Patel himself arrived in the flesh, a bit more flesh than he'd had when he made women weep into their popcorn five years before.

As Cora's stage manager, Lydia met Mr. Patel for the first time on Friday afternoon. He wasn't fat exactly, but his face had lost the angles that had made long close-ups a pleasure to scrutinize. He still had the shining swath of dark brown hair and coffee-with-cream complexion that had helped to make him a household name, but other than that, he was disappointingly average looking.

Lydia arrived at the auditorium at three o'clock and saw Cora perched in the new balcony. Mr. Patel stood gazing up at Cora with pained adoration splashed across his face, his hand raised as if he could stroke her cheeks from eight feet away. Cora was somewhat stiff, and while she, too, did her fair share of gazing, Lydia noticed that she was drumming her fingers on the railing.

"Well, I think that's enough of that, don't you?" She smiled a tight smile at Patel and waved at Lydia.

"We have to *feel* passion for each other. If we don't *feel* it, we can't *express* it. *Really* look into my soul. Let your feelings for me grow as strong as you can *bear*."

"Oh, Nikhil," said Cora, "I have very strong feelings toward you indeed. Really I do."

Lydia eyeballed Cora with alarm and then looked to see if Nikhil Patel had caught anything in Cora's tone other than admiration. From what she could tell, Patel was completely immune to irony.

"Good! Great! Focus down here—*look at me*—and . . . *cut*! Fabulous! Let's take a break."

"Lydia," called Cora. "Thank God you're here." Cora climbed down from the balcony and jumped the last few feet. "Nikhil is trying his hand at directing!" Cora's eyes popped with enthusiasm that was as false as her gazing adoration for Romeo had been. "Nikhil, this is Lydia Boswell. She's the stage manager."

"Lydia. Nikhil Patel. It's really nice to meet you." Nikhil grasped Lydia's hand in both of his and stared long and meaningfully into her eyes. Lydia felt her smile become fixed and struggled to keep panic out of her expression as the eye contact lasted much longer than was comfortable.

"Yes, nice to meet you, too," she said, and when that failed to bring the handshake to an end, she added, "It really is an honor, Mr. Patel. Really."

"Call me Nikhil." Nikhil gave her hand one final squeeze and then, still with a soul-deep gaze, said: "I'll take a skinny latte with two stevia, okay? Thanks."

"Uhh . . . ," said Lydia.

"How about a water, Nikhil?" suggested Cora.

"Juliet, it's like you're reading my mind. Honestly. I should really watch my caffeine intake. But we should stay in character. Call me Romeo."

Cora gave Romeo a dazzling smile and tugged Lydia into one of the wings. "His personal cooler is right there," she said. "If he suggests gazing into each other's eyes again, I want you to hit him over the head with a bottle of San Pellegrino."

Lydia went to the cooler, which was the size of a steamer trunk and was custom-painted with Nikhil Patel's eyes. Inside was a bewildering variety of bottled water, prescriptions, and face creams. She picked a water at random and brought it out to where Nikhil was standing center stage. His arms were held up an imploring manner again, but this time it was a smartphone that he gazed at with pleading in his eyes.

"Is there really no signal on this whole island?" he asked. "That's crazy. Great, really, but I don't know how you live like this."

"Aw, come on, Romeo, it must remind you of when you were a kid. You know, before the Internet," said Cora with a sweet smile.

Nikhil studied Cora before deciding that she couldn't possibly have meant to insult him.

Lydia spent the rest of the afternoon dodging Nikhil's requests for prickly pear juice, extra-hot decaf espresso, California rolls, and a Wi-Fi signal. He tried to get Cora to engage in a series of "acting exercises," but Cora stayed safely up in her balcony, redirecting each of his suggestions until he wore a look of permanent confusion.

Finally, at six thirty, Lydia reminded them both that dinner was almost over and she didn't know when the last ferry was leaving. Nikhil left in a hurry, shouting directions about his cooler and promising to be off book tomorrow. The door of the auditorium slammed shut behind him, and Cora climbed down. She looked at Lydia and then they both burst into laughter.

"Wow," said Lydia.

"Yeah," said Cora.

"Tomorrow's the performance?"

"Yep."

"What are you going to do?" asked Lydia.

"I've got some ideas," said Cora. "Remember how you said I should make it funny?"

"Yeah, but what does Nikhil think?"

"I think old Nikhil is in for a surprise."

Chapter 22

Despite the waning holiday atmosphere, on Friday evening Lydia made a dogged effort to get ahead with her reading, both for her Special and for history. She had gotten a book out of the library that included a time line of modern history, because so much of her reading relied on understanding references to the names of dictators and battles and revolutions that Lydia had never heard of. She was getting a pretty good grip on World War I and all the factors that had led up to it when she fell asleep with the light on and her books tented over her chest.

Around two o'clock in the morning Lydia woke with a start, coming fully awake as if there had been a thunderclap in her ear. At first she didn't know what had woken her, but then she spotted Naomi standing in the corner of her room. Lydia sat up quickly, gathering her covers around her chest convulsively. Her history book slid off the bed with a crash.

"Naomi?"

Naomi's shoulders were back up around her ears, and her head bobbed out in front of her body like a puppet with a broken string on its neck.

She shook her head slowly, as if denying her own name. Her eyes, huge and white within deep blue shadows, stared unblinking and pleading at Lydia. She lifted up one hand with ritual solemnity. She held a small piece of notebook paper out to Lydia and then slowly approached Lydia's bed. The strangeness of it all made Lydia shrink back against the wall as if Naomi were offering her a scorpion rather than a crumpled piece of paper. Naomi took another step closer and thrust the paper at Lydia.

Cautiously, her heart throbbing in her chest, Lydia reached out for the paper and took it with the tips of two fingers.

Naomi nodded and slouched to the door. When she put her hand on the doorknob, she straightened, growing taller by two inches, and turned to look at Lydia with her face crumpled in confusion.

"Did you just kill me again?" she asked, and then slipped from the room.

Lydia couldn't be sure she was talking about Bourne War.

The paper was slightly damp, almost rubbery, as if Naomi had been holding it in her sweaty palm for a long time. Lydia smoothed it out on her knee, then flipped it around. It was a black ink drawing of an ankh, the ancient Egyptian cross that had a loop at the top instead of the straight line of a Christian cross. She looked closer. The ankh was made of hundreds of tiny words, written in minuscule handwriting. Lydia blinked and leaned toward the light on her desk.

Repeated over and over in tiny letters were the words *we are not ourselves*.

Chapter 23

Lydia lay in bed, waiting for the light of dawn, thinking that when the sun rose, she would go check on Naomi. She had put the ankh on her desk and then turned out the light so that she wouldn't have to look at it, and now she was caught in the old childhood dilemma: turn on the light to face the monster, or stay motionless in the dark.

The moon was waning and looked like a teacup knocked on its side. The white moonlight blended oddly with the bronze light from the porch, causing distorted and discolored shadows that slid slowly up Lydia's wall. It wasn't until the light turned gray and then warmed to gold that Lydia fell asleep, despite her intention to check on Naomi.

Lydia woke with a heart-thudding start to pounding on her door. Cora peeked her head inside. "Wake up, Sleeping Beauty, you can't leave me alone with Nikhil 'Romeo' Patel, and he's been here for half an hour."

"Naomi," croaked Lydia.

"She's not in her room," said Cora, misunderstanding what Lydia meant. "And she's not as good a buffer as you are."

Lydia brushed her teeth and struggled to think of some way to keep an eye on Naomi. She wondered if Naomi would even remember their encounter, if she remembered drawing the ankh.

I am not me.

We are not ourselves.

Lydia's brain felt like it had been rolled in sawdust, and her eyes were crusty and hot. She grabbed a dry bagel on her way to the auditorium, wondering where Naomi might be now and how to find her.

In the auditorium the house lights were on and Lydia nearly wept with relief to see Naomi studying the stage halfway down the aisle with her hands on her hips.

"Let me see it again!" she called to somebody at the back of the auditorium.

Lydia, startled, looked around behind her. She saw a window she'd never noticed before lit up on the back wall. It was about the size of a windshield and about fifteen feet off the ground. A second later the house lights went down and the stage lights came on.

"Nope," muttered Naomi. "Okay," she shouted. "I'm just gonna have to do it again."

The house lights came on and Lydia was blinded and stunned all at once. The room with the symbols. There it was in the back of the auditorium. She'd known there was a room somewhere! It just wasn't where she remembered it being.

Blinking, she turned to look at Naomi, who was taking long steps up the aisle.

"Are you okay?" asked Lydia, grabbing her arm.

"Yeah." Naomi puffed out her cheeks. "I just don't like what the stage lights do to my colors. I'm going to have to redo it."

"Today?"

"Yeah. Right now, I guess."

Lydia was so relieved she'd be able to keep an eye on Naomi that she said, "Great," which earned her a strange look.

Lydia walked down the rest of the aisle to find Cora, who looked unbelievably lovely in an old-fashioned nightgown with her hair falling in heavy waves down her back.

Cora held her arms out at her sides for Lydia's inspection.

"You look amazing," said Lydia.

Cora grimaced. "Tell him that. He wanted a skimpy one that he described as avant-garde."

Lydia shot Nikhil Patel a glance. He was massaging his vocal cords and making raspberries with his lips.

"Cora, how do you get up there?" asked Lydia, pointing to the rectangle of light that revealed the inside of a room above the back of the auditorium.

"The sound booth?" asked Cora.

"Yeah."

"You just go through that door back there," said Cora, pointing to the right. "It's usually locked because of all the equipment, but I think the guy is up there now. But you're stage manager. You don't need to worry about any of that."

"Oh, I'm just curious," said Lydia. "I think I'll go check it out."

Excitement was burning through the haze of Lydia's exhaustion and worry. Normally, she would have been a bit timid to knock on a strange door and ask for a tour, but she surprised herself by pounding on the door until a short, bespectacled man with a long ponytail and a baseball cap opened the door.

"Hey," he said without curiosity.

"Hey," said Lydia.

"You want something?"

"No," said Lydia. "I mean, yeah. Can I come see your room? I mean, the room? Up there?"

"You a techie?" asked the man.

"Stage manager," said Lydia.

He pulled off his baseball cap, smoothed his hand over a very bald pate, and replaced the cap. "Come on."

Lydia's heart was stuttering again. She'd *known* there was a room! The stairs weren't how she remembered, but *up* was the right direction.

Lydia stood at the top of the stairs and took in the tiny, crowded room.

"Is this it?" she asked.

"Home sweet home," said the man.

"Is there another door? Another part of this room?" Disappointment was sweeping away all of Lydia's caution.

The man frowned at Lydia from under the bill of his hat. "You never seen a sound booth before?"

"No," said Lydia. All her despair came out with the word, and she sat down hard on the top step. This was definitely not the room in her memory. She felt as though she was drifting further and further from finding the truth.

"You all right, kid?" asked the man. He was surprisingly kind. Lydia imagined telling him that the other members of the school had all been drugged and hypnotized and she was trying to find out why. That dozens of Claybourne students had committed suicide.

"Boy troubles?" said the man. "Girl troubles? Parent troubles? I've seen it all. You spend thirty years in the theater, you know all kinds."

"Yeah," said Lydia.

"Yeah what?" said the man. "Which is it?"

"Just trouble," said Lydia.

"Get it off your chest, kid. Tell me what it is. I guarantee, I heard it before."

We are not ourselves, thought Lydia. *If your friends seem different to you, do not be alarmed.*

"Never mind," she said. "You've heard it all before."

Naomi came back with her paints. Cora installed herself up on top of the balcony and refused to come down. She said she was staying in character, but Lydia could tell she was avoiding Nikhil Patel. Lydia gave up trying to be helpful to Cora, because Nikhil kept her busy doing things she couldn't imagine were actually related to the play. As she sat in the first row of the audience, sorting his receipts, she kept an eye on Naomi.

Watching Naomi paint was like watching magic happen. She painted with the stage lights on now and spent a lot of time getting the colors just right. Once she was satisfied with the colors, she moved over the whole set, daubing paint here and there. She held the brush far back on the handle, and that was the magic part; the paint always seemed to go exactly where she wanted it to go. The daubing looked totally random to Lydia until Naomi stood back, finished, and suddenly Lydia could *see*. Naomi had painted leaves and flowers that looked like daggers and bottles of poison. She'd painted the stones of the tower to look like arguing faces. The piece was, as Cora had predicted, a work of art.

"That is amazing, Naomi, really!" called Lydia.

Naomi shrugged and then turned around to smile at Lydia. "Much better." She waved her arms at the sound booth. "Okay, you can turn 'em off now!"

Naomi began putting the paint away and rolling up the newspapers she'd spread to protect the stage floor.

"Are you leaving?" asked Lydia, suddenly alarmed.

"All done," said Naomi.

"But . . ." Lydia's mind sluggishly attempted to come up with a clever excuse to have Naomi stay. "Will it look different when it dries? Don't you want to stay and see?"

Naomi wrinkled her nose and frowned. "It's mostly dry already."

"Well, do you want to stay and help me? Nikhil keeps giving me all this stuff to do. . . ."

Naomi shrugged. "I could stick around a little bit, I guess."

Lydia nodded and turned back to the receipts. Blocking Naomi's view with her body, Lydia mixed them all up again. "Come on, you can help me with this."

Lydia spent the whole day acting like an anxious hostess, trying to get Naomi to stay within earshot. She waited for Naomi to mention anything about her visit last night, but Naomi didn't even seem sleep deprived.

Cora and Nikhil made it through two run-throughs with the sound and light guy, but Lydia had to lie when she said they were great. Cora was not so wonderful an actress that she could disguise her dislike for Nikhil Patel, and Nikhil Patel looked like a thirty-year-old man trying to be a teenager, which was exactly what he was.

Around four o'clock Nikhil finished bowing to an imaginary audience and beamed at Cora.

"All right, everyone, let's take a break. Naomi, fabulous job. Lydia? Where is Lydia?"

Lydia was hiding in the deep shadows behind a curtain. She thought if she was asked to do one more mundane task, she'd either scream or burst into tears. She was so tired. She motioned for Naomi to wait for her and stayed hidden until Nikhil Patel's voice faded out the back of the auditorium. Lydia peeked around the curtain and mimed relief to Naomi.

"That guy is something else," said Naomi.

"I was about to stab him with his own fake sword."

"He deserves it."

Lydia linked her arm through Naomi's and gave her her most winning smile, despite being so tired that her eyes burned. Lydia was determined to keep Naomi safe, and she wanted a chance to talk privately about the ankh.

She, Cora, and Naomi all walked back to the dorm together, a limp conversation passing among them like a poorly thrown Frisbee. Cora saw Charlie and peeled off.

"Where to now?" Lydia said brightly.

Naomi gave her a pained smile. "Actually, I think I'll go for a walk or something. We've been inside all day."

"Okay," said Lydia, though inwardly she was drooping with fatigue. "Just let me change my shoes."

Naomi grimaced. It was supposed to be a smile, but Lydia pretended she couldn't tell that Naomi wanted to be alone.

"I'll be right back," said Lydia, and she lumbered up the stairs to her room.

Lydia sat down on her bed to tie her sneakers. She lay back with a groan and closed her eyes for just one moment.

For the second time that day, Lydia was awakened by pounding on her door. Also for the second time, her first thought was of Naomi. She stumbled out of bed and whipped the door from Cora's hands.

"Where's Naomi? Have you seen her?" Lydia said.

Cora recoiled from the door. "Uh, no, but we have a play? In, like, ninety minutes?"

"Yeah." Lydia blinked at Cora with eyes that wouldn't focus properly. "I just need to check something."

Lydia slipped past Cora, strode down the hall, and pushed open the door to Naomi's room with a bang.

Naomi was sitting at her desk, looking at a pile of shells. She gave Lydia a quizzical glare. "Yeah?" she said.

"Oh." Lydia swallowed. "Hey. Um, you want to come to dinner with us?" Cora appeared at Lydia's shoulder.

"We have to eat early," Cora explained.

Naomi gave Lydia another searching look. "Nah, I'm good. Break a leg, though," she said to Cora.

"Thanks," said Cora. "Lydia, I'll be ready in two minutes." Cora turned and walked down the hall to her room.

Lydia stared at Naomi, wishing she could force her to come with them.

"You're coming to the play, though, right?" she asked.

"Yeah, of course." Naomi turned around in her chair and looked directly at Lydia. "Are you okay, Lydia? You're, like, all jumpy or something."

"Are *you* okay?" countered Lydia. "I mean, do you remember?"

"Remember what?"

"The drawing you gave me? Last night, in the middle of the night?"

"What drawing?"

"You don't remember?"

Naomi shook her head and squinted at Lydia. "I don't know what you're talking about. If I gave you a drawing you can keep it, whatever it is. I mean, I've got literally hundreds." Naomi waved proudly at the stack of drawings that had begun to pile in drifts in every corner of her room.

"No." Lydia slumped with frustration. "It was a symbol. I'm worried—"

Cora poked her head into the room again.

"Ready?" she asked.

Lydia nodded. Then she said to Naomi, "Promise you'll come to the play?"

"Yes!" Naomi made shooing motions with her hands. "I promised already. Go. Eat. Cora, you'll be great!"

Lydia hesitated in the doorway. She knew that Naomi was beginning to tire of her vigilance, but how could she explain what she was worried about? She didn't really know herself. Lydia tapped the doorframe and said as lightly as she could, "Let me know if you need anything."

In the dining hall Lydia ate mechanically, Cora picked at a pile of noodles, and Pilar tried to keep a conversation going. In the end, Pilar decided that Cora must be too nervous to chat. She gave her a big hug and told her she'd be great, but Lydia wasn't sure that nerves were Cora's problem. If anything, Cora seemed to be deep in thought. Every once in a while a wicked grin lifted one corner of Cora's mouth, a grin that almost made Lydia feel sorry for Nikhil Patel.

Lydia went backstage to find that Nikhil had completely emptied the contents of his cooler all over the wings of the stage, and now nobody could pass from stage right to the stage. Evidently, the facial toner he'd wanted had been at the bottom of the cooler, and he couldn't be bothered to return everything once he'd found it. She spent the first twenty minutes putting all the bottles of everything back in the cooler and then wiping up the slippery pools of melted ice and condensation. By the time she found Nikhil, he was in costume and also apparently in character, because he was peeling an apple with an absurdly long knife that Lydia had thought was just a prop. She wasn't really sure she trusted Nikhil Patel with a real blade. He glanced at Lydia.

"I require nothing," he intoned in the quasi-British accent he used for Romeo. He went back to peeling his apple.

Lydia organized Romeo's props and then checked on Cora. She was sitting up in the balcony with her back to Lydia, concealed from the audience by the balustrade. Lydia noticed a small bag that hadn't been there before, but just then Romeo called for a Band-Aid, a big one, and so Lydia didn't see Cora again until just before the show started.

Lydia had never before experienced the keen excitement in the air before the start of a show. The audience was heat and noise that grew until it sounded as if the whole ocean were crashing about on the other side of the curtain. There had been a special ferry from the mainland and Lydia knew that the students, at least, were excited by the presence of actual technology on the island, because tonight's performance would be recorded. The heat of all those bodies rose, and Lydia found herself stripping off her black sweater, glad she had a black T-shirt on underneath.

Suddenly it was seven o'clock. There would be a piano performance first, then a quartet, and then Cora and Nikhil. Lydia signaled to the sound guy and the house lights blinked. The audience hushed and the performance began.

Another time Lydia might have enjoyed the music, but she was too nervous and exhausted to do more than huddle backstage and wait. She helped roll the piano behind a scrim and then fold up chairs when the quartet had finished. Finally it was time. Cora gave her a thumbs-up from the balcony and Nikhil gave her a terse nod. Lydia signaled the guy in the sound booth and the lights went down. The audience hushed except for a few coughs, then the curtains came up. Romeo stepped out onto the stage opposite where Lydia was hidden in the wings and began his first monologue.

Lydia winced. The presence of an audience had made Nikhil Patel even worse. His voice rose and fell dramatically but without enhancing the meaning of what he said. He made his gestures so huge that Lydia could hear him struggle to catch his breath as he flung his arms wide. *Poor Cora*, thought Lydia, *this is like watching a train wreck. Bad enough from backstage, but Cora is right out there, tied to the tracks.*

Lydia shrank back into the wings to bite her nails and fret, but then there was a great gout of laughter from the audience. Lydia peeked out again.

Romeo looked a little confused by the laughter but was gamely trudging through the monologue as if it hadn't happened. More laughter erupted from different spots of the audience, making Lydia twitch the curtain aside and look up at the balcony from behind.

Cora was up there. When she moved, Lydia saw that she was applying a thick, goopy mud mask to her face, stopping to inspect a zit in a mirror. When Romeo said, "See, how she leans her cheek upon her hand! / O, that I were a glove upon that hand, / That I might touch that cheek!" Juliet raised one haunch over the balustrade and scratched vigorously at her buttock.

A surprised laugh escaped Lydia's mouth. Juliet inspected her waistline in the mirror and said, "Ay me!"

The audience sounded like a thick stew, bubbling with occasional spurts of laughter. Romeo looked very confused, but that worked with the humor Juliet had created. He continued tentatively at first, but soon he was getting laughs too. Now the audience believed that his overwrought expressions were intentional, and their laughter had a wash of relief in it.

Lydia felt her shoulders relax. Cora was incredible. Her timing was as flawless as if they had practiced it that way for weeks. She stuffed her bosom with round cushions, and when one fell out while she was leaning over the balcony, it hit Romeo directly in the face. With a disgusted look at the moon-shaped cushion, she threw the other one away, saying, "Swear not by the moon, the *inconstant* moon." And that one was a direct hit as well.

At first Lydia was too relieved to really laugh, but by the end, when Juliet was leaning over the balcony and calling that parting was such sweet sorrow, Lydia was laughing with the rest of the audience.

The curtain went down, the lights went out, and there was a delicious, electric quiet like an inhaled breath before a courtroom verdict. The breath was exhaled in a roar of applause, loud as hail on a tin roof. Lydia grinned. The cheering and shouting grew, whistles piercing the wash of noise until Lydia remembered she was supposed to open the curtain again. Cora was shining with mischief and delight; Nikhil was slightly stunned, as if he was trying to figure out what had just happened.

Cora and Nikhil bowed and blew kisses, and then suddenly the backstage was flooded with friends and strangers, all shaking Lydia's hand and hugging Cora and then going to stand in a little awed circle around Nikhil Patel.

Pilar grabbed Lydia's waist and spun her around. Gus came and punched her in the shoulder, and then Seth was there with his mouth quirked up and his eyes sparkling. Naomi slipped in too, Lydia noted with relief, and then somebody handed her a heavy backpack.

"To the rock," Seth spoke loudly in her ear to be heard above the noise.

Lydia felt as if she were riding a wave of bubbles, bouncing and floating to the top of a giant flute of champagne. She wasn't tired anymore. Elation sparked and pricked in her chest as if she had breathed it in like a gas. Seth had one of her hands in his warm, dry hand. Pilar was cackling behind her. Ben was shouting up ahead, and then they all exploded out of the hot crowd into a crystalline night on the main lawn.

Giggling and pushing one another like a pack of puppies, Lydia and her friends trotted across the lawn into the sweet-smelling pine woods. They all hushed instinctively as their footsteps were swallowed by the thick carpet of needles and sand. Somebody giggled. Someone else snorted, and then they were all running and laughing.

Lydia burst out onto the silver expanse of rock above the sea that Seth had shown her on the first day of classes. The moon was globular and heavy. It seemed to wobble like a drop of milk about to fall from the platter of the sky. An undulating trail of gleaming water led back to the moon, uninterrupted by islands or boats.

Lydia breathed, her face turned up to the blanket of stars overhead. Seth came and put his arm around her shoulders and then, more intimately, her waist. He squeezed her against his side, and she turned so that she could press her front against the warmth of his body.

Lydia heard a pop and cheering, so she pulled away from Seth, but the heat of him lingered like a fingerprint.

Ben held up a bottle of champagne. "Ladies and gentleman, I offer you Nikhil Patel's finest vintage."

Pilar punched Ben in the arm. "You stole that?"

"No," said Naomi, "I did. We earned it today, Lydia and I."

Lydia laughed. She took off her backpack and found a second bottle inside, wrapped in her sweater. Raising it up, she clinked it against Ben's bottle. "To Nikhil Patel, may I never set eyes on him again!"

Ben drank out of the open bottle and passed it to Lydia. Lydia tipped up the bottle and allowed the frothy liquid to fill her mouth. It expanded as she swallowed so she coughed, then wiped her chin sheepishly. There was laughter as she passed the bottle to Seth, who managed to drink without choking. Lydia worked open the bottle from her own backpack, and a few more bottles appeared out of backpacks and bags.

Lydia, Seth, Sorcha, and Pilar sat in a tight circle, sharing a bottle of champagne. Lydia felt like she had never loved a group of people more than she loved her friends at this moment. It was so beautiful; the laughter, the moon, the sighing waves. How fortunate they were, all of them, to be alive, and how sad, piercingly sad, it was that Matthew was not here right now. He would be throwing rocks into the sea with Ben and Gus, thought Lydia. Or writing, maybe, somehow finding the marrow of this moment so that later they all could see it from the inside out.

Lydia stood up and wobbled a bit, then went to look over the edge of the cliff. Even her sadness was beautiful tonight.

She felt Seth come up behind her right shoulder. She turned, and he held up a bottle.

"Where'd you get that one?" she asked. By the weight of it, it was nearly full.

"I am a strategist. I have my ways."

"What are you strategizing now?" Lydia slouched her hip forward to bump Seth's side. She looked up at him and gave him a nudge.

When he laughed, Lydia felt a gentle buffet of warm air from his mouth. "I'm strategizing—well, I'd like—I'm trying—"

Lydia slid her thumbs over the tops of his hip bones and kissed him.

They kissed until Seth chuckled, a soft huff on the side of her mouth. Lydia laughed too and stepped back so she could see his face.

"Good strategy," said Seth.

"Good stragedy," agreed Lydia. They both laughed.

At that moment Cora and Charlie burst into the moonlight from the woods, and everybody cheered. Lydia had that untethered bubble feeling again. Cora spotted her and hugged her, twirling and laughing. Lydia felt chosen. She handed Cora the almost-full bottle and then found Seth's hand.

The talk and the laughter of her friends was layered atop the waves; rising, falling, foamy, moonlit. Lydia floated through the crowd, anchored by Seth's warm hand. There was Charlie squeezing Cora's shoulders and bending in to kiss her temple. Ellie Martin's laughing profile seemed ready to take a bite out of the moon. Sorcha was either describing something large with her hands or attempting to swim up through the air. Marin was there too, pulling needles off a small pine branch and dropping them over the edge.

Time hiccupped forward. Lydia was kissing Seth. He was so warm, and the scent of him was like a food she could live on for weeks.

Another hiccup. The large, flat rock wasn't crowded anymore. Most of the juniors and seniors were gone, and bottles had stopped circulating. Lydia sat next to Seth, their legs stretched out in front of them. They wagged their feet so that their shoes knocked together, and Lydia's head was bouncing gently on Seth's shoulder with each knock.

Lydia looked up. The moon was overhead now and there was no trail on the water, just fragmented horizontal daubs of light. Somebody stood alone at the edge of the rock, leaning forward.

Lydia focused on the silhouette and then sat up quickly. It was Naomi.

"Naomi!" Lydia scrambled to her feet and lurched forward. "Don't!" Lydia made a desperate grab for Naomi's arm and dragged her back from the edge. She felt curls of Naomi's skin come up under her fingernails, and Naomi shrieked in pain. Naomi fell on top of her, and her hip connected hard with the rock below her.

"Oww!" said Naomi. "Lydia! Jesus! Leave me alone!"

"I got you," panted Lydia.

"That really hurt!" Naomi scrambled up and backed away from Lydia. "You scratched me!" Naomi held up her forearm and peered at the dark beads of blood appearing there.

Ben came up behind Naomi and turned her arm toward the moonlight. "Whoa. You're bleeding."

Naomi hissed, "What was that for, Lydia?"

"You were going—I don't want to you die."

"Nobody's going to fall off the cliff, Lydia. Don't be ridiculous," said Naomi, holding her arm out in front of her.

"I'm not ridiculous." Lydia was hurt, then angry.

"You've been acting crazy all day," said Naomi, squeezing her arm. "You have a problem. You know that?"

Lydia lurched to her feet, and her head snapped back as if she'd been slapped. "I don't have a problem," sputtered Lydia. "You guys don't know what he did to you. It makes you want to kill yourselves."

"Who makes you want to kill yourself?" asked Ben. He laughed, hoping that Lydia was joking.

"Dr. Gaddify! He drugs you and hypnotizes you and does something in a secret room. . . ." Lydia heard herself gibbering but couldn't stop. "Now you're geniuses, but—suicide . . ." The words that Lydia wanted were far out at sea, arriving too late on the shore of her mind, like flotsam. "My friend Matthew, he came here, and now . . ." Tears burned hot trails down Lydia's cheeks.

"What are you talking about?" asked Naomi, bewilderment and hurt making her voice crack.

"You've all changed, right?" Lydia turned to face Gus. "Gus, you used to be funny—goofy, I mean. And Cora"—Lydia swung around and found Cora, who'd walked cautiously forward—"you used to be really vain. Then we had orientation and everybody's smart all of a sudden." Lydia flung her arm out to Seth, who was standing uncertainly a few feet away. "Seth used to be depressed and now he's not." Lydia gulped in a breath of cold night air. It had grown cold suddenly, and she shivered so hard that her teeth chattered together.

"This is not like you, Lydia," said Cora. Her voice was bewildered.

"It's true!" shouted Lydia. "Twenty-one Claybourne students have committed suicide!" Lydia felt somebody grab her arm above her elbow and tug her toward the woods. "You're all in danger! Please believe me!"

Lydia found herself tripping across the rock. Seth was at her side, propelling her, not gently, to the path in the woods.

"Does she even have a *real* Special?" said Ben.

"I guess not *everyone* here is a genius," said a voice Lydia couldn't recognize.

Seth pushed her onto the path and Lydia tripped. It was dark under the trees, and tears blurred her vision. Seth held her steady until she could stand upright, and then dropped her arm. Lydia's bicep felt cold where Seth's hand had been.

"Do you believe me?" whispered Lydia. "Seth? Do you believe me?"

"I really don't know what to think," growled Seth. "But I guess everybody knows I used to be depressed."

"I'm sorry." Lydia took a shuddering breath.

"Yeah," said Seth. "You are. Let's go."

Lydia tripped again and Seth caught her, but she wrenched her arm away from him. "I can walk back by myself," she said. She was shivering again, even harder than before, so the words came out like cold pebbles between her teeth.

Seth stopped walking. Lydia paused too but then took a wobbling step and then another. She walked off into the night feeling Seth's eyes like hot needles on the back of her neck.

Chapter 24

The next morning Lydia woke early and lay in bed touching her lips, which were a little tender from so much kissing, and then touching her arm where Seth had dragged her away. She stood slowly and went down the hall. The bathroom was empty because it was barely dawn. She stood at the mirror for a long time trying to see herself, but her features were out of focus and changing. Back in her room, she lay down again, rolled over to face the wall, and curled up like one of those mummies from South America.

She was not asleep; she heard noises and voices and was aware of the thin sunlight on her back. But neither was she awake. Around noon hunger drove her into a sitting position. Lydia had the thought that maybe everybody would think she had just been drunk, that she hadn't really meant it. She felt shrunken.

Lydia hurried across the lawn to the dining hall, half tiptoeing, half scuttling. Inside she stayed close to the walls, blindly piled a plate with food, and then stood just inside the door of the dining room. There was a group of sophomores Lydia knew from Regulars to her left and some freshman girls from her floor on the right. Lydia decided that the freshmen were less likely to have heard about last night and headed that way.

She was almost to the table when she heard somebody snigger the words "Dr. Gaddify's secret room," followed by laughter. She ate alone with her back to the room.

Lydia left the dining hall and turned away from the dorm, taking the hallway past Dr. Gaddify's office and exiting the main building out the back. The library was there, solid and comforting as an armchair.

Lydia haunted the cottony silence of the library, reading snippets of pages here and there for about an hour. Finally she realized what she was looking for. She had been too complacent, she thought. She'd gotten caught up in Bourne War and the play and Seth, but now it was time to do what she'd come for.

There was a large bay window on the third story of the library that looked out over the tops of the trees to the south. You couldn't really see the ocean, but you could detect the horizon through the trees, and it was very sunny there. Lydia brought a pile of books up to a golden pine table and started to read.

The ankh was found throughout ancient Egypt and into the Mediterranean and Mesopotamia. It symbolized life and afterlife. Lydia studied pages of ancient Egyptian paintings that showed gods giving ankhs to pharaohs. Scholars believed an ankh could be meant to represent male and female genitalia, with a female circle and a male trinity below, or it could be the cross section of an ox vertebra from a culture that highly valued cattle. Lydia could not imagine what it meant coming from Naomi.

She also found a lot about hypnotism, its medical uses and uses for entertainment, but there wasn't anything that suggested hypnotism could unlock potential intelligence or change a person's personality as dramatically as Lydia had witnessed.

The sun slowly swept the table until it left the big window altogether. Lydia put all the books back on the shelves where they belonged. She trudged down the stairs and saw Ms. Alton in her small glassed-in office behind the main desk.

"Hello, Lydia," said Ms. Alton. She was wearing a beige cardigan and burgundy corduroy pants, which Lydia guessed were what Ms. Alton thought of as casual.

Lydia walked over to her office door. "Hello." The word came out croaky. It was the first thing she'd said all day.

"I think you and I were the only two people here all day," said Ms. Alton, looking at Lydia over her glasses. "It's good. I have a lot of shelving to catch up on." Ms. Alton gestured to three rolling carts filled with books.

"I can help," said Lydia. "I mean, I know how. If you want." Lydia shrugged, hoping that she didn't sound desperate.

"Well." Ms. Alton studied Lydia. Lydia could tell she was wondering why she didn't have anything more important to do, but Ms. Alton nodded and said, "That would be lovely."

It took Lydia an hour to shelve the books. She was a little relieved to discover that her classmates, geniuses though they may be, read a lot of mysteries, romances, and fantasy novels. When she was finished, she rolled the last empty cart back to Ms. Alton's office and waited for her to finish writing something down.

Ms. Alton capped the pen neatly, slid the paper into a pile, and removed her glasses to look at Lydia. "Lydia, I can't tell you what a help it has been to have you this afternoon." Ms. Alton smiled at Lydia and swept her hand at a small chair that was tucked in a corner of the tiny office. "I think we've earned a treat."

Lydia pulled the chair out from the corner and put it down facing Ms. Alton's desk. Ms. Alton got up and went to a small refrigerator that was under a counter behind her desk. "I can make us some tea if you like, or would you prefer lemonade?"

"Lemonade, please," said Lydia.

Ms. Alton chatted comfortably while she made herself tea from an electric kettle and then poured some lemonade from a bottle into a glass, which made it seem much fancier. They talked about books and writers, and Lydia told Ms. Alton about her mom's library and her job over the summer. For one whole hour Lydia didn't think about her friends at all.

On Monday, Lydia learned that her outburst had had two effects: First, none of her friends would talk to her or look her in the eye, though she felt their stares whenever she walked across the dining hall to sit alone in a dim corner. Second, the population of the school seemed unanimous in their verdict that Lydia was crazy. The student body was divided as to whether this proved she was a genius or not.

In math, Seth sat down across a table from her and bluntly asked if she'd meant it.

"I mean, did you drink too much champagne? Do you really think all that stuff that you said?"

It would have been so easy for Lydia to lie. She could have covered her face with her hands and giggled and acted embarrassed, and the whole thing might have gone away. She could kiss Seth again. Talk to her friends. But if she lied, her friends would think they were safe.

"It's true, what I said." Lydia looked at Seth steadily. "I don't have proof yet, but I can show you what I've found."

Seth shook his head. He looked genuinely sad.

"I'm not crazy," said Lydia. "Yet." She smiled, holding out the joke like a peace offering.

Seth ignored the joke and studied her face so intently Lydia could almost feel his gaze as it traveled across her skin.

"If you want my advice," he said, "even if it is true, *especially* if it's true, you had better act like you made it up. Better yet, act like it's something you read somewhere." Seth looked away and frowned.

"I'm sorry that I told people about . . . what you told me. I shouldn't have said you were depressed."

Seth snorted. "That's the least of it! You said Cora was vain, Naomi's suicidal, and Gus *used* to be funny but now he's not!" Seth's jaw worked, and then he whispered, "I really liked you, Lydia."

"I'm not lying, Seth. I'm worried about you. All of you."

Seth looked away and swallowed. Lydia saw his face change. He turned his eyes back to her and sneered. "Worry about yourself, Lydia. You're literally nuts."

Tears pushed at the backs of Lydia's eyes. Seth got up and walked to the other side of the classroom, where Sorcha was sitting. Sorcha gave Lydia a curious look and then turned her back. It was the beginning of a very long day.

Lydia thought about what Seth had said. Even if Seth hated her, it was good advice. What would happen to her if Dr. Gaddify or his mysterious helper heard about her tirade? Would he get rid of her somehow? Discredit her? Expel her? Murder her? That wasn't even the worst part. The real problem was that she had insulted all of her friends. She needed them to believe her so that they could be on guard. Lydia didn't think she could bear it if they all committed suicide one after the other. Lydia couldn't take back what she'd said and couldn't pretend she'd made it up. She desperately needed proof that something was wrong.

As they were leaving their Special, Gus gave Lydia a puzzled, hurt look that squeezed her heart painfully. She opened her mouth to apologize, but he moved so quickly away from her that she would have had to shout. Lydia slouched, exhausted, in the middle of the hallway and turned in the opposite direction. She walked down the rear staircase and found herself back at the library. She helped Ms. Alton glue cards into the fronts of books that had been donated, and was rewarded with another glass of lemonade.

At dinner Lydia sat alone at one end of a table. Jay, the architecture kid, was sitting a few chairs away by himself. He seemed to be absorbed in a sketchbook that he was drawing in with a ruler and a compass, but abruptly he pushed his notebook away and turned to face Lydia.

"What you said . . ." He cleared his throat. "I wasn't there, but I heard you said something about a secret room."

Lydia stabbed up a forkful of mashed potatoes and looked at Jay from behind it as if the tubers might protect her somehow.

"As a matter of fact, there are three holes in the main building. Not holes, per se, but blank spaces or 'secret rooms,' if you will."

Lydia lowered her fork. "What do you mean?"

Jay frowned, thinking. "There is a depression in the third floor—in the ceiling, that is—so that a section of it is about eight inches lower than the rest of it. It's a perfect square, about forty feet on each side, right in the center of the building. The structure beneath it suggests something heavy."

Lydia looked at him, searching his face for signs of mockery. "What about the other two?"

"On the second and third floors there are gaps between the classrooms that are big enough to be large closets or maybe a staircase." Jay focused his eyes and frowned more deeply. "It's not ductwork or anything to do with utilities." He said it defensively, as if Lydia had suggested it.

Lydia nodded.

"The third is right next to Dr. Gaddify's office, between his office and the kitchen. It's not so big. Probably a safe."

Lydia nodded again, still trying to figure out why Jay was talking to her.

"You're not the only one to notice things, you know," he said, defensive again. "I noticed it first." Jay stood and snatched up his notebook. He walked away without clearing his tray.

Lydia finished eating and wearily cleared both trays. She stepped out onto the main steps and saw Pilar, Cora, and Naomi coming. She stood on the top step, watching them. They ignored her so strongly that she felt as if they couldn't see her. It made her unabashed in her staring. When they got to the bottom of the steps, they stopped talking, looking at Lydia with carefully neutral faces.

"Pilar," said Lydia.

Pilar stopped but shifted her gaze down. She was not committing to a conversation. Cora and Naomi paused, then walked through the doors to the dining hall.

"I think you took some pictures with your plane during Bourne War," said Lydia.

Pilar said nothing.

"If you have any of the top of the main building, I'd appreciate seeing them."

"Dr. Gaddify made me stop taking pictures of the buildings. And he accidentally exposed my film when he was looking at my invention," Pilar blurted out, seeming as though she had spoken against her will.

"Did you get any photos of the buildings?"

Pilar looked fiercely up at Lydia. "Does this have to do with your crazy theory?"

Lydia paused. "Yes." She paused again. "I want to know if there is something on the roof. A square room. With a lot of windows, I think," she said, remembering the light for the first time.

Lydia waited. After a few seconds Pilar looked down again and then brushed past her roughly.

Lydia walked out onto the main lawn and turned around to study the main building. It was three stories high and had a flat roof. You couldn't see the roof, and there seemed to be a decorative wall all around it that blocked the view of anything on top of the building.

Inside the dorm, Lydia went to the top floor and tried to see the top of the main building from there. The dorm was also three stories high, but it had shorter stories, so even from the highest point the roof of the main building wasn't visible. Lydia considered all the other buildings on campus. None of them were any taller than the dorm. Another dead end.

That night in her room Lydia was studying similarities in the grammatical structure of romance languages. There was a hiss and a scratching noise, then a thick piece of paper slid under the door and wafted across the floor until it hit the rug. Lydia turned it over. It was an 8 x 10 black-and-white photo that was out of focus and hard to make out. A sticky note with messy handwriting scrawled across it read: *I took a roll of film before Dr. G. stopped me.* In different ink, looking like an afterthought: *I don't think he knows about this roll.* Lydia put the sticky note aside and turned the photo ninety degrees, then turned it again. She recognized the brickwork that was out in front of the library. The part of the photo that was most in focus must be the roof on the south side of the main building. Lydia studied it harder. There wasn't much to see except a flat roof and a large shadow in the shape of a triangle.

There was a second photo underneath the first, stuck to it by a ring of condensation from a glass. Lydia pried the two photos apart and studied the second one. This one was less out of focus, and the whole frame was filled with a flat gray roof and what looked like a pyramid made entirely of glass. Three facets of the pyramid were opaque because of the light, but the fourth offered a sliver of the floor inside. The floor was light colored but had the corner of a dark pattern painted on it, and at the tip of the corner, barely discernible, was an ankh.

All week Lydia felt as if she were one of the secret rooms that Jay had talked about—a hole, a blank spot. She wasn't exactly invisible; she was simply a space where nobody ever went. The only place that she felt visible was in the library with Ms. Alton. Lydia helped with shelving, late notices, and loan requests. Anytime she was in the stacks, she opened books at random, hoping one might explain what she had seen in the pyramid room. She ate dinner early, alone, and afterward she would check the auditorium to see if she could snoop around for the spiral stairs she remembered. She was sure they led up Jay's secret staircase and into the pyramid room.

She dreamed the anger dream so often that her teeth seemed permanently clenched. Matthew jumping off the cliff on the island, Matthew stepping off the top of the swing set at home, Matthew letting go as they hung from the side of a building. Always, always, always the anger.

On Thursday, after a little shelving, Ms. Alton brought out a tin of cookies, homemade oatmeal raisin. Lydia ate five before she even realized what she was doing. She stopped and blushed when she caught herself reaching for the sixth.

"Go on, dear," said Ms. Alton.

Lydia, who was still chewing the last cookie, shook her head and looked away, embarrassed.

Ms. Alton carefully brushed the crumbs on her desk into her palm and then tipped them into the garbage. "If you don't mind me saying, Lydia, I've noticed that you seem troubled by something."

Lydia opened her mouth, but what could she say? Ms. Alton studied her for a moment and then smiled kindly. "If I can help, please let me know."

Lydia was horrified to find that her vision had started to wobble because of the enormous tears that sprang to her eyes.

"Oh dear," said Ms. Alton. She stood up and went to a bookshelf. She ticked her finger along the spines until she found a yellow book. Lydia wiped her eyes on her sleeve and sat up straighter in her chair.

"Here," said Ms. Alton, turning back. "I find it immensely comforting." She handed Lydia a well-loved copy of *Little House in the Big Woods*, by Laura Ingalls Wilder.

Lydia was so touched by the kindness and concern in Ms. Alton's eyes that tears swam in her own again.

"And you'll let me know if I can help you with whatever it is you're researching upstairs?" said Ms. Alton, frowning with concern.

"Yes," croaked Lydia. "Thank you."

"Is there anything else I can do?"

"Actually," said Lydia with a weak smile, "I'm late for extra help with Mr. Harcourt. Could you write me a note or something?"

"I'll do you one better. Mr. Harcourt, you say? In his office?"

"Yes."

Ms. Alton moved aside a stack of folders, revealing an odd speaker-looking box lodged in the top of her desk. She saw Lydia's curious look and smiled. "It an old-fashioned intercom. It works with wires instead of radio waves. Apparently, it doesn't violate Dr. Gaddify's rules about tech." Ms. Alton ran her finger down a list that was taped to her desk. She tapped her finger twice and then pressed a two-digit number into the keypad on the intercom. Lydia heard faint static. After thirty seconds Mr. Harcourt's voice scratched out of the speaker, barely recognizable but clear enough to be understood.

"Harcourt."

"Mr. Harcourt, I've got Lydia Boswell here at the library, and I've accidentally kept her late. Do you still have time to see her if she comes right over?"

"Yes. I suppose. Send her over."

"Thank you for your understanding," said Ms. Alton. She pushed another button and the static stopped.

"One for the road?" Ms. Alton held out the tin of cookies.

"Thanks, Ms. Alton," said Lydia.

"You take care now."

"I will."

After dinner, more out of habit than hope, Lydia checked the auditorium again and was surprised to find it both open and empty.

Beyond the trapezoid of light from the door, the room was filled with inky shadows. Lydia slid inside and walked a few steps before the door fell closed and she was in the pitch dark. Instead of turning on the house lights, which might give her away, Lydia felt for the floor with her feet and stepped slowly down the aisle until she bumped up against the stage. Lydia's breathing seemed loud and intrusive in the dark. She could smell the dusty, old-sneaker smell from backstage and wondered if she could find the light switch she knew was back there somewhere to the left.

Lydia kept one hand on the stage and blinked. Her eyes were starting to pick out shades of blackness. She could see the shape of the stage now, a slightly grayer rectangle of air. The only light came from the exit signs on three sides of the auditorium and an electrical box to the side of the stage. Lydia decided to try to find the light panel. With luck she could turn on just the backstage lights.

Lydia crawled up onto the stage and stood cautiously. She slid her feet along the gritty floor, making loud rasping sounds, and walked forward with her arms out in front of her. She found the curtain, heavy and musty, and pushed it around her body, so that it fell about her like a heavy gown. It was even darker back here, and that was the only reason Lydia didn't miss it.

A narrow sliver of light lay like a silver épée along the base of the wall. Lydia knew the wall was painted black and covered in strips of electrical tape. She had never seen a door in the wall, but the strip of light was about as wide as a door.

Lydia's heart began to knock against her ribs. She knelt and ran her fingers along the line of light. It was the narrowest of gaps, but her fingers encountered cool air. She followed it all the way to the edge and felt a corner. The space between the corner and the wall was covered with rubbery tape.

Lydia had found it. The way up to the pyramid room.

Chapter 25

Lydia had a plan. Saturday was the sophomore trip to the mainland and the pizza party. She'd find her way to the hardware store and buy electrical tape, a box cutter, and a disposable camera. She'd get into the auditorium, cut open the door, and take pictures for proof. Maybe the hardware store would have lock-picking stuff, in case the door was locked, though Lydia wasn't sure how you could ask for such a thing. Maybe a screwdriver would work.

Saturday morning was gray and drizzly. Lydia walked through the dripping woods down to the ferry, alone again but between two groups of sophomores who were all chatting and laughing, their shoulders hunched against the drizzle.

Lydia pretended that she was a part of one group, as if their jokes were meant for her ears. She hadn't showered in three days now, and the rain heightened the doggy smell of her dirty hair. She was beginning to wonder if Matthew and all the others had discovered something the way she had. Maybe they'd felt ignored and half crazy too. Maybe she should get off the ferry on the mainland and hitchhike back home.

Lydia found a quiet seat on the ferry and looked out the window the whole way across. It wasn't raining where the boat was anymore, but she could see rain far away. It looked like hair, as if a giant gray corpse were lying on a slow-moving gurney in the clouds.

Captain Whelk let them off at the boathouse with the standard warning about bringing tech to the island as well as a promise that anyone who wasn't on board by four o'clock would have to swim back to school. Ms. Windham told them all to meet at Scruffy's Pizza on Main Street in two hours, and then they were free.

Despite everything, Lydia couldn't help but feel a little lift of anticipation as she stepped off the boat. Seth and Sorcha were in a group that was already disappearing around the corner of a building. Lydia squashed a little tug of longing and pulled up her hood. The rest of the sophomores were wandering off in groups of two or three. Marin and Malia walked off together, stiff as a couple on a blind date. Lydia sighed and climbed up the steep hill to Main Street alone.

She wandered past a pet store that seemed to be on its last legs, an antiques place, some law offices, and a thrift store called Unique Boutique. The sidewalk ended and up ahead was a boatyard, so Lydia turned back. In the opposite direction there was a coffee shop that was packed with Claybourne students and then Scruffy's Pizza. Lydia wondered if there was a library in town where she might get on the Internet, so she asked a harassed-looking mother and got directions to go two blocks up the hill and it would be on the right.

"I think half your school is there now," said the woman, who was out of breath from rocking a giant stroller.

Lydia thanked her but hesitated. She should have guessed she wouldn't be the only one with a burning desire to use "Google" and "e-mail" as verbs again.

Instead Lydia walked down the rest of Main Street. She remembered the church and the general store from arriving with her mom, but that seemed like ancient history. The hardware store was right where she remembered, on the uphill side of the street.

The store was called Riendeau's Hardware, and it had a long, low porch along the front. Stacked up against the back wall of the porch were ceramic planters, buoys, lobster traps, snow shovels, leaf rakes, beach pails, a lone toboggan, rolls of chicken wire, a large motor, and, right by the door, the very old woman in the rocking chair.

Lydia walked up the steps, trying to gauge if the old woman was asleep or, for that matter, alive. She had on the same dark, round glasses Lydia remembered from her first day, and she was wrapped in several layers of colorful material. As she got closer, Lydia saw that the old lady's jaw was making small chewing motions, but she couldn't see through the lenses of the glasses to tell if the woman was awake. Lydia waved just in case and walked into the dim interior of the store.

The building had been built at least a century ago, Lydia guessed, because the ceiling was low and dark, and the floors were so warped that she tripped over a bulge as she walked in.

A compact, dark-haired man was stacking boxes into a pyramid. The boxes held garbage bags that would look like giant pumpkins when filled with leaves. He looked up and gave Lydia a nod, then went back to work. Lydia lifted her hand to acknowledge the nod and slunk into one of the aisles. There was something about a hardware store that always made her feel like she was crashing a formal party.

Lydia found a box cutter and three sizes of electrical tape. She brought all three up to the counter and waited uncomfortably for the man to stand up and brush off his knees.

"How can I help you, miss?"

"Well, um, I was told to get electrical tape, but I don't know what size. Is one of these more, uh, normal?"

"You probably want the three-quarter inch."

"Okay." Lydia paused and sucked in a breath. "I know this sounds . . . bad—but do you have anything for picking a lock?"

The man smiled and raised his eyebrows. "I do actually have a lock kit." He moved out from behind the counter and disappeared into an aisle. A minute later he was back with a small plastic-sealed package in his hand. "Now, I don't want to hear about a crime spree in Stillbay." He forced his smile into a stern expression.

Lydia smiled sheepishly. "No. I live on the island anyway. It's not that smart to steal when you're stuck on an island."

"You're from the school?" The man seemed surprised and maybe alarmed.

Lydia was a little annoyed. Was she so obviously lacking in genius potential that this man couldn't believe she went to Claybourne? "Yeah. I'm a sophomore."

The man peered at Lydia and then suddenly shouted over his shoulder into the back room. *"Julien, ou est Maman?"*

A voice came from the back. *"Dans sa chaise!"* A man, who was also dark and compact, came from the back room with a rag in his hand. *"Il y a un probléme?"*

Lydia was delighted to find that she had followed the exchange in French: "Where is Mom?" "In her chair! Is there a problem?" But then the first man burst into rapid French that Lydia couldn't follow. All she heard was the word "Claybourne," which came at the same time he jerked his head in her direction. The second man walked quickly around the counter and peered out onto the porch.

"Elle est la."

She is there.

"Est-elle morte?"

Is she dead?"

"Maman?"

Lydia heard a voice that was old and brittle, like the rasp of dry leaves over pavement, but couldn't make out the words.

"Did I do something wrong?" asked Lydia.

The first man recalled his attention to Lydia and frowned. "No, not at all. It's just that Maman does not usually allow students from Claybourne into the store. She makes a terrible fuss. Scares 'em away."

"Really?" asked Lydia. "How come?"

The man shrugged. "She calls them *les hantés*. Won't let them near the place." The man studied Lydia doubtfully. "Maybe we should sneak you out the back."

"*Les hantés*?" said Lydia. "'The haunted'?"

"*Oui*," said the second man, coming halfway back inside from the porch. "Maman has the Sight. She can tell everyone who comes from that school, even the alumni, and she says they're all haunted."

Lydia got the sense that the first brother didn't like to talk about their mother, but the second brother did. She turned to the second brother and tried to look innocently curious.

"Haunted how? Like, literally haunted? With ghosts?"

The second brother, Julien, shrugged and held up his palms. He seemed to enjoy spooking Lydia. "Don't ask me. The Sight only goes through the women in our family. But she knows you're here. I guess you're just not haunted." He smiled mockingly, as if this might be embarrassing for Lydia.

The old lady on the porch said something again, and Julien ducked his head out the door to catch it. "The woman has ears like a cat," he said, shaking his head. "She says you *are* haunted.

But *your* ghost is not angry." Lydia could tell that Julien was hoping for a big reaction, so she kept her facial expression polite.

The woman said something else, and Julien faced Lydia again. "She says that, also, you are not dead."

Lydia wasn't sure how to receive this pronouncement, other than to take it as an obscure compliment.

"Can I talk to her?" she asked.

Julien smirked a little. "How's your French?"

"Okay," said Lydia. "I'm learning. I just want to know what she means."

Julien shrugged and jerked his head toward the porch. Lydia left her things on the counter and followed him outside.

The old woman was bent over like a shell curled in on itself, so Lydia squatted down in front of her to be on eye level.

"*Bonjour, Madame,*" said Lydia, feeling stupid. "*Je m'appelle Lydia.*"

The old lady lifted one shrunken hand and used the whole thing to brush her glasses down her nose. When Lydia caught sight of the woman's eyes, she lost her balance from her squatting position. The eyes were almost entirely white, like two closed barnacles. The irises were nearly covered over by translucent clouds. At some point they may have been a very pale blue. Lydia sat down hard and tried to make her surprise seem unrelated to the woman's eyes.

The old lady cackled, not fooled, and spoke in rapid French.

Julien was smiling broadly now that Lydia had fallen over in surprise. He was like the zookeeper in the reptile house who relishes telling squeamish visitors how many rats the snakes eat every day.

"She says that eyes that look on the dead lose their color. Bleached by spirit energy."

"Je suis hantée?" asked Lydia, pointing to her chest and speaking carefully.

"Oui." The old lady sank her chin into her chest and then said something else. Lydia looked up to Julien for a translation. He shifted his eyes left and cleared his throat, looking apologetic for the first time. "It's the boy who is like a brother."

Lydia looked back at the old lady, who spoke again.

"Il te protége de la femme avec les yeux comme les miens."

"'He's protecting you—'" Julien started to translate.

"I know," said Lydia. "He's protecting me from the woman with eyes like hers."

"Il y a quelq'un qui aide M. Gaddify?" Lydia asked in slow French. There is a someone who helps Mr. Gaddify?

"Oui. Avec les yeux comme ca." The old woman pointed again to her own eyes.

Lydia studied the woman's white eyes. They were set deep into the sockets. They weren't piercing—it wasn't as if the woman could see through Lydia—but it felt as though she could see all of Lydia at once. Lydia shuddered.

She thanked the old woman and stood up slowly, wondering why she wasn't more surprised or skeptical. It was nice, actually, to imagine that Matthew was with her. Lydia opened her mouth to ask one of the questions that had popped up like mushrooms, but the old woman made shooing motions and hitched one of her many shawls around her shoulders.

"She's tired now," said Julien. "You had better go."

"I just have one more question," said Lydia. She turned to the old woman before Julien could protest.

There was a light film of condensation on the painted porch floor, and Lydia used her finger to trace an ankh onto a patch of smooth painted board. *"Qu'est que c'est?"* What is this?

The old woman shouted and stomped on the ankh, scrubbing it out with her small, slippered foot.

"I'm sorry," said Lydia, standing up and backing away. "I'm really sorry."

"You should go," said Julien. His eyes were dark and hard.

"I'll just pay for my things."

Julien hesitated. His mother was rocking back and forth and chewing rapidly.

"Get your stuff."

Lydia paid for her purchases with the feeling that if she didn't get out soon, one of the two brothers was going to toss her down the front steps. She hurried back to the street, stopping at the sidewalk for a quick look back at the old lady. She was motionless again, her glasses staring off the porch like two sightless eyes.

As she walked away, Lydia noticed a sharpness to her perceptions. The wet edges of all she saw were backlit in a way that made everything more real, more defined. She stopped and put her left hand out in the air across her chest. She changed her mind and laid her hand on her own shoulder.

"Hello, Matthew," she whispered.

It might have been her imagination, but she felt the skin on her back tighten as if she had a sunburn, then the sensation went away.

For the first time in a week Lydia didn't feel alone.

Chapter 26

Lydia wandered around Stillbay until noon, all the pieces of information she had learned buzzing like static. She was almost surprised that nobody else could see the dark cloud of thoughts that swarmed around her head.

At noon she went to the library, waited out the stragglers who were furiously typing in a few last words before the pizza party, and then sat down at a computer.

"There's a fifteen-minute time limit," said a very large woman with a name tag. She said it in a way that let Lydia know that she was prepared to enforce the fifteen-minute rule with the last of her strength.

Lydia logged in to her e-mail and skimmed through the inbox. Life, apparently, was going on without her back home. Her friends had sent a flurry of messages at first, but the last one was dated five days ago and said, "Just checking."

Lydia didn't have the time or the energy to think of something to say to everyone back home, so she used the camera on the computer to take a picture of herself smiling and sent it to all her friends with the caption "Proof I'm alive."

Then she got down to work. She searched "the Sight" and got a completely overwhelming barrage of information that seemed to be mostly made up.

She searched "ankh," spelling it wrong twice, and when she finally got it right, she noticed something odd in the drop-down menu. The fifth option on the menu was "ankh inverted." Since she already knew the basics of ankhs, she clicked on that.

The sites that came up were all strange and mystical sounding like Third Eye Socket, Beloved Dead, and Finger Knuckle Coven. An inverted ankh, she learned, was a symbol that was most commonly used in necromancy.

Lydia looked up "necromancy." It was magic having to do with the dead. It seemed to run the gamut from spirit communication to creating servants out of corpses and grave dirt. Lydia had the sense that each website she clicked on fell into one of two categories. The first was a factual reporting of mystical beliefs. The second type was made by people who liked to pretend to believe in necromancy and had something to sell. It was enough to make her think the whole thing was made up.

Lydia took her fingers from the keyboard and thought hard. She had four minutes left.

"Protection from haunting," she typed, then hit search.

Lydia skimmed over offers of amulets and crystals and exorcism and stopped on an article about how to make a circle of protection with salt.

> Find a small, flat area where you will not
> be disturbed. Starting in the east and
> moving clockwise, pour a thin line of
> blessed sea salt—

The large woman came and loomed over the back of Lydia's chair.

"Time's up."

Lydia strained to look around the considerable bulk of the woman's stomach.

"There's no one else waiting."

"You're supposed to be at a pizza party or something. Not ordering sacred amulets online." The woman snorted, causing her whole torso to contract upward four inches and then wobble back into place.

Lydia was irritated but kept herself from saying the biting retort that was on the tip of her tongue.

"I just met the old lady at the hardware store," she said, hoping the snide and superior librarian would offer an opinion.

Another snort. "She run you off?"

Lydia shrugged, which wasn't a lie exactly.

"She's crazy as the day is long. Her own daughter doesn't even talk to her anymore."

"Does the daughter still live around here?" Lydia remembered that the Sight ran through the women in the family.

"She sure does. She gave you a ride over here this morning."

"Captain Whelk?" said Lydia, surprised.

The librarian raised an eyebrow to indicate that Lydia was right. She folded her arms over her bosom and glared over the tops of them. Despite this intimidating posture, Lydia could tell that the lady was enjoying knowing more than one of the snotty little geniuses that came over from the island.

"Martha used to get seasick, you know. Couldn't even sit on a dock without turning green. As soon as she washed her hands of her mother, she wasn't seasick anymore." The librarian looked around loftily. "Some people say that her mother cursed her with seasickness. It's just lucky that Dr. Gaddify gave her a job, because no one around here wanted to risk getting on the wrong side of her mother." The librarian checked Lydia's reaction, found it suitably awed, and went on. "Course, it's just superstitious nonsense. Like that website you've got there."

"Do you mind if I read this last part?" asked Lydia. "That lady really freaked me out."

The librarian snorted again. "Five more minutes, not that any of that garbage is going to help."

Lydia quickly skimmed through the article, which turned out to be about possession. According to Mother Shipton's Archive, the best way to rid yourself of possession was to destroy anything that may have belonged to the spirit. Of course, if you lived in the spirit's house, that might not be possible. There was a link to read the spell for exorcism.

The librarian came back and hovered.

"Oh, well, I guess I better go," said Lydia, getting up.

The librarian shifted to one side to let Lydia pass. "Don't want to miss out on the pizza." She sounded wistful.

"Yeah," said Lydia.

Lydia gathered up her bag and flipped her hood over her head. It was drizzling again. She realized she was hungry, and more than anything she wanted somebody to talk to. She trudged down the slick, wet sidewalk toward the water. Leaves, plastered like stickers on the gray rock of the sidewalk, had made prints of themselves here and there. It was fall, Lydia realized. It didn't seem possible that Matthew had been dead for nearly a year. Sometimes she forgot. Not that he had died, but sometimes the feeling she'd had since he died went away and she would feel normal again. Then she'd realize, would remember, and it was always a surprise how painful it was when the feeling came back.

Lydia felt the pressure of grief building in her throat and forced it down. She swiped at her eyes with the back of her hand and turned her face up to the drizzle to cool the burning.

Suddenly she was just plain tired. Tired of trying to solve this mystery, tired of being by herself, tired of trying to understand things that were beyond her.

She passed behind the church and walked alongside the very steep cemetery she had noted on her first day. There was a flicker in the murky light. A ghost? No, Nurse Proctor. She was kneeling in front of a headstone, oblivious of the drizzle. She wasn't even wearing a raincoat, just her usual gray uniform with the crimson belt like a mortal wound. She fussed about the base of the stone, patting and wiping the grass like a woman cleaning up a kitchen counter.

Lydia slowed but did not stop. *A woman with eyes like Maman's who helps Mr. Gaddify.* She thought of the articles she had just skimmed and remembered everything they claimed you could do with grave dirt. She shivered in the cold and hurried on, suddenly terrified that Nurse Proctor would look up and see her there.

Slightly out of breath, Lydia tugged open the door of Scruffy's Pizza, which was sticking from the humidity. The hot, pizza-smelling air that rushed out to envelop Lydia was so comforting that she felt her knees wobble with relief.

Scruffy's was a single large room that was dominated by a long black bar facing the windows. There was a mirror behind the bar with a painting of a boat in a storm right in the middle. The mirror reflected the meager light of the day, making the place seem even more welcoming. Past the bar were two rows of booths with a long table in between. What was left of the pizzas was scattered along the long table in the middle. Lydia's classmates were stacked in the booths, shouting and laughing, their faces glowing with pizza grease and happiness. They didn't look like people who were haunted.

Lydia found a plate and three pieces of pizza. She sat down in a chair by the edge of a booth where a girl named Blair, Marin, and some others were sitting. This booth was definitely the least boisterous, but Lydia didn't mind. She listened to them talking about what foods they missed eating because they lived on an island.

"I miss real french fries."

"Burgers with pickles."

"The bakery next to my house makes amazing croissants."

"I miss my friends," said Lydia. Everyone turned to look at her. They had ignored her when she sat down, and now they were surprised that she was drawing attention to herself. She'd broken nerd code.

"I miss my friend Matthew from home," said Lydia. It felt good to say his name. "I miss all my friends." Lydia meant her Claybourne friends and didn't care if these people knew it. There was another silence.

"I miss my cat," said Marin. "I guess."

"My car," groaned a boy Lydia knew only as Bunt.

They turned away from Lydia again. She ate all the pizza on her plate and then one more slice. Without speaking to anyone, she helped herself to some Diet Coke from a pitcher on the table and gulped it down. She belched and left.

Rain was making the streets all but deserted. Lydia scurried along the empty sidewalk to the general store. She bought a disposable camera, some candy bars, and a large bag of Doritos for comfort. *She's just a crazy old lady,* Lydia told herself a hundred times. *Who somehow knew about Matthew.* At the counter was a bin of cheap plastic ponchos. Lydia added one to her pile, paid, and put it on.

There was still two hours before she had to be at the ferry, and there was one more thing to do in Stillbay.

Lydia trudged back up the hill to the side entrance of the cemetery. It was empty now of people. Living ones, anyway. Lydia tried to remember which stone Nurse Proctor had visited. It had been uphill, almost at the top wall of the cemetery. Lydia let herself in the black iron gate, wincing at the squeal of rusty hinges. The steady rain had already found a way in through her poncho. A thread of icy water ran down the side of her neck and into the front of her hoodie. Risking even more drenching, Lydia lifted her head to look all around. Nobody was in sight. She made her way, squelching through the grass, up to the second-to-last row of stones and immediately found one that had a mat of crushed grass in front of it.

MOSES B. JOHNSON
GONE TO THE ANGELS
MAR. 19, 1977–AUG. 4, 1990

Lydia lingered only long enough to memorize the name and the dates. She thought that if anyone was watching her, she wouldn't want anyone to know which grave had interested her, so she went and stood in front of a few other tombstones. She wandered, staring blindly through the rain and trying to fight the feeling of unseen eyes. After fifteen more minutes in the pouring rain Lydia left.

Lydia got down to the ferry early. It seemed deserted. Lydia tried the door to the boathouse, but it was locked. Though the rain had slowed to a drizzle Lydia didn't relish the thought of standing in her leaky poncho for half an hour or more. She walked tentatively up the ramp onto the boat. Nobody stopped her, so she went to the door and called inside.

"Hello?"

There was a clank from somewhere.

Lydia stepped all the way in and eased the door shut behind her.

"Hello?"

"Hello!" The voice came from the staff office in the center of the boat.

Lydia walked over to the door and knocked.

"Come in."

Captain Whelk was sitting in a small, crowded room with her feet up on some sort of console. She had a Styrofoam cup of coffee in one hand and was flipping through papers on a clipboard with the other.

"Oh. Hi," said Lydia. "Um, I'm early, so is it okay if I just hang out?"

Captain Whelk looked Lydia up and down and then, as seemed to happen often lately, decided that Lydia looked a little worse for wear.

"Why don't you pull up a chair in here. I got the heat on and you look wet through."

"Thanks." Lydia put her bags down and looked around. The only other chair had a big stack of rolled charts on it.

"Just lean those over against that wall. Do you drink coffee?"

"Not really," said Lydia. "Thanks, though."

Captain Whelk settled into her chair and nodded. She looked a lot like her brothers except that she had pale blue eyes that were barely visible in their deep sockets. She had the wrinkles of a woman who squinted a lot but also smiled. Lydia liked her.

"Have a good pizza party?" she asked.

"Yeah," said Lydia. "The pizza was really good."

"Mike knows what he's doing. That's Scruffy. We went to high school together, on the mainland." Captain Whelk studied

Lydia. "You from a city? I guess it's funny to you that we all know each other."

"Actually, I met a lady today in the library who said she knows you. She told me you used to get seasick." Lydia grinned as if she'd never believe that the captain of a boat could get seasick.

Captain Whelk smiled ruefully into her coffee. "It's true. Certain days, just the sound of waves was enough to put me off my feed. You know who cured me, though?"

Lydia shook her head.

"Your Dr. Gaddify came and talked to me. After that I could ride a rowboat through a hurricane and not get sick."

"He just *talked* to you?" asked Lydia. "Do you think he hypnotized you or something?"

Captain Whelk smiled indulgently. "Could be. Whatever he did, I'm grateful."

Lydia used her lips to smush her face into a smile, but inside her head she was desperately trying to figure how to ask Captain Whelk about her mother and if she had the Sight too.

"Does seasickness run in your family?" Lydia asked.

Captain Whelk stiffened slightly. "I wouldn't know. I don't think my mother ever set foot on a boat. My brothers have a boat they share. Dad was fine."

"I met your family today," Lydia confessed. She couldn't think of a way to smoothly introduce mystical elements into the conversation, but Captain Whelk obviously knew where Lydia was going.

Captain Whelk shook her head in disgust. "I hope you didn't believe a word that woman said. She just likes to scare people, is all. I keep telling those boys to get her off the porch before she runs their business into the ground!"

Just then the radio crackled, making Lydia jump.

"You better go get comfortable somewhere else," said Captain Whelk. "I've gotta get ready to cast off."

"Thanks," said Lydia. "Thanks for letting me warm up."

Captain Whelk swallowed the last of her coffee and stood up.

"You get yourself a good raincoat now that you live by the sea, okay?"

"All right," said Lydia, backing out the door. "I will."

Lydia found a seat right by a heater that was tucked out of the way. She scribbled down the information from the tombstone on her receipt from the general store. Captain Whelk clearly didn't believe in the Sight, even though she'd grown up with it. But there was also a chance that she'd been hypnotized by Dr. Gaddify. Curing seasickness seemed to fall within the possibilities of what one could do with hypnotism, but why had Dr. Gaddify singled out Captain Whelk? Unless Captain Whelk did have the Sight. Or maybe it was all made up. It would be easy to say that the old lady was just trying to scare people, except for the fact that she had known about Matthew. Lydia had another startling thought. The old lady had also known that Lydia was different from everyone else at school. So it was true, then; Lydia wasn't a genius.

Absurdly, this depressed Lydia even more.

By the time Lydia had trudged back up to her room at school, she was exhausted. She lay down on her bed and wanted to fall asleep, but instead she listened, tracking the progress of her former friends as they went down the hall, collecting one another for dinner.

Lydia lay curled up on her side in a tangle of covers. Snatches of voices played through her head as if she were passing through a party. *You have a problem. You know that?*

Does she even have a real *Special? Leave me alone! This is not like you, Lydia. I really don't know what to think.*

She squeezed her fists into her eyes as if that could block the memories of her friends' voices.

A knock on her door made Lydia's whole body jerk with surprise. Stupid, humiliating hope bloomed in her gut.

"Hello?" she called.

The door opened slowly and Marin's thin, rabbity face peered into the room. She looked at Lydia, waiting, and when Lydia didn't say anything, she stepped inside.

Marin stared at Lydia with impersonal hostility that reminded Lydia of how a child looks at strangers.

"You want to sit?" asked Lydia doubtfully.

Marin pulled out the desk chair and perched on the edge of it. Lydia sat up and smoothed the covers around herself, as if that could disguise the fact that she had done no personal grooming for three days.

"You're Wid?" asked Marin. "Matthew was your friend, so you, you're Wid?"

Lydia was so surprised that it took her a minute to figure out what Marin meant. She remembered the moonlight, Marin stripping needles off a branch and Lydia shouting how her friend had committed suicide. Only three people in the world called her Wid.

"You knew Matthew? Matthew Hafford?" asked Lydia.

"Matthew Hafford was my boyfriend," said Marin, a shade of defensiveness in her voice. "But you . . . you're—"

"I'm Wid. He's called me that since he was three."

Marin nodded. "He told me that."

The silence stretched like hardening glue through the room.

"He talked about you. He said you were like a sister." Lydia could sense that Marin was asking her a question with her last statement.

"He was like my brother. He and Abilene, they're half my family."

"I used to be jealous of how he talked about you. I thought—"

"Don't be." Lydia smiled. "I mean, you shouldn't have been."

"Yeah."

Both girls looked into opposite corners of the room and sniffed. Lydia wiped her nose on her sleeve and saw Marin blot her cheeks with her shoulders.

"So, tell me what you meant," said Marin. Her voice was back to its usual stiff commands. "When you said that about everyone being hypnotized and stuff."

"You believe me?" asked Lydia, straightening up.

Marin shrugged. "Not really. But what Matthew did—it didn't make sense. You said there have been others."

Lydia scooted forward on the bed, hope stirring in her gut.

"Do you know that at least twenty-one Claybourne alumni have committed suicide?"

"Yeah. You kind of shouted that last part."

"It's true. I found out right after Matthew—I looked everybody up." Lydia could feel the same jabbering that had happened out on the rock begin to build up. She stopped and took a breath, trying to figure out the best way to prove to Marin that she wasn't making this stuff up.

"Okay, Marin," said Lydia, calming herself with another deep breath. "How old are you?"

Marin sneered but answered: "Fifteen."

Lydia got out her list of new moons, counted back fifteen years, and looked up at Marin.

"Okay, so which one of these days is your birthday?"

Lydia showed her the list and Marin pointed. "I'm a Scorpio. But how did you know it would be one of these days?"

"I'll explain in a minute. You know Matthew's birthday?"

Marin pointed to one of the dates farther up the page.

"What other birthdays do you know?" said Lydia

"Students."

Marin studied the list. "That's Blair. Kent, he's a sophomore too, we have the same birthday." Marin studied the list again. "I don't know any others."

"Okay," said Lydia, flipping through her notebook. "This is a list of the dates of new moons."

"So we were all born on a new moon?" Marin shrugged but looked interested.

"All of us," said Lydia. She got out her suicide spreadsheet. "These are the birthdays of the people who committed suicide. The birth *dates*, I mean. The years matter. Every single one of these people was born on a new moon. All the birth dates I could find, all new moons. You're a new moon, Matthew, Blair, Ken. . . ."

"Kent."

"Whatever. Everybody here, everybody who ever came here, *all* born on a new moon."

Marin squinted at Lydia. "Are you sure?"

"All the ones I could check. I couldn't check them all, but at least"—Lydia did a quick estimate—"at least thirty birthdays check out."

"And your birthday?"

"New moon," said Lydia. "That's how I knew I'd get in. So I applied. I came here to find out what happened to Matthew and to all those other people." Without realizing it, Lydia had scooted closer and closer to Marin. Now their faces were less than a foot apart and Marin was leaning all the way back in her chair. Lydia stood up and began to pace.

"On orientation morning I woke up with a warning in my mind. It was just one word: 'truffle,' but the way it was in my head, it was like 'TRUFFLE!'" Lydia almost shouted the word and realized she was freaking out Marin even further. She sat down and took a deep breath. "I didn't eat it. I spit it out in one of the rows, and then we sang the school song, which, by the way, is totally creepy." Marin frowned in thought and then nodded with concession. "We sang the song twice, and I looked around to see if anyone else thought that was weird, but everyone else looked drugged."

"Drugged how?"

"Staring ahead. Singing the song like robots."

"Except you."

"I didn't eat the truffle. Dr. Gaddify told everyone to obey his voice and said for us to stand up. I did, to fit in, but a couple of people didn't. He went around to each of them and hypnotized them individually."

"Hypnotized?"

"Yeah. I think. What else would it be? Everybody just did what he said after that. So then another person came out on the stage—"

"Who?"

"I don't know. Our eyes were closed. They took nine students, and that's when I decided to get out of there, but I was standing up and this . . . *feeling* . . ." Lydia made a motion with her hands to indicate exploding.

Marin sat forward and blinked. "I felt that too. Three times. I thought I was sad about being back here without Matthew."

"You felt it?"

"Yeah. Like being knocked over by a freezing-cold wave. But I don't remember it that well. It's fuzzy."

"Yes!" Tears of relief pricked at Lydia's eyes. "He tells you not to remember."

"He gave us all a truffle at the start-of-year check-in," said Marin. "I came away from my meeting feeling . . . awestruck, maybe? Dazed? Now I wonder."

"He could be rehypnotizing you."

Marin shook her head, still not wanting to agree with anything Lydia said. "So then what?"

"Dr. Gaddify came back onto the stage, so I decided to fake being hypnotized so I could find out what happened to Matthew. He took me and eight others up some stairs behind the stage, but he put sacks over our heads so I couldn't see much. There were a lot of stairs and then a room, really bright. I remember the floor had all these symbols and candles, and we lay down inside the patterns, and then the other person, a woman, I am pretty sure, gave me a shot, and I don't remember anything until we were all back in the auditorium and he was telling me to wake."

"But it didn't work on you? Whatever he did?"

"Whatever they did, I don't think it changed me. I'm not— I'm not a genius." Lydia looked down and felt shame drench her body.

Marin shooed it away. "Ben and the others, they were mad that night on the rock. They didn't mean it."

"No, it's true, but it's okay." Lydia shook her head to clear it. "For a long time I looked for the room with the symbols in it.

I couldn't even find the door to the room. But then a few days ago I found it. The door's hidden backstage. I think if I can get in there, I can see what we're dealing with."

Marin raised an eyebrow and leaned back in the chair with her arms crossed. "Humph." She snorted dryly.

"I know. Crazy."

"Crazy," agreed Marin.

"I haven't even told you the craziest part yet." Again Lydia paused to think of the best way to present her information to Marin. Marin's expression had an uncomfortable amount of amusement in it. "Okay, look at these." Lydia pulled a folder out from under her bed. She stood and laid out the photo of Dr. Gaddify's desk, the photo of the glass pyramid, and the note from Naomi. Finally, she smoothed Matthew's last words—*I am not me*—onto the desktop and stepped back.

Marin reached for Matthew's words and frowned. "Who wrote this?"

"Matthew."

"That's not his handwriting." Marin pulled a small leather wallet out of her back pocket and withdrew a folded piece of notebook paper. She unfolded it and covered up all but the top line. "Don't read it," she ordered, though Lydia had already read: *Marin—Don't tell Ms. Windham, but I'd rather describe the way the light is illuminating your profile than consider—* The handwriting was a little strange, a blend between a teenager's scrawl and script such as you might see written in the Constitution.

Lydia brought over her postcard. "He was younger, but this is his writing too." The writing on the postcard matched *I am not me* but was markedly different from Marin's letter.

"You're sure they're both Matthew?"

"Positive. But . . ." Lydia paused and sat down. "It makes sense. Everyone changes, but I didn't know it would affect—did your handwriting change after orientation?"

"A bit," said Marin, "but not in an alarming way."

"Alarming! That's what Dr. Gaddify says—not to be alarmed by changes in yourself or your friends. 'Alarmed.' That's his exact word."

Marin frowned, then bent over the desk and studied Naomi's drawing of the ankh. "Okay," she said.

"Okay? Okay what?"

"Something's weird. The birthday thing is weird. It's weird they both said they were not themselves."

"Here's the room," said Lydia, sliding over the photo. "It's on top of the main building. Pilar took these with her plane for Bourne War." Lydia was talking too fast again, and Marin was drawing away. Lydia stopped and took a deep breath. "It gets weirder."

Marin cocked an eyebrow.

Lydia told her about the witchy old lady at the hardware store.

"So I think . . ." Lydia paused again, then she said aloud what she had been thinking all afternoon. "I think that they're doing something witchy. With spirits, I mean."

Lydia's words sounded strangely flat, as if sound wouldn't work to echo such a strange statement.

Marin sighed and studied Lydia's tense face. Lydia knew she was waiting for her to say "Just kidding" or start laughing, but after thirty seconds Marin's expression changed to pity. "Come on, Lydia."

Lydia sat up and leaned forward. "I know. I know. But look at this list. I took a picture of it in Dr. Gaddify's office."

Lydia handed Marin the list of names.

Marin read it at her usual lightning pace. "So, what does this mean? You think that Gus is haunted by Joshua Lawrence Chamberlain, and Cora is haunted by"—she consulted the list again—"Julia Child?"

Lydia rubbed her face with both hands. "I don't know. I've never thought anything like that was real before." She flopped back on her bed.

"And now you do?"

Lydia thought about Matthew and the words: ** *river* ** and ** *truffle* **. She thought about the sunburn feeling on her back, but she couldn't bring herself to try to explain it to Marin. Instead she just sat up and looked Marin in the eye. "I do believe it's real. Something is."

"You think we're all haunted because we all have new moon birthdays, we all changed during orientation, there's a crazy old lady, and it has something to do with this list on Dr. Gaddify's desk."

"And the room," said Lydia. "With the symbols. That definitely exists."

"So how come nobody's noticed this before?"

"He changes the teachers every two years. Nobody sticks around long enough to get suspicious. I think he's gotten to Captain Whelk somehow, so she doesn't say anything either." Lydia punched her bed. "I'll bet they read our letters home. If anyone gets suspicious, they just get another hypno session with Dr. Gaddify."

Marin was squinting suspiciously again. "I'm not saying that I believe in witchcraft. . . ." Marin paused. "Or spirits or whatever this is, but I do think something doesn't add up."

"Okay. Great. Oh, Marin, thank you." Lydia sat up again and scooted toward Marin. "Half the time I think I'm crazy."

"I haven't ruled that out either."

Lydia paused and looked at Marin. "Marin, did you just make a joke?"

Marin smiled a crooked smile. "Weirder things have happened."

Lydia laughed out loud for the first time in a week.

Chapter 27

Lydia and Marin spent all of Sunday arguing about what to do first: get into the pyramid room or find the woman with white eyes.

"I saw Nurse Proctor in the graveyard in Stillbay," said Lydia. "She visited the grave of somebody name Moses Johnson. He's not on any of my lists, but he was born on a new moon."

"So what do we do?" asked Marin. "Squirt Proctor in the eyes and see if her contacts fall out?"

Lydia laughed. "That's one idea." She was aware that when she laughed with Marin, there was a tinge of hysteria to her laughter, mostly because she was so relieved to be talking to somebody again.

Lydia's sense of isolation was further lifted on Sunday because Corbin Palisin had to be taken to the hospital for severe burns to one of his retinas. He had been studying medieval alchemical texts and believed that he might actually be able to turn base metal into gold. Unfortunately, while he was studying the composition of some metal under a microscope, there was a small explosion. He was the new official mad genius of Claybourne, and Lydia was no longer headline news.

Sunday evening Lydia was studying in her room when Marin barged in.

"We should break into Gaddify's office," she said without preamble.

"What? No. I already did."

"Right, but you only saw the one page. There's probably more. What if we find something that explains everything?"

Lydia was reluctant to add another complication to their plans, so she hesitated before telling Marin what Jay had said about the safe.

"See!" said Marin. "I knew it. We should go there first. We'll be able to find out who the woman is, and who knows what else."

Lydia frowned. "I have everything we need for the pyramid room. If you just borrow Cora's auditorium key—"

"That's too risky until we know who the woman is." Marin was developing a mulish look to her face. "Plus, that stairway is probably locked."

"That's why I got the lock-picking set," Lydia argued.

"Okay, let's see you pick the lock to this room." Marin put her hands on her hips.

Lydia sighed, exasperated. "I can practice. Besides, how are you going to get into Dr. Gaddify's office without picking a lock?"

Marin gave Lydia a superior smile. "I have a plan."

The next evening just before dinner Lydia heard raised voices down the hall. She didn't think much of it until Marin swept into her room without knocking.

"We're going to do it tonight," she announced.

"What?"

"Dr. Gaddify's office. We can get in tonight."

Lydia sat down hard on her bed. "How?"

"I just had an unfortunate accident with Pilar's plane."

"What?"

Marin shrugged. "I borrowed her plane because I needed to describe something for my novel." Marin wrapped her arms around her waist. "I'm not a very good flier, it turns out. The plane hit Dr. Gaddify's office window and shattered it."

Lydia took a moment to absorb this.

"Pilar's pretty mad," said Marin, looking the slightest bit guilty. "I broke the camera and the propeller."

"Okay," said Lydia. "Wow." Lydia studied Marin and then smiled a little. "Remind me not to get on your bad side."

Marin nodded.

"I still think we should do the pyramid room first. It's easier," said Lydia.

Marin shook her head. "Right now the window is covered with nothing more than a sheet of plastic duct-taped to the outside wall. It's perfect. We don't know when they'll get a new window in, so it's got to be tonight."

"Right," said Lydia. "So what do we need?"

At one o'clock that morning Lydia stood inside the door to her room with the lights off. The door was just the slightest bit open, and Lydia was listening for the sound of Marin's footsteps in the stairwell. Twenty seconds ago she'd heard three steady thumps on the ceiling, which was the signal to meet Marin.

Lydia was dressed all in black. On her back was a backpack that had a flashlight, a notebook, a towel, the camera, and duct tape. Lacking panty hose, she and Marin each had one leg of a thick pair of black tights to use as a mask. Lydia's was rolled down over her face, and she was finding it very hard to breathe. She wasn't sure if the headache she could feel building in her temples was from worry or from the elastic fabric squeezing her brain.

The small taps of sneaker-clad feet reached Lydia's ears, so she took a deep breath and eased out of her room, shutting the door gently behind her.

Marin was in the stairwell, also dressed in black, but with her face mask in a tight roll around her forehead.

"I can't breathe in this thing," she whispered.

"Me neither, but I think we need them on."

Marin sighed and pulled her stocking roughly into place.

They moved without speaking down the stairs onto the main floor and out the door to the front porch. Lydia had never noticed before how loud the door was or how the third stair down sounded like a sneaker on a gym floor when you stepped on it. Once they were on the walkway, Lydia and Marin stopped and looked around.

The moon was in its last quarter and was casting the shadow of the boys' dorms onto the main lawn. The wind was up and leaves rushed in little cyclones along the pathways. Lydia was glad of the noise. In the stairwell her breathing had seemed loud enough to wake the dead.

Across the green there was one light on in the third floor of the underclass boys' dorm, but nobody else was outside. The lamp from the porch and the lamp from the front of the main building formed rings of bronze that did not meet. Lydia touched Marin's shoulder, and they started forward together in the shadow of their dorm. There was a bright gap of moonlight in between their dorm and the main building. Marin and Lydia jogged lightly across and stepped into the shadows with relief. Now they were in a bit of a tunnel between the upperclassman girls' dorm and the main building. The wind was even louder, and the bare lilac bushes outside Dr. Gaddify's office were

218

bowing and springing energetically. Lydia and Marin stepped off the path and into the deeper darkness next to the evergreen bush and a lilac.

Lydia got the towel out of her backpack and handed it to Marin. It was too dark to see much, but if Lydia had to guess, Marin was wearing a determined scowl under her face mask. Lydia shivered with fear, glad that Marin couldn't see her convulsions.

Lydia got on all fours right below Dr. Gaddify's window. The evergreen needles stabbed her hands and knees, so that she had to brush them flat before she could comfortably settle into position. She gritted her teeth to make herself stop shivering.

Marin put one foot into the small of Lydia's back and did a little hop. For a second Lydia felt Marin's weight, but then she tipped backward into the bush. Marin gave a small cry.

"Sorry," they both whispered at the same time.

Marin tried again, and this time she got her second foot up and stood there wobbling. Lydia wished Marin had thought to take off her shoes. She could feel a very uncomfortable grinding on her spine, and now that she couldn't scratch, the face mask was driving her crazy.

Lydia heard the wet sound of duct tape and then plastic flapping overhead. The towel fell and landed on Lydia's head.

"Sorry," said Marin again. She stepped painfully onto Lydia's kidneys and retrieved the towel. More wiggling and sawing on the backbone, and then suddenly Marin's shoes were up and scrabbling away at the wall. Lydia stood quickly and pushed at Marin's bottom. Marin was grunting and muttering to herself.

"Hang on!" said Lydia as loudly as she dared. Marin stopped struggling and Lydia found Marin's foot. She guided it to her shoulder and then braced herself. Marin put her weight on

Lydia's shoulder, eased herself up, and managed to get the top half of her body inside the window. There was a truncated scream and then a crash.

Lydia stood, panting and achy, looking up at the window. After a long silence Marin's head appeared, silhouetted against the sky.

"Okay?" asked Lydia.

"Yeah. Here."

Marin dropped one end of a bedsheet out the window. "It's tied," she whispered harshly.

Without much confidence, Lydia wrapped the sheet around her forearm and leaned back. She braced one foot against the gritty wall and then hopped tentatively and struck out with the other foot. Her footing and the sheet both held. Panting and terrified, Lydia worked her feet up the wall, taking in more sheet as she went. Before she knew it, her foot reached the window and she was almost horizontal to the ground.

"Help!" she gasped.

Marin grabbed her leg and guided it over the windowsill, then grabbed the straps on Lydia's backpack and hauled her inside.

Lydia slithered to the floor and sat down hard, breathing heavily. "Oh man," she whispered.

The windless office was quiet compared with outside, and Lydia's panting sounded loud enough to wake the dead. Holding her breath, she listened hard for signs that they'd been heard, but there was nothing except the flap of the plastic and Marin's frightened breathing.

A small beam of light appeared from Marin's flashlight.

"Wait," said Lydia. The light clicked off. "Hang up the towel over the hallway window. I'll put the sheet over this one."

Time seemed to be galloping dangerously by as the girls fumbled about in the dark, covering the windows. Lydia was still breathing heavily when the sheet was finally in place and the room was even more muffled. Marin turned on the light again and trained it over the wall to the right of the window.

"Jay said between the office and the kitchen, right?" whispered Marin. "If there's a safe, it'll be on this side?"

"Yeah." Lydia gave up trying to breathe through her face mask and pulled it up to her forehead. She got out her own flashlight and studied the bookcase in front of her. Marin's beam of light was traveling over the spines of books as quickly as windshield wipers. Lydia tried not to be distracted and instead concentrated on looking for hinges or gaps.

"Ah," said Marin. "I think I found it."

"What?" asked Lydia. The books on the shelf were all old, bound in either leather or cloth. Lydia couldn't see what distinguished the book that Marin was pointing to. It was a washed-out blue and said *The Complete Works of Søren Kierkegaard* in gold embossed writing.

"This one's out of place," whispered Marin, stroking the cover with one finger. She glanced at Lydia and then pulled up her own face mask.

"'Cause he's Swedish?"

"No, he's Danish, and he's an existentialist."

"So?"

"All these others are early enlightenment."

"Right." Lydia paused. "Nothing else is out of place?"

"No." Marin was abrupt and confident.

Lydia studied *The Complete Works*. "The top of the binding is sort of squashed." She pointed to the small accordion pleats in the blue fabric.

"No dust," said Marin.

Lydia reached up and slid her finger along the pages at the top of the book. She felt nothing unusual, so she hooked her finger inside the top of the binding and pulled.

There was a slight resistance and then a jolt as the book tilted forward: a creak and a huff of air, then a section of bookshelf the size of a large TV swung forward two inches.

Marin took a deep breath, and Lydia paused with her hand suspended over the book.

"Okay," breathed Lydia.

"Okay."

Marin reached forward to the top of the free section, but she paused. "I'm afraid of what we're going to find back here," she whispered.

"I know," said Lydia. "Creepy dolls."

"A bloody scepter."

"Human heads." Lydia huffed out a mirthless laugh and then grabbed the top of the bookshelf and pulled.

"Journals," whispered Marin.

Inside the bookshelf was another bookshelf. One shelf had a dozen fabric-bound journals and then two composition notebooks. The shelf below had an assortment of glossy catalogs, all of which had several bookmarks. Lydia picked one up and showed it to Marin.

"Auction catalogs," said Marin. "Weird."

Lydia replaced the catalog and picked up one of the composition notebooks. She flipped it open at random.

On the page in front of her were two columns of names, just as she had seen on Dr. Gaddify's desk that very first day. Lydia checked the dates on the front of the notebook. This notebook went up to five years ago. She picked up the next notebook and flipped to the last used page. It was familiar.

Angus McCracken   Joshua Lawrence Chamberlain
Bethany Ming   Fanny Mendelssohn Hensel
Sophia Nowel   Norma Merrick Sklarek
Corbin Palisin   Linus Pauling
Benjamin Loi   John Templeton
Calliope Smith   Agnes Arber
Trenton Stuart   Edwin Land
Frances Trombly   Julia Child

She flipped to the page before it and found her name:

Lydia Boswell   Nancy Wake

Nancy Wake. Dr. Gaddify hadn't been telling her to wake. Wake was the last name.

Lydia glanced at Marin. She was reading one of the journals with a look of terrible intensity. Lydia decided not to bother her. She groped around in her backpack for her notebook and began scribbling down the names. She tried not to pause as she discovered that Naomi was paired with Georgia O'Keeffe. Pilar with Kalpana Chawla. Sorcha with Hedy Lamarr. She found Marin and Seth and then Matthew. . . .

The next hour dissolved into a blur of scribbling and breathing. Marin chewed through notebook after notebook, only making choking noises sometimes or closing her eyes in pain.

Lydia was bent over another page of names when suddenly the light in the office got brighter.

"Marin!" she gasped. The light coming through the sheet was now several shades brighter. Was somebody coming outside?

Lydia checked that her face mask was still on top of her head and crept to the window. She twitched the sheet aside and looked out. The moon had come up over the top of the main building and was shining into the headmaster's office.

"We better go," said Lydia.

Marin's eyes were wide and haunted. She didn't speak, only put the last journal away and stood as slowly as if she'd aged fifty years.

Working together, the girls put everything back, removed the towel from the hallway window, dropped the sheet and backpacks outside, then slid out the window, using the towel as protection from the jagged broken glass. Lydia landed hard, then stood, listening. Marin was tugging the towel out of the windowsill. There was that noise, but also something else. The wind carried sounds to Lydia's ears and then snatched them away. Did she hear footsteps?

"Marin, run!" Lydia pushed Marin toward the path.

"The window. I have to tape it up!"

"No time! Go!" Lydia shoved hard now, and Marin stumbled onto the path. Lydia tugged her face mask down but could see out of only one eye. She turned back toward the library. Someone was coming. Lydia grabbed Marin's hand and tugged her along the path.

"Stop!"

It was a male voice. Marin stopped abruptly, but Lydia gave her another shove. They ran. The girls wheeled around the corner to the front of the dorm, and Marin started for the steps. Lydia jerked her back from the steps and dragged her past the porch out to some hydrangea bushes at the far end of the building. With another shove Lydia sent Marin to her knees, then she dove in after her and pulled her to the ground.

Again Lydia was grateful to the wind. It masked both their terrified breathing and the crunch of leaves as they scuttled back into the darkness beneath the bush.

"Keep your face down," hissed Lydia. Marin's pale skin shone like a moon because she hadn't replaced her face mask. Still peering out of only one eye, Lydia watched the corner of the building.

The figure came on. It stopped and lifted its head, turning from side to side like a wolf sniffing the breeze. The light on the porch gilded the edges of the person's face, and Lydia saw clearly who it was. Dr. Gaddify.

Dr. Gaddify walked carefully up the steps and out of sight. A new band of light cut the darkness, so Lydia knew he had opened the door. Had he gone in? Lydia waited, frozen. Dr. Gaddify reappeared. He stepped slowly down to the lawn and turned toward the place where Lydia and Marin lay hiding. His face was in darkness, but menace poured off of him like a scent. He took a step toward them.

Suddenly he turned as if a noise had startled him. A new figure appeared. Nurse Proctor. They spoke, but Lydia couldn't hear what they said. After a few seconds they both turned and went back around the corner of the building. Lydia shook Marin's shoulder.

"Let's go. Quick." Hunched over, below the height of the porch, Lydia scurried forward and peered around the edge of the building. Dr. Gaddify and Nurse Proctor were headed back toward the main building. Lydia and Marin ran up the steps, yanked open the door, and tiptoed at a sprint up to Lydia's room. Lydia shut and locked the door, and then her knees gave out.

Chapter 28

Marin sat down hard on Lydia's bed and stared into the space in front of her, twisting the thick black tights of her face mask in her hands. She was barely visible in the dark. Lydia sat on the floor with her head between her knees for a few minutes and then got up and started moving around the room needlessly. She checked that the shade was pulled all the way to the bottom, checked that the door she'd just locked was still locked. She pushed her sweatshirt up against the bottom of the door so that no light would leak out and then moved the desk light to the floor and turned it on. After that, she pulled out the chair and sat down, clasping and unclasping her hands. She took her notebook out of her backpack, put it on her desk, and adjusted it so that it was perfectly square to the corner. Finally she looked at Marin.

"So," she whispered.

"Jesus," whispered Marin. She squeezed the bridge of her nose and took a deep breath. "Okay."

Marin stared at Lydia as if she were trying to remember who she was.

"I forgot to take pictures," said Lydia. "Stupid. I should have gotten proof . . ." She stopped, looking at Marin. "Are you okay?"

"I'm okay. It's just—"

"I am right? Are we right? Are they—"

Marin closed her eyes and held up a hand to ward off questions. Lydia jiggled her knee in the long silence. She looked at her palms and realized that she had two cuts in one. A small piece of glass winked at her from inside her own flesh. Lydia plucked at it with trembling fingers.

"They started off with séances." Marin's voice sounded far away. "There were three people. Dr. Gaddify must be one, and there were two others." Marin gulped and glanced at Lydia. "It was all written in the third person, and there's J., L., and H. H. is Henry Gaddify, I'm guessing. I think L. is a woman."

Lydia accidentally pushed the shard of glass deeper into her palm. A drop of blood oozed out.

"L. is a necromancer."

"She works with spirits? The dead?"

"Yes. H. did the hypnotism. J. did the research." Marin shook her head to show that Lydia shouldn't interrupt. "So they would do séances to learn about the past. I guess they were all history nuts, so . . . It was slow going. The spirits"—Marin shook her head again, this time in disbelief—"the spirits were vague and hard to talk to. One night L. was holding a ring that belonged to one of the spirits, and it, well, the spirit possessed her."

Lydia nodded, staring intensely at Marin.

"It was much better," Marin went on. "I mean, much clearer. The spirit was able to answer questions directly. J. was really excited. He got loads of stuff for a book he was writing about the flu epidemic. L. was excited too, but being possessed was . . . 'unpleasant' was the word Gaddify used. Headaches, double vision, nightmares. They took turns being possessed and they learned a lot. J. was really eager to get information for his book. L. was interested in the spirit part. They got good at it.

Figured out the symbols, the rituals." Marin swallowed hard and shook her head again. "They found some guy, maybe a homeless guy, and they made him be the one who was possessed. It was a huge improvement, according to Gaddify, anyway. The guy was possessed for three days before he went crazy and jumped through a glass window. Bled to death. Having him for three days, though, they made 'enormous strides' with their research. They thought maybe a younger person would be 'more flexible' in accepting a new spirit, so they found a teenager, a runaway from Bangor, and tried it on her. They gave her the spirit of one of the second-class passengers on the *Titanic*. Got a whole book out of her, but she was confused. Didn't understand about technology half the time, didn't know who she was the other half of the time. She made it four months before she jumped into the sea. Drowned a second time."

Marin held her head in her hands for a moment, then took a deep breath and continued.

"They didn't get the recognition they thought they deserved for their historical research because they couldn't cite their sources. They tried to use a vague 'firsthand account,' but they got skewered by academics. They were accused of making it all up when they couldn't produce sources. But by then they were more interested in perfecting the possession, seeing how long a person could live. They worked with hypnotism to try to smooth out the transitions. There was a lot of"—Marin waved her hands vaguely—"mistakes. They believed they were making 'great strides for science and history.' It gets a little sick."

Marin closed her eyes. Lydia tried not to imagine what exactly the mistakes were. She could tell that whatever came next was going to be awful.

"There was a newspaper clipping in one of the journals. A terrible fire in an orphanage on the mainland southwest of

Stillbay. Only the bodies of the caretakers were found. The police thought that the fire had been hot enough to burn even the bones of the kids."

"But?"

"But they had taken the kids and lit the fire to cover their tracks. I think they must have used hypnotism somehow. That's when they moved out to this island, because they brought all the kids here and perfected the technique."

Lydia and Marin both shuddered. It must have been horrifying for those kids.

"Teens worked best," Marin spit out bitterly after a moment. "Two of the kids had new moon birthdays, and they worked even better. So that's when they tried to implant their first genius."

"Who?"

"It's predictable."

"Einstein?"

"Yup. Now, this is sort of interesting: Apparently, some neurosurgeon had stolen Einstein's brain. Einstein was supposed to be cremated, but the guy couldn't bring himself to do it. He wanted to study the brain of a great genius. For all that he was obsessed with the brain, he was pretty careless with it. He'd put it in a cooler and bring it out at barbecues. That sort of thing. It was easy to convince the surgeon to give them some slides of the brain. They took in three teenage foster kids with new moon birthdays. But the kids, they didn't work. They thought the kids weren't smart enough. Childhoods were too tough. Too much brain damage from trauma. Plus, the foster kids were too suspicious, too canny. So they kidnapped a kid from a boarding school."

"What about the foster kids? Didn't anybody worry about them?"

"Another fire. A real tragedy out on the island. All three kids died."

"Jesus," said Lydia.

"Yeah. So they got this kid. Smart, new moon birthday, teenager."

"Did it work?"

"You ever heard of Joseph Weisner?"

"The guy who is supposed to be *this* close to inventing a time machine? With the scars on his face?"

"That's him."

"Einstein?"

"Yup."

Lydia squinted at Marin without really seeing her. Could she admit to the thrill she felt at the idea that Einstein was at work again, plumbing the secrets of the universe? She made another pinch at the glass in her hand. But what about the real Joseph Weisner? What if he could have been a genius all on his own?

Marin flopped back on the bed and recited what she'd read to the ceiling. "They scarred up his face, hypnotized him, and told him he'd been in a car accident that had killed his parents. Got some professor to teach him quantum mechanics. It took only a month for him to learn everything the professor could teach him. He helped them to design the pyramid room. They told him it was theoretical, and he figured out the perfect wavelengths and resonances for spirits. He never suspected anything. His theories about wavelengths are why there is no tech allowed on the island. They believe it interrupts the spiritual vibrations."

Lydia found herself squinting at Marin as if her eyes were the thing she was having trouble believing instead of her ears.

"When the Einstein guy got famous, he started a scholarship in memory of the foster kids who had died in the fire. He actually sounds really nice." Marin sat up again and shook her head in disgust. "The next two years was experiments. They tried athletes and singers, but that failed because those people rely too much on their bodies. They traveled around the world collecting things owned by geniuses, or parts of their bodies if they could get them. They had fantastic results with the spirits who took. The money started coming in from alumni. You know the rest."

"The suicides?" asked Lydia.

"They noticed that, and they think it happens when the spirit doesn't take. Or maybe because the original spirit is too strong."

"I'm worried about Naomi," Lydia blurted out. "She talks about how sometimes she thinks she's working on one painting but then finds she's doing another. And that night she came into my room and gave me the ankh? She was all slouchy again, like she was before orientation."

Marin nodded. "They also think it might have to do with interference from technology, or maybe being back at home brings up too many of the original memories. Luckily, everybody thinks that geniuses are crazy anyway. The technology bit also helps explain why the Claybourne Method doesn't work elsewhere. No one has suspected anything. Except you."

"Okay," said Lydia, picking her words carefully. The idea was too strange for an everyday sentence. "So. They take teenagers and stuff the souls of dead geniuses into their bodies?"

Marin's chin twitched. It was barely a nod.

"And that means . . . ," Lydia faltered. "Everybody in the school is possessed?"

Marin just closed her eyes.

"So what happens to the original spirit? What happened to Matthew?"

Marin scrubbed at her eyes. She was crying. "I don't know. They don't even really mention it."

"That's like murder, right? Kicking somebody's soul out of their body?"

Marin wiped her nose on her sleeve and stared at Lydia miserably.

Is that what the old lady meant by "haunted"? Maybe the original souls are still attached somehow, haunting their own bodies.

Marin dropped her head into her hands and mumbled something.

Lydia knew what she was asking. She paused, looking at her notebook.

"Just tell me," said Marin.

"E. M. Forster."

Marin's head twitched to the side; half a denial.

"And Matthew?"

"Virginia Woolf."

"Oh God." Marin's face crumpled with misery and despair. Lydia moved over to the bed to sit next to her, but Marin shrugged off the arm Lydia tried to put around her shoulders.

Lydia patted Marin's back awkwardly, tears making silent tracks down her own face. "We have to stop this," Marin whispered. "We should get all the journals—bring them to the police. Maybe the lady at the hardware store would help. . . ."

"Who would believe us? Gaddify can just say it's all fiction. I don't even know how we could get off the island without permission. We can't call anyone." Lydia chewed her lip and looked at the postcard from Matthew. "Is there anything from the journals we could use to stop them? I mean stop them and fix everybody? We have to help Naomi."

Marin swiped furiously at her tears. "Yeah. One of them died. J. died and they did something to fix his spirit in death so that he couldn't grow a conscience and stop them from the spirit world. They mentioned a bunch of spells and rituals."

"Does it say how to do the spells in the journals?" asked Lydia.

"No, but I know where it does."

"Where?"

"In the pyramid room."

Chapter 29

Marin spent the night in Lydia's bed, while Lydia slept fitfully on a pile of blankets on her floor. It was only fair to take the floor, she thought, since Marin had just learned that she was actually a long-dead writer from the early twentieth century. On the other hand, wouldn't it be nice to know you were a genius? To not have to figure out what to do with your life? Lydia entertained the notion. *But what is the point of being alive then?*

When Lydia woke, she stretched the kinks out of her neck and checked in with herself. There had been no dream. She felt . . . better. Despite the lack of sleep and the cold, hard floor, she felt as if after months of stumbling around in a dark room, her fingers had finally hit a doorframe. She didn't know how to open the door yet, but she knew that there was a door, and even better, a friend was in the dark room with her.

She sat up farther and checked on Marin. She lay curled up on her side, her face slack with sleep. Lydia thought it was safe to leave her for a few minutes.

She showered, brushed her hair and teeth, and cleaned out the cut on her palm. For the first time in weeks, she faced the day with something that might have been described as optimism. When she was clean, she went back to her room and found

Marin still sleeping. Lydia sat carefully on the bed and shook Marin's shoulder.

"Marin?" she whispered.

"Call me E. M."

"That's not funny."

"I know."

"Also, I don't know what the *E* or the *M* stands for."

"Um, Edward Morgan, I think."

"Show-off," said Lydia.

Marin opened her eyes and squinted at Lydia from the pillow.

"Are you . . . ?" Lydia asked hesitantly.

"Am I going to commit suicide?"

"Well, yeah. I mean, should I stay here with you?"

"Thanks, but I'm okay."

"Really?"

Marin frowned and seemed to be taking stock. "Yeah. I'm okay. I mean, it's weird, but I like that Matthew and I knew each other in our other lives. Our spirits' lives, I mean."

"Really?"

"Yeah. E. M. Forster and Virginia Woolf were part of an intellectual group called the Bloomsbury Group. They believed that art was an important part of life. Very philosophical."

"Cool."

It was quiet for a minute, with only the sounds of the other girls slamming drawers and dropping books coming through the walls.

"Who were you supposed to be?" asked Marin suddenly.

"Oh. Nancy Wake? I don't know who she is—was."

"Nancy Wake?"

"Yeah."

"I've heard of her. She was an Australian, I think. World War Two."

"What did she do?"

"Oh, you'll like this." Marin grinned weakly for the first time. "She was a spy."

Lydia digested that for a moment. "Okay, so what should we do? We have to get into the room, and we have to stop them, but I don't know how."

"It's okay," said Marin. "I know a couple of geniuses who might help."

All day Lydia imagined she could see ghosts. Each of her classmates had lost his or her soul. All of those souls were— what? Floating around the classroom? There was a constant prickle on Lydia's skin, but she wasn't sure if it was from ghosts or from knowing she was on an island with Dr. Gaddify and a necromancer.

The plan was that Marin would talk with the others after Specials. Lydia was supposed to wait in her room, but she couldn't bear waiting, so she went to the library and helped Ms. Alton shelve books. After an hour Ms. Alton seemed to sense that Lydia was distracted rather than sad.

"Time for our lemonade?" she asked, even though there were still a dozen books left.

Lydia smiled. "Sorry, I'm kind of spacey today, I guess."

"I could recommend a good thriller, if you like."

"A thriller, Ms. Alton? I wouldn't have thought you read those."

"Strictly medicinal. It helps focus the mind." Ms. Alton smiled and held open the door to her office.

Lydia took a step to go in and glanced up at the same time. There was Seth. He was standing at the top of the steps in the vestibule, looking at Lydia like a lost puppy.

Lydia paused and studied Seth's face. She couldn't tell if he was looking at her or right through her.

"Um, will you excuse me, Ms. Alton?"

Ms. Alton followed Lydia's gaze out to Seth and smiled again.

"Of course, my dear. I think that a resolution is much more satisfactory than even the best thriller."

Lydia smiled at Ms. Alton and then threaded her way slowly through the tables and chairs to where Seth was standing.

She stood in front of him while he studied her face.

"You okay?" she asked after a good minute had passed.

Seth's lips twitched up into a smile that fell woefully short of happiness.

He cleared his throat and shook his head. "You, uh, know any good books about Winston Churchill?"

Lydia looked at him sharply. "You sure?"

"Yeah." Seth spit out the word.

Lydia thought a minute. "Books about him or by him?"

Seth threw up his hands. "You pick."

Lydia touched Seth's shoulder, and then, before she thought too hard about it, she kissed his cheek. "I'm sorry," she whispered.

Seth jerked his head and frowned. "Yeah."

Lydia sensed that he didn't really want to talk about anything. He was too shocked. She straightened her shoulders and pointed up the stairs.

"This way," she said.

Seth took out four books about Winston Churchill and two written by him. Gus came in and found a book about Joshua

Lawrence Chamberlain. Lydia passed Naomi in the art section with a stack of Georgia O'Keeffe books out on a table.

She left the library and walked back to the dorm, then up to Marin's room.

Marin looked pale and exhausted, but she smiled at Lydia when she knocked and came in.

"They're going to help us," she said.

Chapter 30

"First of all, I want you to know that I am doing this not because I believe you"—Cora looked hard at Lydia—"but because I want the chance to decide for myself."

Lydia looked around Naomi's studio. It was lunchtime the next day, and they had borrowed stools from some other studios. Seth, Marin, Naomi, Cora, Gus, Sorcha, Pilar, and Lydia were perched in a small circle. Ben was the only one who'd refused to take part. He'd called them all a bunch of lunatics but had promised not to tell.

There were paintings everywhere; on easels, stacked against the wall, propped on shelves. About half of the ones that Lydia could see were extravagantly colored, textured abstract paintings. The other half were large, voluptuous-looking shells that filled the whole canvas. Lydia knew that Georgia O'Keeffe was famous for her large flowers and that she had lived in the Southwest. It made sense that if O'Keeffe had lived near the ocean instead of in the desert, she would have painted shells, but it was an uncomfortable reminder of what they were dealing with.

"Okay," said Lydia to Cora. "It's fine if you don't believe me, as long as you realize how dangerous these people are."

"If you don't want to believe that every student who has ever gone here has had their soul replaced with the soul of a genius, then think of the twenty-one students and alumni who killed themselves," said Marin.

In the silence that followed, Lydia tried hard not to look at Naomi. She wasn't sure if warning Naomi about suicide would save her or give her a bad idea.

"Okay," said Lydia. "Where do we begin?"

"'The first quality that is needed is audacity,'" said Seth in a British accent.

"Oh God," Cora groaned. "You're not quoting Winston Churchill, are you?"

Seth raised an eyebrow. "'True genius resides in the capacity for evaluation of uncertain, hazardous, and conflicting information.'" His accent was pretty bad.

Naomi groaned. "Don't worry," she said. "We've got another strategist if this one's gone round the bend." She swiveled on her stool to face Gus. "Any thoughts? Original thoughts?"

Gus swallowed and looked around at each face. "He believed in this, you know. Chamberlain, I mean. I guess a lot of people believed in spirits back then, but he believed that a ghost came and saved his company one night. He believed that his daughter Grace was his soul mate. He thought that even before she was born. He—I—"

"It's okay to say 'he,'" said Marin.

"He was a good man. He made all his soldiers salute when the Confederates marched by to turn in their surrender."

"Great." Cora snorted. "You're a war hero, and I'm a— what? A cook? A TV personality? Why bring me back?"

Marin cleared her throat. "According to the journals, H. and L. agreed to allow two 'moneymakers' in each class. They have their own twisted form of ethics that involves the belief that bringing back geniuses will improve the human race, so they only bring back geniuses who might be useful in the course of history. But probably you, being so beautiful, and Julia Child, being personable, are one of the moneymakers."

Cora tsked in disgust. "'Our wealth we will share with the school that we love.' I should have picked that out right away."

"Well, you didn't. I didn't. None of us did," said Naomi.

"Except Lydia," said Seth.

Lydia felt all the eyes in the room swivel toward her. She shrugged. "Okay, so we need to break into the pyramid room. You need to see it so that you can believe—or not. I want pictures for proof. We need to find the notes on necromancy so that we can figure out how to stop these people."

"We also need to figure out who L. is," said Gus. "It seems logical that H. is Henry Gaddify, but who is L.?"

"I think it's Nurse Proctor," said Lydia. She and Marin had argued about this.

"Her name is Constance. Constance J. Proctor. There's not even an *L* anywhere in her name," said Marin.

"But what about the bloody bandage and the grave?" said Lydia. This was old territory between her and Marin.

"You saw the bloody bandage too?" asked Pilar.

"Yeah, the first day," said Lydia.

"Yesterday, too," said Pilar. "Her hand was all wrapped up just yesterday."

Lydia shot a look at Marin.

"There's only one teacher who has a name that begins with *L* and that's Laura Kennedy," insisted Marin.

"Dr. Kennedy? Seriously?" Cora snorted. "Come on, guys. Plus, she's only been here for two years."

"Nurse Proctor definitely gives me the creeps," said Naomi.

"It makes sense if it's one of the staff," said Gus. "All the teachers come and go too much."

"I'll find out the names of the staff and see who has been here for a long time," said Marin. "All we can guess is that she might be wearing colored contacts to cover up the fact that she has white eyes."

"So we're sure it's a woman and we can eliminate anyone who doesn't wear contacts?" asked Gus.

"That's our best guess," said Marin.

"I'd like to see the door before we try to plan how to get inside," said Seth.

"I can let you into the auditorium anytime," said Cora.

"Gimme your lock picks," said Sorcha to Lydia. "I'll practice."

"Okay," said Lydia. "We'll meet here again tomorrow? Same time?" Nods rippled around the room.

"There's something else," said Marin with uncharacteristic hesitation. "I'm no expert on possession, and the journals didn't go into specific technique. But, Lydia, you read that one way to get rid of a spirit is to destroy anything that belonged to it, right?"

Lydia nodded.

"And they need something that belonged to the spirit to make sure that we're possessed by the right spirit, right? Lydia and I found a shelf full of auction catalogs. They search the whole world looking for belongings or body parts to use in the ritual. So what do they do with those things?"

"You mean they buy Mozart's wig and Benjamin Franklin's socks and then use them to possess us with the souls?" Cora snorted. "Oh please. I already said I don't believe any of this."

Seth held up a hand to stop Cora's tirade and looked at Marin. "So you think we all have something that belongs to our . . . spirit? Or whatever you want to call it?"

Marin shrugged.

"Maybe they put it in our rooms," said Gus.

"What about uniforms? It makes sense if it's something we wear," said Pilar.

"Too complicated," said Seth, shaking head. "We have too many pieces of uniform to be sure that we're wearing whatever it is. Shoes maybe . . ."

Naomi held up her hand. Lydia thought for a moment she was waiting to be called on, but then she saw what Naomi meant. It was her bracelet with her keys on it.

"Our key bracelets?" asked Pilar. She closed her fist protectively around her bracelet. "I love mine." Everyone besides Lydia nodded.

Lydia scrabbled around in her backpack for hers. "I've never liked wearing this." She stabbed up the bracelet with a pencil and dropped it on the table without touching it. Everybody stared at her, bewildered. "Is it weird that you all *love* yours?"

"Oh, come on," said Cora, picking it up. "They're just cool, that's all." She palpated the bracelet, considering it and holding it up to the light to inspect it. "It's thick. All of them are. I suppose there could be something hidden in between the leather and the embroidery." Cora's tone left no doubt that she thought the idea was ridiculous.

Lydia picked up her bracelet and felt along the seam where it was thickest. "There's kind of a bump here."

Naomi handed Lydia an X-Acto knife. Lydia worked the blade in between the leather and the embroidery, sawing until she felt the first thread break. She did another and another, opening up the short edge of the bracelet. She stuck her finger inside and felt something hard and smooth. Carefully she worked it loose and then tipped the bracelet over her hand. Out fell a small, oblong object, pale yellow, like a dirty pearl.

It was a human tooth.

There is no way to encounter a human tooth outside of its natural setting and not be alarmed.

Cora and Pilar screamed and jumped back from the tooth. Marin knocked over her stool, and Lydia banged her knee, hard, on the table. The tooth dropped to the floor and lay on the dirty tile. It wasn't short and hollow like a baby tooth, but long and jagged. An incisor, tugged from a skull or a living mouth. Naomi was panting quick, high-pitched breaths, which reminded Lydia to breathe. Cora started to scrabble at the bracelet around her arm, trying to force it over the knobs of her wrist.

"Get it off," she growled. "Get it off!"

Lydia grabbed the X-Acto knife off the table and took Cora's hand.

"Hold still."

Cora froze, holding her breath while Lydia slid the blade along the delicate skin on the bottom of her wrist and then jerked the blade upward. The bracelet dropped open like the arms of a person falling backward and hit the floor.

Everyone looked at it in silence. After a minute Sorcha coughed. "I want to keep mine." Sorcha's voice was scared.

"Yeah," said Gus, looking at his bracelet. "I don't think I want to know, actually. What's in here, I mean."

Naomi pressed firmly along the seams of her bracelet and then wiped one finger along its length. "Mine's not a tooth, at least."

"But the tooth," said Cora. "It means—"

"Yes," said Seth. "We all know what it means."

The air in the room went absolutely still.

Seth bent forward and picked up the tooth. "This is real."

Cora's head twitched involuntarily. Gus exhaled. Pilar's head dropped forward on her neck.

"This *is* real," Lydia repeated softly. She paused, wondering if she should go on or give everybody a chance to think their own thoughts. She took another deep breath and continued. "We need to find a way to make this right. But most important, please stay safe. If you're feeling . . ."

"Suicidal," provided Pilar.

"Say something to one of us, okay?" Lydia looked each person in the eye. "I know this is really, really hard."

"'If you're going through hell—'" started Seth.

"Yeah, we know," said Naomi. Her British accent was a lot better than Seth's. "'If you're going through hell, keep going.'"

Chapter 31

The next day Lydia was carrying a stool down the hall to Naomi's studio when Pilar came up behind her and grabbed her arm.

"Come on," said Pilar, taking the stool from Lydia. "I've got big news."

"What?" said Lydia, increasing her stride to keep up with Pilar. "What is it? Did you find L.?"

"No," said Pilar. "I'll tell you when everybody gets here."

In Naomi's studio, Sorcha was demonstrating her improved skills at lock picking.

"I can do doors and padlocks now," she said proudly. Sorcha was the only one of Lydia's friends who showed no curiosity about discovering who she was. She had asked Marin not to tell her. Lydia wondered if it wasn't better that way. Sorcha was the only one who seemed well rested and cheerful.

"Well, I am not having much luck finding L.," said Marin. "Lenore Pritchard works in the kitchen, and she goes by Lee. But she doesn't strike me as a criminal occult mastermind."

"I'm on it," said Cora.

"How?" asked Marin.

Cora shrugged. "I'll talk to her. Ask if contacts help when she's cutting onions. If she doesn't wear contacts, we can eliminate her, right? If she does wear them, I'll think of something. Don't worry."

"Well, do it soon!" Pilar looked around the group, her face tight with suppressed excitement. "This morning I found out that Dr. Gaddify is going to a conference in Boston tomorrow."

Gus's head whipped up, and he and Seth grinned at each other. "That makes this almost too easy," said Seth. "Gus and I had elaborate plans to distract him while the rest of you went into the room."

"You have a plan, then?" asked Lydia.

"We have something in mind," said Seth. He had a superior tone to his voice that both annoyed Lydia and made her feel relieved. Seth must be feeling better if he was smug.

Everyone got settled and looked from Seth to Gus. Seth nodded at Gus, who cleared his throat and stood.

"We thought it would be safest to do this in plain sight, as it were. Cora, do you have a play you're working on?"

"Yeah," said Cora. "I've got something."

"So we'll have you, Lydia, and Naomi rehearsing onstage while Sorcha works on the lock."

"Since we don't need to keep Gaddify away, we can help Sorcha," Seth pointed out. "Plus, I really want to see that room."

"We have to keep an eye on Proctor," said Lydia.

Gus nodded. "One of us will fake a concussion. There is an hour-long interview in the concussion protocol, so she'll have to spend at least an hour with that person." Gus paused. "I can do it. Kit told me about the interview, so I'll learn what I can from him. I think it's mostly just questions to check your mental functioning and assess if you have a concussion or not."

Lydia wanted to protest. Now that Gaddify was out of the picture, dealing with Proctor would be the most dangerous task. "Someone should go with you, Gus."

"I can check in on him," said Naomi.

Gus nodded again and went on. "We will set up lookouts in the auditorium and have a code word. If anyone comes in while Sorcha's working on the lock, just yell 'Project!' to Cora. Everyone should think that you're just trying to get her to speak louder."

"We need lookouts in place for a while before the operation begins," said Seth. "It wouldn't do any good to get into the room and find L. in there."

"There might be another way in," said Marin.

"I don't think so," said Sorcha. "I checked those blank spots that Jay was talking about on the second and third floors. They're there, all right, and there isn't any way through those walls that I could find."

"Good thinking, Sorcha," said Gus.

Sorcha nodded.

"So, Marin, Lenore is the only person whose name begins with *L* on the staff, and Dr. Kennedy is the only teacher?" asked Seth.

"Before you ask, there are no female teachers or staff whose name begins with *H*, so that is almost definitely Dr. G. Also, I was able to ask Ms. Windham her middle name, Goodson, but I don't know anyone else's middle name." Marin looked defensively around the room.

"'Success consists of going from failure to failure without loss of enthusiasm,'" Seth intoned in his British accent.

Everybody groaned.

"We could always go back to our squirt gun plan," said Lydia, hoping to help Marin relax.

Marin grimaced.

"Well, we'll keep working to find L. Let's plan to carry out the attack tomorrow," said Seth.

"I don't think we should do anything until we know who L. is," said Marin. Lydia recognized the stubborn set of her face from her short time as Marin's friend.

"We have all the tools we need," said Seth, "and Gaddify will be out of the way. We don't know if there is some alarm system in place, but if Gaddify's gone, he'll never be able to get back to the island in time even if he does find out somebody broke in."

Heads bobbed in agreement.

"But L. might know if we break in! She could call Gaddify or he could call her," said Marin. "We have no idea what a necromancer can do." Marin's voice began to climb the scale. "What if she can get a *spirit* to guard the door? What if all she has to do to stop us is poke a pin in a voodoo doll or something? What's the plan for that?"

Marin's eyes were wide and panicky. Seth looked as though he wanted to disagree, but Gus shook his head and stood up.

"You're right, Marin," he said. "We are operating in the dark here." Gus put his hand on Marin's shoulder, and for a second Lydia thought that Marin was going to swat it away.

"I can't help imaging the worst," she said.

"I know," said Gus quietly. "Me too."

There was a quality to the exchange that was intimate, so that everybody else held his or her breath and tried to disappear. Lydia was struck by the different qualities of leadership Seth and Gus displayed. Seth sort of swept you up in his own confidence. Gus made you feel understood. He squeezed Marin's shoulder and then turned back to the group. "Marin's not wrong, but we can't be sure that anything we try to do to protect ourselves from spirits won't work against us. Because we're spirits. I think. Except for Lydia, I mean."

The room seemed airless for a moment and then Gus continued.

"I think we should put all our efforts into finding L. in the next twenty-four hours. If we don't find her, we take the risk and use Dr. Gaddify's absence to get into the room."

Lydia's eyes slid over the faces of her friends, looking for dissent and finding none.

"How's everybody doing?" asked Lydia. She made a point of not holding Naomi's gaze any longer than anybody else's. She was rewarded by a faint smile.

"Still freaked out," said Cora.

"I don't really get this stuff," said Pilar. "I wish I'd read more witchy novels."

"I wish I'd read fewer," said Gus.

Seth and Gus had decided that it was important for everybody to continue as if nothing were different, and for Lydia, that meant the library. After Specials that afternoon she dropped her books in the dorm, got changed out of her uniform, and headed over to the library.

She hurried through the tasks that Ms. Alton had set aside for her and presented herself in Ms. Alton's office after just half an hour.

"Do you have time for a lemonade today, Lydia?" asked Ms. Alton.

"Thanks, but I'm meeting a friend soon," said Lydia truthfully.

"Is it the boy from the other evening, by any chance?" Ms. Alton eyes were as close to teasing as Lydia had ever seen them.

"Yup." Lydia grinned.

"Well, good." Ms. Alton patted a stack of papers into neatness on her desk. "Have a good evening."

Lydia said good-bye to Ms. Alton, pulled up her hood, and went down the steps of the library into the sharp, cold air. Seth was waiting for her, sitting on the back steps of the main building, opposite the library.

"I think my butt might have frozen to these steps," he said, getting stiffly to his feet.

"Is that another Churchill quote?" Lydia teased.

Seth pouted. "No sympathy, eh? I deserve that, I guess."

Lydia didn't say so, but she agreed.

"You once told me that you would do anything for a peanut butter and jelly sandwich," said Seth. He squinted up into the bright sky and then looked hard at Lydia.

"I did."

Seth pulled a slightly battered-looking sandwich out of his backpack. "Would you listen to a total boob apologize if he gave you this?"

Lydia looked at the limp sandwich and then up at Seth. "I'll do you one better," she said. "I'll forgive you."

Seth put the sandwich down on the steps and faced Lydia. He tucked a strand of hair into her hood and then lifted her chin. He took a deep breath.

"If you're about to quote Churchill, don't," said Lydia.

Seth let out his breath and laughed at the same time.

"How did you know?"

"'Cause you're nuts."

"Yeah, well." Seth sighed.

"Don't worry," whispered Lydia, just inches from Seth's face. "I'll never, never, never give up."

Chapter 32

The two other times that Lydia had done a secret mission, there hadn't been time to get nervous. Now, with hours and hours to contemplate all the ways things could go wrong, and armed with the information of exactly what type of people she was dealing with, Lydia felt like there was a steel band around her chest that squeezed tighter and tighter every time she thought about the plan. She saw Dr. Gaddify striding across the main lawn early in the morning, and Lydia got so nervous that she had to sit down and breathe with her head between her knees.

It didn't help that when Lydia looked around at her classmates, she marveled at who they really were. She wasn't seeing Kit with the severely tilted bangs; she was marveling that Niels Bohr, a Nobel Prize–winning physicist, was teaching *her* about sine waves. In real life, Niels Bohr had helped figure out the structure of the atom and made discoveries about radioactivity, but here he was impatiently correcting her math homework, punching Seth in the arm, jostling to get out the door first when class was over. Slightly chubby Pilar was actually Kalpana Chawla, an aerospace engineer who had died in a space shuttle crash. Sorcha, even though she didn't know it, was Hedy Lamarr, a famously beautiful actress who also invented technology that proved important for communications.

At lunch Cora came over to the table where Lydia, Pilar, Seth, and Gus were sitting, her eyes streaming.

"Lenore Pritchard is definitely not our L.," said Cora, grabbing a napkin and dabbing at her eyes. "She just showed me how to chop an onion and then demonstrated how to use the eyewash station to stop the burning. Nobody with contacts would do that, right?"

"Brilliant, Cora," said Gus.

"Julia Child wanted to be a spy, you know," said Cora. "Maybe she was."

Seth's mouth was too full to say anything, but he looked impressed too. Lydia's nerves were making it hard for the peanut butter and jelly sandwich to go down, so she just nodded.

"Marin said she's going to follow Ms. Pritchard to the ferry this evening just to make sure," said Cora. She seemed a little annoyed at Marin's paranoia.

Lydia swallowed a particularly sticky bite of peanut butter. "She's also going to talk to Captain Whelk and confirm that Gaddify left this morning."

There were more nods and Lydia was getting the feeling that she wasn't the only one who was nervous. Seth had started humming again, and Cora kept picking up things from her tray, looking at them, and then putting them down.

"It'll be all right, guys," said Gus. "In the meantime, I highly recommend the white chocolate macadamia nut cookies today."

Lydia and Gus finished their Special but lingered at their desks while Mr. Harcourt packed up his stuff and left. After a minute Gus inhaled and turned his body to face Lydia.

"Lydia?" said Gus.

"Yeah?"

"We have to get our spirits back, right? I mean, Gus McCracken's soul is still out there."

"I think so," said Lydia. "I think that's what the old lady meant by 'haunted.'"

"So if he's still out there, then we can save him, right?" Gus twirled a pen through his fingers. "I have all his memories, you know. He seems like a decent guy, and I've been thinking about it." Gus put the pencil down gently. "I think I—*he* deserves to come back."

"Okay," said Lydia slowly.

"I mean, everybody does, right? All the kids who came here. We need to figure out how to get their spirits back into their bodies."

For a moment pure joy flooded Lydia's body like a current of light. *Matthew could come back.* But no, Matthew no longer had a body to come back to. The joy was extinguished so harshly that Lydia clutched her stomach as if she'd been punched in the gut.

"So," Gus continued, "this mission we're on. It's a suicide mission, in a way."

Lydia stared at Gus, horror rising up her spine. "We don't have to—switch you—right away!" she protested. "We need you. How you are, I mean. We just have to stop them from doing more! Gus—"

"You know I'm right," said Gus firmly. "Joshua Lawrence Chamberlain had his life. Angus McCracken deserves his shot."

"But . . . ," said Lydia. "But *you* are my friend. The you you are now. The mix of Gus and Josh. You're—I love you. I can't bear if you all . . . if you all die!" Hot tears splashed off of Lydia's cheeks and splattered onto her lap. "Don't say that, Gus. Please."

"It's the right thing." Gus looked up into a corner of the ceiling, trying the same tactic that failed Lydia's mom so often. Sure enough, a tear slipped out and Gus swiped it away. "Think of Naomi. She was born to be an artist, a really good one. What could the *real* Naomi teach us if she had a chance?"

"No—"

"She's clearly having issues. Half her paintings are Georgia O'Keeffe and the other half are Naomi."

"Okay, we have to save Naomi. I agree, but—"

"It's okay, Lydia. I think Marin's figured it out too. And Sorcha. She's been saying good-bye to the world. Haven't you noticed?"

The sound that came out of Lydia's mouth was a mix between a sob and a bleat. Another time she would have been embarrassed, but now, for the first time since Matthew died, Lydia grieved unreservedly.

"I don't want you to die," she hiccupped.

Gus squeezed her hand. "I don't either. I mean, I'm scared. But I know it's right."

"None of this is right!" Lydia choked, tears burning down her cheeks. "Promise you won't leave—you won't leave without saying good-bye."

Gus took Lydia's other hand and looked at her through his own tears. Lydia could see that whoever he was, he was a good man and a wise one. She believed that if she had to follow someone into battle, this man's character would give her strength and resolve.

"Lydia, I promise, whatever happens, you won't be alone."

The plan was for Lydia to confirm that Pilar had Dr. Kennedy occupied and then take over for Seth watching the door backstage until after dinner. When Lydia checked in the lab, Pilar gave her a tight smile.

"We finally just got this set up," said Pilar, her voice heavy with significance as she waved at a very complex-looking experiment that took up three of the tables in the lab. "It will take at least three hours."

"If everything goes well," said Dr. Kennedy without looking toward the door.

Lydia nodded to Pilar, who gave her a thumbs-up, and then hurried over to the main building and into the auditorium.

Only the stage lights were on, and Seth was lying on his back with his backpack for a pillow when Lydia came in. He stopped humming and sat up when he saw her, then waited until she'd walked down the aisle to the front of the stage.

"Nothing happened here from three until now," he said. "Cora was here from one to three, and she also said that nobody unusual came in."

The muscle that Lydia had first noticed during the Bourne War battle was twitching in Seth's jaw.

"Go eat," she said. "I'll see you in two hours."

Lydia passed the next two hours in a fugue state, sitting in the front row of seats, pointedly ignoring any thoughts of what she had discussed with Gus and not allowing herself to think about the evening ahead. Her heart stuttered and stopped when two seniors opened the door with a bang. Lydia guessed they were looking for a private spot to make out, because when they saw Lydia, they jumped apart and retreated.

Cora was the first to arrive. She had a stack of scripts, and her voice seemed jarringly loud after the tomblike silence Lydia had endured.

"Lydia?" called Cora. "Ready to rehearse?"

Lydia cleared her throat and stood up shakily. "Yeah," she said. "I'm ready." This was code too. It meant that neither Lydia nor Seth had seen anything wrong.

Marin came next, nodded grimly, and took a seat in the front row of the auditorium. "All clear," she muttered to Lydia. So Lenore Pritchard and Dr. Gaddify were both confirmed off island.

Sorcha and Seth arrived together. Sorcha was whistling and Seth was humming. Neither one seemed to notice that they weren't on the same tune.

They all milled around in front of the stage, waiting for Naomi and growing more anxious every second she was late. Naomi was supposed to bring Gus to the nurse and explain that he might have a concussion. Everybody jumped when she opened the door and walked quickly down the aisle.

"Pilar managed some delays," she said. "Dr. Kennedy's pissed, but now they will be at it until at least nine. Gus had an accident in my studio, as planned. I took him to see Proctor, and they had just started the concussion interview when I left."

There was a pause and everybody looked at Seth.

"Okay, kids," he said. "We've got about forty minutes. You know what to do."

Cora ran up the aisle and locked the auditorium doors. If Gus or Pilar had to get in, they would use a special knock. Cora gave her keys to Sorcha and then handed Marin, Naomi, and Lydia some scripts. Sorcha and Seth vaulted up onto the stage and disappeared to the left.

"All right," said Cora brightly. "Who wants to be who?"

Lydia was so nervous she was having trouble focusing on the words in front of her, but she was not the only one. Time passing seemed overbright; the volume of conversation was alternately too loud and too soft.

Lydia asked for the third time who she was reading, when Seth poked his head out from behind the curtain.

"We're in," he said.

Cora stopped speaking in midsentence. Lydia dropped the script and scrambled up onstage. Marin seemed to have forgotten she was carrying a script and walked, trancelike, toward Seth. Sorcha appeared, looking solemn but girded for action.

They all stood in a bunch, crowded into the wings outside the door.

"Wait," said Lydia. She looked around at the avid faces of her friends. "I'm so sorry," she whispered. "I didn't think it through—what this would mean for you to find out." Each face took on a careful blankness, so Lydia knew that they knew what she was talking about. "You figured it out, but you helped me anyway. So . . ." Lydia's chin began to tremble. "So, thank you for believing me."

Lydia scrubbed at her cheeks with her palms. Cora's lips were twisted up into a half smile. Seth's mouth was set and firm. Lydia had thought she loved her friends that night out on the rock. That had been effervescent love; bubbly and light. The love she felt now was solid and heavy. She was grounded by it and fortified.

"Good luck," said Sorcha. She gave Lydia a quick hug and patted Marin's shoulder. "If anyone comes in who you need to worry about, I'll just yell, 'Hurry up, your audience is waiting.'" Sorcha went and scooped up the script Lydia had dropped, and pressed it into Lydia's chest. "You'll need this if someone comes."

Lydia stowed the script outside the opening in the wall, and stood up. Naomi nodded solemnly. Seth saluted, and everybody except Sorcha started up the stairs.

The dark, twisting staircase seemed to last forever. Lydia felt nausea roiling in her stomach that was a combination of spiraling and anxiety. Cora kept her hand on Lydia's back the whole time, and when Lydia reached the top, she turned and pulled Cora up into the room.

The floor of the room was a perfect square of light-colored wood. The evening sky pressed purple-gray and heavy against the glass overhead, and Lydia had the feeling of being underwater. Underwater in a shark-infested sea. Sound reverberated strangely inside the pyramid, and the small noises of people moving echoed against all the hard surfaces.

Seth was standing at the edge of a square that had been painted onto the floor with a dark red paint. To his left was the point of another square, which had been drawn at cross angles to the first, making an eight-pointed star. At every point of the star was an upside-down ankh, so thickly painted as to be black.

Runes and symbols ran along the edges of each square, so dark and malign that they seemed to squirm in front of Lydia's eyes. She could see drops of wax, the color of old blood, pimpling the smooth wood around the points of the star.

Every instinct told Lydia to get out of that room. She had to suppress the urge to run straight through the glass of the pyramid and into the suffocating night, to stop breathing the poisonous air of the room, to scrape the sight of it from her eyes. She mastered herself by looking away from the pattern and along the base of the pyramid.

"They laid us down on our backs," she said quietly. "There were nine in each group, so I'm guessing eight around the outside, with our heads at each point, and one in the middle."

Everybody looked at the pattern briefly, but their eyes all skittered over it as if they could avoid forming a memory. Marin spotted some notebooks and started edging along the sides of the pattern, careful not to step foot inside. Cora, who had brought her camera, held it protectively up to her eye and was doing her best to take pictures in the dim light. Every time the camera flashed, Lydia winced. She followed Marin around one edge of the squares. She could see a small refrigerator and wondered what was inside.

Like people in a crypt, Lydia's friends were silent with equal parts reverence and fear. They spread out along the edges of the pyramid, drifting around the neat piles of candles, avoiding the pattern in the center of the room. Lydia crouched down under the slant of the ceiling and opened the fridge. Inside were two racks of syringes. Wondering if this was what she'd been drugged with, she picked up a syringe and read the label. The top rack was sodium thiopental. She grabbed a handful of syringes from the bottom rack. It was all epinephrine, which she recognized as something you gave to somebody who was having an allergic reaction. Maybe she'd been given the sodium thiopental, whatever that was.

From her squatting position, Lydia looked around. Seth was kneeling in front of an elaborate antique cabinet that had hundreds of small drawers. He slid out a drawer and held up a lock of gray hair. He read the label, replaced the hair, shut the drawer, and wiped his hand on his shirt. Naomi was squatting in front of a black-velvet-lined tray where a pair of scissors gleamed wickedly.

Marin picked up a notebook and then let it fall back into her lap. "I can't do this," she whispered to Lydia. "I hate being here in this room."

"I know," said Lydia quietly. "It's okay."

She stopped. "Quiet, everyone!" She stood up, still holding a handful of syringes. Now the others heard it too.

Footsteps.

Up over the edge of the stairs came the smiling face of
Nurse Proctor.

Chapter 33

"I knew it." Nurse Proctor's harsh whispering voice echoed around the glass pyramid like bats fluttering. She stepped into the room, and Lydia saw that she was carrying a gun.

Seth lunged forward. "You did this!"

Nurse Proctor pointed the gun at Seth.

"No! It's not me. I didn't do this."

Lydia and her friends spread out around the edges of the room. Nurse Proctor couldn't shoot them all at once.

"If you shoot," said Lydia, "you'll break the glass. I wouldn't risk it if I were you."

"I'm not going to shoot you," said Nurse Proctor. "I'm on your side."

Nobody moved.

"I've been here for fifteen years, trying to figure out what happened to my brother." Nurse Proctor's protruding eyes glistened with tears. "Last year I figured out that Dr. Gaddify had me hypnotized, and I started carrying my pins." Nurse Proctor held up her palm. It was covered in small scabs and scars. "He can't get me again as long as I have my pins."

Seth cleared his throat. "So you've been trying to uncover the same thing we have?"

"Yes," croaked Nurse Proctor. "They told me that my brother burned up in the fire at the orphanage, but I was there. I know he wasn't in the fire because I went in to find him. None of those kids were in the building when it burned."

"Your voice," said Cora.

"Smoke inhalation. I nearly died," said Nurse Proctor.

"Is your brother Moses Johnson?" asked Lydia.

"Yes."

"And your middle initial. J. Is that for Johnson?"

"Yes. Proctor is from my adoptive family. I never believed about the fire, so when I was old enough, I started looking into it. A lot of things didn't make sense, but it took me years to piece it all together. I traced it all back to this island and came here when I got the job, but Dr. Gaddify kept me hypnotized for *fourteen years*. I forgot what I was looking for until last year, when he missed our start-of-the-year appointment. It was like coming out of a dream."

"So, you're not L.?" asked Lydia.

Nurse Proctor frowned. "No, but I am on your side if you're trying to stop these people." She held up the gun and put it carefully on the floor. With her shoe she slid it behind her, under the slope of the pyramid.

"What did you do with Gus and Sorcha?" asked Seth.

Nurse Proctor grimaced. "I'm sorry about them. They will be fine, but I needed them out of the way. I've had my eye on Lydia since I first caught her taking pictures of Dr. Gaddify's office. I suspected you were all up to something, and Dr. Gaddify's been suspicious too. He tried to hypnotize me after he saw that someone had broken into his office, but I had my pins."

"You were there that night," said Lydia.

"I was. I had the same idea as you, actually, but I saw someone was in the office when I went to get in. I met Gaddify by the library as I was leaving and I tried to stall him, but he almost caught you. I told him that I'd seen people in the main building to draw him away."

"What about Gus and Sorcha?" growled Seth.

"It was obvious that Gus was lying about his concussion, so I knew something was up. Naomi mentioned something about the auditorium before she left, and I've suspected that this is where they do whatever it is, so I took a chance. I gave him some sodium thiopental."

"What is that?" asked Lydia. It was the same stuff as in the syringes.

"Truth serum," said Seth and Nurse Proctor at the same time.

Nurse Proctor went on. "He told me where you were and about your special knock to get in. Sorcha unlocked the door. I pulled her out of the auditorium, took her keys, and told her that Gus needed her help, then locked her out. She didn't even have time to yell."

"She probably went to help Gus," said Cora.

"Gus will be okay in an hour or so," said Nurse Proctor. "Please, let's get some pictures of all this and get out of here. I can bring the evidence to the police tomorrow."

Nurse Proctor stepped up into the room and did a slow circle around the pattern. Lydia and her friends watched her, still unsure. Her voice, the grave, her scarred palm, it all pointed to her innocence.

"Okay, Nurse Proctor's not L.," said Marin. "I told you guys! But if she's not L., then who is? We're still safe, right?" said Marin, convincing herself. "We've covered our bases. Pilar has Kennedy, and I talked to Captain Whelk myself. She said I shouldn't be alarmed, Dr. Gaddify will return Sunday. As if I care when he comes—"

"Wait," said Lydia. "What did she say?"

"Captain Whelk said Dr. Gaddify left this morning on smooth seas."

"What *exactly* did she say?" Lydia stepped forward, the syringes rattling in her fist.

Marin's brows drew together. "Dr. Gaddify was on the seven-thirty boat. Seas were smooth as glass."

"What about 'alarmed'?"

"Oh, yeah. She said: 'Don't be alarmed. Dr. Gaddify was on the seven-thirty boat, but he'll be back Sunday night.'"

"*'Don't be alarmed'*? Those were her exact words?"

"Yes," said Marin. Her features suddenly stretched with fear. "Captain Whelk was hypnotized?"

"Guys!" called Lydia. "Hang on. Something's weird."

"What?" said Nurse Proctor. "I heard it too, that Dr. Gaddify left."

"But what if he didn't? You said he was suspicious, so what if this is a trap and he hypnotized Captain Whelk—" In her panic Lydia started across the middle of the room, forgetting about the terrible pattern on the floor.

"Very good, Lydia." Dr. Gaddify's warm voice came from the stairwell.

Seth dropped the drawer he was holding and lunged for Dr. Gaddify. Naomi snatched up the scissors and lifted them over her head.

"I command you to STOP!" shouted Dr. Gaddify. Everybody else froze, but Lydia kept moving, leaping up behind Seth. For half a second she inhaled, ready to yell at everyone to attack, and then she realized. They were all under Dr. Gaddify's thrall.

"Put down everything you are holding," commanded Dr. Gaddify. Naomi lowered the scissors. Marin replaced the notebook, and Lydia carefully slipped the syringes into the kangaroo pocket of her hoodie. She prayed that Seth's body had blocked Dr. Gaddify's view of her movements enough to disguise the fact that she had stopped a full second after everybody else. She glanced at Nurse Proctor, whose face was entirely devoid of expression. She hadn't had time to use her pins. Lydia forced herself to breathe through her nostrils and prayed that Gaddify wouldn't notice that she wasn't in his thrall like the rest.

She could hear his breathing, which was also accelerated. *Good. He's nervous too.* He took a slow step up the last stair and moved out onto the floor as if he were walking among a flock of rare birds that might easily be frightened away.

"Very good."

Lydia felt Dr. Gaddify's eyes study her face and then slide away to Cora's. "We will walk down to my office," he said calmly but forcefully. "Seth, you will discuss Winston Churchill's cabinet during World War Two. The rest of you will listen. Look agreeable and walk in front of me. Now go."

Lydia glanced at the gun, still under the edge of the pyramid and out of reach. Her friends shuffled into a ragged line and spiraled down the stairs one by one, like water going down a drain. Nurse Proctor was in front, Seth was last. Lydia could hear him saying something about Clement Attlee, but she bent all of her attention to thinking about how to get everybody out in one piece. Her first thought was of Sorcha and Gus. Were they okay? Would they come?

Lydia's friends stepped silently out onto the stage. Lydia noted with despair that Sorcha had left the lock-picking kit on the edge of the stage.

"Walk in pairs," said Dr. Gaddify. He was panting a little. "Go straight to my office. Seth, keep talking."

Lydia was not sure that anyone who was paying close attention would be fooled by their strange parade through the hall. They passed a group of three students, and she begged them with her eyes to notice something weird, but she also knew that with one word from Dr. Gaddify any student they met would be useless. They met two more groups of students, but each group just moved to one side and let them pass through. Lydia thought about running away to get help, but she didn't want to leave her friends helpless like this.

Lydia and the others walked into Gaddify's office and waited, quietly listening to Seth, while Dr. Gaddify locked the door and drew down new sets of blinds over the window in the door and the window to the outside.

"I got the idea for these blinds from whoever it was who broke into my office the other night," said Dr. Gaddify in a conversational tone. "Who was that, anyway?"

"That was Lydia and me," said Marin.

"Ah," said Gaddify, studying Lydia. "How upsetting for Elle."

Dr. Gaddify moved through the statuelike group of students and went over to his desk. He cleared some papers away from the intercom and stabbed a number, then leaned over and spoke clearly into the speaker. "I've got them. It was Lydia Boswell and Marin Blodgett. There are three others, plus Proctor. What should I do?"

The voice that came through the speaker was too garbled to be recognizable, but it was definitely female. "Get rid of Boswell, Blodgett, and Proctor. Suicide, if they are suitably submissive. Reprogram the others."

"Okeydokey." Dr. Gaddify jabbed another button and then turned and sat on his desk, facing the students.

"Listen to me," he said.

Lydia was beginning to recognize a certain weight in his voice that he used to give them commands, but she felt no compulsion to obey. Instead she began to work the protective covers off the tips of the syringes in her pocket. If she could get close enough to Dr. Gaddify, maybe she could stab him and it would be enough of a distraction to get everybody out of the office.

"Lydia Boswell. Nancy Wake."

Lydia froze.

"When we are finished here, you will leave the main building out the back and walk to the big rock on the east side of the island," Dr. Gaddify continued. "You will wait until no one is around, and then you'll jump onto the rocks below."

An odd sort of shudder went through Lydia's friends, which gave her the strength to keep her face expressionless.

"Marin Blodgett. Edward Forster. You will return to your room. You will write a beautiful note explaining why life is not worth living after the suicides of your boyfriend, Matthew Hafford, and your best friend, Lydia Boswell. You will not leave your room until tomorrow evening, when you will walk into the ocean and drown." Dr. Gaddify paused and then continued. "You will write that all of the writing you've done in the past two years is the property of the school."

Again the odd little shudder in her friends saved Lydia from betraying herself.

"Constance Proctor. You will go to the nurse's office and inject yourself with three syringes of sodium thiopental." He looked at the side of Nurse Proctor's face. "That should make you good and crazy. Too many suicides would be suspicious, but we'll get you out of the way."

"As for the rest of you," said Dr. Gaddify. He began to move through the motionless students. "You will understand that

Lydia and Marin were two *deeply* disturbed young women. They were haunted by insecurities and jealousy."

Dr. Gaddify threaded his way between Lydia and Marin. He studied the side of Lydia's face. Lydia wrapped her fist around the collection of syringes in her pocket. Dr. Gaddify leaned close to her ear. "Lydia had a dark imagination. She told lies." The word hissed against Lydia's cheek with a wet stream of air. Dr. Gaddify paused and then turned to Marin.

"Marin Blodgett was a talented writer, but she had no real frie—"

Dr. Gaddify never finished the word.

Lydia plunged the fistful of needles into his shoulder and then slammed her palm against the plungers. He fell clumsily against Marin, crying out in pain and surprise. Marin crashed forward and hit the desk, her head making a wet smack against the edge.

The other students shifted, as if a gust of wind had blown through the office, but otherwise didn't move.

"Lydia Boswell," Gaddify hissed from the floor. "I command you . . ." Suddenly his eyes flickered open and shut and then rolled back, showing white. His entire body began to jitter and jerk, his heels beating a rapid tattoo against the floor. The syringes still in his back clicked and rattled.

Lydia heard thick choking noises come from deep within Gaddify's throat as she raced to Marin's side. She didn't know if she should touch her or not, so she looked around for help.

Dr. Gaddify's face turned pale green and then blue, his eyelids fluttering weakly, the jerking of his body lessening until there was one last choking noise and he was still.

Chapter 34

Lydia looked in horror at Dr. Gaddify's swollen blue face on the floor, at the spreading puddle of dark liquid beneath Marin's head, at her friends' expressionless faces. She lurched to her feet and jiggled Seth's arm.

"Wake up," she begged.

Seth did not blink.

Lydia looked around the office again and darted to the door. She fumbled with the handle for a moment then fled down the hall with only one thought in her head: *Get help now.*

Her feet brought her careening out the back door and up the library steps without asking permission from her brain. The lights in the library were out except for a soft glow coming from Ms. Alton's office. Lydia flung open the front door and hurled herself up the steps to the office.

"Help! Help! Ms. Alton!"

"Lydia dear, you gave me fright!" Ms. Alton whipped around from where she was standing in front of one of the cupboards in her office. "What is it? Sit down."

"It's Dr. Gaddify," Lydia gasped. "He has students in his office. He hypnotized them and he told Marin to kill herself." Lydia heard herself wail. "But she's hurt! She's bleeding!"

"Shhh. Shh. Lydia. Okay, in his office, you say? I'll go right away." Ms. Alton strode to the door and then whirled on the spot. "No. I need to stay with you. You look like you might faint." Ms. Alton leaned over her desk and pressed some buttons on the intercom. "Nurse Proctor! This is Ms. Alton. There are children in Dr. Gaddify's office who need help!"

"Nurse Proctor is with them," said Lydia. "She's not in her office."

"Is she okay?"

"No," wailed Lydia.

"I'll call Dr. Kennedy, then."

"No!" Lydia lurched forward. "Dr. Gaddify's working with someone. A woman. I don't know who she is, but he called her on the intercom, so she's on the island." Lydia collapsed into a chair.

"You have no idea who she is?"

"No, the voice was garbled."

"Dr. Weatherby, then." Ms. Alton pressed some numbers on the intercom pad on her desk and leaned over to talk into the microphone. "Dr. Weatherby. It is Mary Ann Alton in the library. I need you and Mr. Harcourt to go to the headmaster's office right away and check on several people who may be in distress. One needs medical attention. I believe Dr. Gaddify may be with them, and I'm not sure he's in his right mind. Please report to me here in the library as soon as possible." She hung up before Dr. Weatherby could reply and stood blinking at Lydia for a moment.

"Marin needs help," Lydia urged. "We should go to her."

Ms. Alton froze, poised over the intercom. "Too risky, I think." She inhaled deeply and stood up. "Are you all right, Lydia? Did he hurt you?" Ms. Alton looked out into the dark library and hugged herself.

"No, no, he didn't hurt me," said Lydia. She sat up and scanned the office for a first-aid kit. Ms. Alton bustled around behind her desk and turned with a lemonade bottle in her hand.

"Oh, I don't know what I'm doing." Ms. Alton looked at the open bottle of lemonade as if surprised to see it in her hand. "A student is hurt, you say? I do hope they hurry." Ms. Alton collapsed into her chair, looking lost. She put the lemonade on the desk with a thunk. "Have some lemonade, dear, you might as well."

Lydia reached forward obediently and drank a mouthful of lemonade. *I might be in shock*, she thought. Her leg was bouncing up and down.

Ms. Alton sat up in her chair across the desk from Lydia and peered over her glasses. "Start from the beginning. Tell me everything."

Lydia put the bottle of lemonade on the desk and moved to stand up. "But my friends—"

"I know. I'm worried too. But they are in good hands." Ms. Alton glanced about fretfully. "I'm sorry, my dear, but I am afraid I would not be much good to your friends in any sort of confrontation. I'll locked the door to this office, so you are safe, and that is what is important."

Lydia blinked back tears. She felt a little woozy. "It's Dr. Gaddify. He's really, really bad. We found his journals." Lydia's voice faltered.

"You found journals?" Ms. Alton returned from locking the office door and sat.

Lydia nodded, then remembered something important.

"I stabbed him," said Lydia. She took another long drink of the lemonade just to hide her face.

"Dr. Gaddify? You stabbed Henry Gaddify?"

"Yes, with some syringes. Epinephrine. He collapsed. I think—I think he could be dead." The lemonade was bitter on her tongue.

Ms. Alton's eyes grew large behind her spectacles. "Oh. I see." Her eyes twitched to the door. Lydia thought that she looked nervous, now that she knew a potential murderer was sitting across from her. "That does change things." Ms. Alton stood up and took off her glasses. She studied Lydia for a long moment. "We must get ready."

"Yes," said Lydia. "My friends."

Ms. Alton held up the bottle of lemonade and shook the remaining inch of liquid. "You must be tired, dear. The night you've had. Don't go to sleep on me just yet." Ms. Alton turned and unlocked a cabinet that was below Lydia's line of sight.

Exhaustion swirled around Lydia like a mist, but something was bothering her. What had Ms. Alton said that jiggled a line in her brain? There on the desk was the list of numbers for the intercom.

2 – Whole school
3 – Headmaster's office
4 – Cafeteria
5 – Auditorium

It went on, but Lydia was tired.

Where was number one? Who was more important than the headmaster? More important than the whole school? Lydia scanned the list and couldn't find the one.

"Are you sure Dr. Weatherby is enough? What if Dr. Gaddify isn't dead? He's powerful and evil," said Lydia. She spoke, hoping it would reel in the thought that eluded her.

"Hank Gaddify is a greedy fool," said Ms. Alton. Lydia studied the bottom of her lemonade bottle. She felt very tired, but something in Ms. Alton's tone made her look up.

"My friends," Lydia begged. "Please." Ms. Alton tsked and turned back to the cupboard that was out of sight. Lydia could hear things being moved about, but Ms. Alton's body was blocking her view.

Lydia looked at the old-fashioned intercom on the desk. Two was the whole school. Three was the headmaster's office. Who was number one? Her friends were in three. Could they hear her? Maybe she could hear them. Lydia pushed the three, and the little red light went on with a very faint buzz. She couldn't hear voices, though. Lydia's brain felt sloshy. Something tugged on her memory, but she couldn't pin it down. Ms. Alton turned and put a box on her desk.

"So," said Ms. Alton. "You found my journals."

"Your journals?" Lydia's tongue was thick and unwieldy. "But you're Mary Ann. M."

"Ah." Ms. Alton smiled. "I call myself L., for Lazarus." Ms. Alton seemed to enjoy the slow spread of terrified comprehension on Lydia's face. "Really, Lydia, I thought you were a *genius*."

Ms. Alton's tone was light and mocking. The word "genius," a slap.

"I'm not," Lydia blurted out. "It didn't work on me."

"Really?" Ms. Alton looked at Lydia with professional interest. "We wondered, you know, but you were proving to be *such* a spy."

"You wondered?"

"Yes, I met you before orientation, remember, Lydia? The transition seemed remarkably smooth. And there was that hiccup in the procedure."

"What do you mean?" whispered Lydia.

"Hank is supposed to use the truth serum, hypnotize you all, and get you into a trance state. Your pulse was racing. I knew you weren't ready for the ritual."

"Ritual! You mean murder!"

Ms. Alton clucked her tongue as if Lydia had just made a mistake in the Dewey decimal system. "Not murder. It's just a little switch."

"A switch? You cast the souls from their bodies. That's murder."

"But we replace *them*, a bunch of lonely, sad children, with *geniuses*." Ms. Alton had a look of fanatical passion in her eyes. "The world needs geniuses, Lydia. Now more than ever. Our students will be the ones to take this world into the future we deserve, but we need to act now! We can't just wait around, hoping a great thinker will be born. These minds, minds that come along once a generation, we're gathering them, bringing them back. Just imagine what they can all do together!" Ms. Alton looked at Lydia, almost as if she were waiting for her to agree.

"Actresses?" Lydia accused.

"Hank was in it for the money," said Ms. Alton. "I let him have his big earners, and he let me have my artists."

"Naomi *is* an artist. I mean, she was even before. You switched her before she could become a real artist."

"Regrettable, but I think still worth the risk. It's one in a million."

"And the suicides? Matthew Hafford?" Lydia's voice wobbled and a sob burst from her mouth like a cough.

"Matthew was a friend of yours? That accounts for the attractive depression in your application. We look for that, you know. And single parents. No siblings or more than four. New moon birthday. It's a formula we've perfected over decades, and you were the complete package."

"Why?" whispered Lydia, but Ms. Alton ignored her.

"What I want to know is *how*. How did you slip under the sickle, as it were? You said it didn't work on you?"

"No," said Lydia. "I'm not anyone but myself."

"But you have two spirits. An animating spirit and a haunt. I check everybody when we're done."

Ms. Alton peered over the desk at Lydia, looking like a cobra sizing up a mouse. "I see I need to inspect you properly." Ms. Alton sat at her desk and pulled out the top drawer. She put a small contact lens case on the desk and then squirted some solution into the two sides.

Even though Lydia knew what was coming, she was still horrified as Ms. Alton carefully pulled down the bottom lid of one eye and removed a small, dark lens. She poked her slender finger into the second eye and then blinked exaggeratedly. "Ahh," she said.

Lydia shrank back in her chair, transfixed. The balls of Ms. Alton's eyes were completely white. Only a tiny crackled pinprick of darkest red marked the pupil. Without the color of the iris, Lydia could see the bulge where the iris should be, so it seemed like there were something moving beneath the surface of the eyeball when Ms. Alton looked about.

The eyes, bulging predatorily, moved closer to Lydia. "You see," said Ms. Alton quietly. "When a soul is in the body it was born in, it fits exactly. I see now that your soul fits you"— Ms. Alton touched Lydia's nose playfully—"to a tee." She sat back on the desk. "I was fooled because the souls we cut away often haunt their body. Not always, but if I can see two souls near one body, it's usually a sign that possession worked."

Ms. Alton's eyes bulged, sweeping over Lydia. "You, my dear, have a spirit companion, just as you would if your soul were haunting your own body. That's what tricked me. I see *now* that the companion spirit is not yours *and* that your animating spirit fits too perfectly to be possession. So who's your companion?"

Lydia thought about evading her, but she was too tired.

"Matthew," she said thickly. "We grew up together." Two big tears dripped down Lydia's cheeks.

"Ahh," said Ms. Alton, widening her ghastly eyeballs even further. "My mistake. I won't be so careless again."

Something occurred to Lydia. "You're number one. On the intercom. You're in charge."

"Who? Little old me? The librarian?" Ms. Alton blinked her grotesque eyes coquettishly. "Guilty as charged."

"Please," begged Lydia. "My friends are in trouble. Marin is bleeding. We need to hurry."

"We do need to hurry," Ms. Alton agreed. "Stand up. We're going for a walk."

"No."

Ms. Alton froze. "Ahh." She circled Lydia in her chair. "I see." She sat down on the desk in front of Lydia, and the tiny pinpricks of red in the centers of her eyes bored into Lydia. "I am surprised to find that I miss the newly departed Dr. Gaddify already. No matter. I have other means of coercion." Ms. Alton smiled, her mouth like a cut breaking open. "You are worried about your friend. Marin. I will send someone to her *if* you cooperate."

Lydia realized that Ms. Alton had only pretended to call Dr. Weatherby. "Okay," she said.

"Good. Let's go."

"Call first."

"I will call when we get there."

"No. She needs help now."

Ms. Alton sighed and leaned over Lydia in her chair. "Do you know that I can have you haunted for the rest of your life? Every moment of your consciousness will be filled with pleading, begging, moaning, and screaming. Every second of your sleep will be spent dreaming the worst moments of peoples' lives. Accidents, rapes, murders, the deaths of children. Perhaps Dr. Gaddify could make a special appearance."

"Call somebody. Please," said Lydia. "I swear. I will go wherever you say."

Ms. Alton tilted her head to one side and tapped a finger against her lips. "E. M. Forster *is* one of my favorites. It would be a pity to lose him so soon. I will call."

"The physics lab," said Lydia. "And I want to hear Dr. Kennedy say that she's going."

"No longer worried about Dr. Kennedy?" Ms. Alton gave a very un–Ms. Alton–like snort. She punched in three digits. Nothing happened, so she tried again, and this time the faint crackle of a connection came out of the speaker.

"Physics lab."

"Dr. Kennedy, this is Mary Ann Alton in the library. There is a student in Dr. Gaddify's office who needs medical help immediately. Can you go?"

"Yes. Of course." Dr. Kennedy sounded surprised. "What happened?"

"I'm not sure, but please hurry."

Ms. Alton slammed her finger down onto the keypad. She turned to Lydia, licking her thin lips. "Satisfied?"

Lydia nodded, her head heavy.

"You're a good girl, Lydia. I like you, you know." Ms. Alton picked up a black case. "Let's go. You look a little sleepy, and I'd rather not do this here. Sedation is an inexact science."

"What did you give me? Is it truth serum too?"

"No, just something to make you more cooperative."

Lydia stood and tottered to the door. It took all of her strength of will to keep her balance. Ms. Alton unlocked the door and steered Lydia out by the elbow. She turned off the light and pushed Lydia toward a side door, half supporting her, half restraining her.

Lydia focused her eyes on Ms. Alton. "Do *what* here?"

"I've never tried it before, but it is the next logical step."

"I don't want to go back to that room." Lydia jerked her arm away from Ms. Alton and fell.

Ms. Alton hissed, "You promised to cooperate, and besides we're not going there." She pulled Lydia roughly to her feet. "We're going to my house."

Lydia tripped down the stairs, out to the dark side of the library. Only fear and Ms. Alton's iron-hard grip on her upper arm were keeping her upright. There was a golf cart parked in the shadows, and Ms. Alton pushed her into the passenger seat, then produced handcuffs from somewhere and secured Lydia's wrist to the roll bar. She stowed the small case from her office in the back and got into the driver's seat.

"Not a word, Lydia dear. If we see anybody, you will remain absolutely silent. I hate to damage you, but I will if I have to." Next, she pulled a pair of dark glasses out of her pocket and put them on. She patted Lydia's knee, making Lydia shiver with revulsion.

The path that bisected the island, which Lydia, Naomi, Cora, and Pilar had taken so very long ago, started from behind the library and went immediately into the trees. To Lydia it was only a tangle of blackness punctuated by bumps and jerks as they careened over roots and around trees. Ms. Alton seemed to have no trouble seeing to steer, and it wasn't too long before the golf cart burst out of the trees into the meadow.

An icy gust of sea air buffeted Lydia full in the face, so that her eyes teared up and she shrank into herself.

Ms. Alton stopped the cart, removed the box from the back, and stalked through the gates of the small graveyard. Her thin form was just visible in the darkness. With her white skin and hair and the dark round glasses, she looked like an animated skeleton moving deliberately about the stones. Lydia squinted into the wind and saw a flash of silver. Ms. Alton appeared to be scooping grave dirt into a silver bowl the size of an adult's skull.

Lydia tugged on the handcuffs. She thought of the lock-picking kit Sorcha had left on the stage. If she could start the cart, maybe she could escape. She looked over at the ignition and then around the floor and seats. She ran her free hand over the gritty surfaces, hoping for the clink of metal, the cold kiss of it on her skin.

"Looking for these?" Ms. Alton appeared out of the night, smiling and holding up the keys. She laughed. "Do you know what I've found about geniuses, Lydia? It's not so much their intelligence that makes them geniuses, it's their curiosity and perseverance. Ironic, isn't it, that you should show so much of both? You might have been a genius after all. Maybe we will be. There is still so much to learn about the spirit world, so many books I intend to write about history." Ms. Alton put her things in back and started to drive across the meadow to the house that crouched on the other side, overlooking the ocean. "Your friend Seth. Now, he's a fascinating subject. Sloppy, by the way, for them all to check out books about themselves. We knew somebody had broken into the office, but we didn't know *who* until the books. But anyway, we were thrilled to finally have a chance of collecting Winston Churchill. I have to admit, Gaddify was right about money. It opens a lot of doors."

The golf cart came to an abrupt stop and Lydia tilted forward, banging her knees. Ms. Alton tsked again. She turned and faced Lydia. "I trust you'll stay here and not damage yourself?"

Lydia didn't answer. What did it mean? "Not damage yourself"?

Ms. Alton collected the silver bowl and the black case from the back of the golf cart, then went up the steps of the house and in the front door. A light came on on the first floor and then on the second floor. Finally, a single window up in the attic bloomed bright into the night.

Even on that sunny, windy day back at the beginning of school, the house had seemed spooky. Now, in the darkness, with the wind coming off the ocean in a deafening roar, Lydia felt a smothering sort of dread. It was a fear so encompassing that she was too paralyzed to blink. The old tree overhead soughed and moaned, its branches rattling together like dry bones.

Ms. Alton's silhouette appeared in the doorway and grew bigger until she was there in front of Lydia, unlocking the handcuffs from the golf cart.

"This way, dear."

Lydia stood, clinging to the cart for support, and then lurched away from the house. She tried to run, but after only two steps her hair was yanked backward and she cried out, falling to her knees. Ms. Alton lifted Lydia to her feet by her ponytail and pushed her face close.

"I told you not to make me do this."

Ms. Alton slapped Lydia hard.

Hot metallic liquid spilled into Lydia's mouth and she went to her knees again.

"Get up," Ms. Alton growled. "You think I won't kick you?"

Lydia moaned and curled into a ball. Ms. Alton cursed, bent over, and grabbed Lydia's chin.

"You see this?" she asked, holding up a small, gleaming knife. "I'll do your eyes one at a time if you don't get into that house now."

Lydia crawled. Not one of her limbs was working the way she needed them to, and her mind held nothing but a high whining sound. She crawled up the porch steps and then more steps inside and finally steps that were almost a ladder. She collapsed onto the floor of the attic and curled onto her side.

Lydia concentrated on staying conscious. She heard the shriek of metal and a thump. *Ms. Alton has pulled up the ladder stairs on the trapdoor.* She heard a long hiss and faint patter she couldn't identify. *Concentrate.* Lydia uncurled enough for a view of the room. Ms. Alton was pouring dirt from the bowl into a circle on the floor. *A ritual.* Lydia's vision wobbled, then shrank inside a gray cone. She forced it open again and sat up, wiping a smear of blood from her cheek and chin.

"Feeling better?" Ms. Alton looked up briefly from her work. She had taken the glasses off again, so her eyes were demonic. Lydia looked away. *A ritual for what?*

"I don't want to be Nancy Wake," said Lydia.

Ms. Alton smiled and lit a match. She touched the flame to eight black candles before turning back to Lydia.

"You won't be."

Now she knelt before the little black case and pulled out a smaller flat leather box. She opened it the way another woman might open a jewelry box. Inside was a silver sickle resting on a black velvet tray. Ms. Alton stroked it and turned to Lydia. She advanced, picking up a syringe and her silver knife. Lydia flailed at her and tried to claw the syringe out of her hands, but Ms. Alton stopped her with a brutal kick to the gut. Lydia felt the needle in her arm and began to cry.

"I don't want to be Nancy Wake," she wept.

"I told you, silly girl," hissed Ms. Alton. "You won't be." Ms. Alton held up the knife and Lydia screamed. Wincing, Ms. Alton pressed down on the inside of her own wrist. Blood welled up around the knife and began to drip onto the floor. Ms. Alton held her wrist over Lydia and let the blood splash onto Lydia's pants, then her shirt, then face.

"You won't be Nancy Wake," said Ms. Alton softly.

The blood was hot and sticky.

"You'll be me."

Chapter 35

Lydia saw her body lying in the center of a large circle made of grave dirt. The candlelight flickered and bounced over her own face, giving the appearance of movement, but when she shouted to herself to *move*, nothing happened. Ms. Alton was sitting up, facing Lydia, with her legs entangled with Lydia's. Lydia could see only the top of her head, the pale part in her white hair. She was bleeding freely from a deep cut on her wrist. Ms. Alton took the silver sickle out of the velvet box and raised it to her own forehead. She tilted her head back and seemed to see Lydia where she was hovering in the peaked ceiling. She grinned at Lydia then and suddenly sliced through the air in front of her own torso.

It was as if Ms. Alton were a puppet and had cut the stings that held her up. Her body dropped heavily to one side. Lydia was distracted for a moment, watching the blood pool up against the line of grave dirt, and then she noticed that a wisp of something foul and dark was forming over Ms. Alton's chest. The wisp grew and coalesced, taking the rough form of a small human. Only Lydia's eyesight seemed to be working correctly, because she couldn't say if she tasted or smelled or felt it, but the gleaming form below was the most repulsive thing she had ever encountered. The form stepped out of Ms. Alton's body as if it were slipping out of a pair of trousers and slid toward Lydia's body below. It was murky green, then blackish red, then dirty purple, but Lydia could see the outline of things on the floor right through its foul, hunched figure. The thing crouched over Lydia's body and then reached out an oily finger to Lydia's breastbone. The finger touched Lydia's chest, and Lydia could feel it where she was in the air above the whole scene. Then the finger entered Lydia's breast.

The pain was searing, radiating out from Lydia's solar plexus to every extremity of her body. She shrieked noiselessly and saw the thing turn its face up to the ceiling.

It had two empty pits for eyes and a hollow, sucking void for a mouth, but it was still recognizably Ms. Alton. Even without lips, the void curled into a triumphant smile before turning again and plunging its finger farther into Lydia's breast.

Again, pain. Pain like scalding static.

*** I am here. ***

And Matthew was there and they were working together, diving at the thing, trying to rake it back from Lydia's body. Lydia's spirit hands clutched at the thing but only rippled the oily surface of it. Matthew plunged right into it but only came howling out the other side.

But there were others. Hundreds of others. Together, like a storm of light, they charged the creature, a soundless ** *NOOOOO* ** vibrating the air in the attic.

The creature removed its fingers from Lydia's breast and stood up. It swatted at the cloud of souls, causing the ones it touched to scream. The souls swirled around the creature in a glinting cyclone, and for a moment Lydia thought they might do it, they might actually stir the creature's substance into nothingness. She pushed all of her will and strength into the task, ignored the occasional searing brush, but then the pain in her breast was renewed.

The creature's hand was fully immerged in Lydia's chest. It slid the other hand in and then began to thrust its head inside, as if it were trying to crawl into a sleeping bag.

The pain.

The pain was so bad that Lydia felt as though she were shattering. She looked up, away from her body, and saw through the roof. Up through wisps of clouds, through dust and atmosphere. Up through stars and a moonless night. Up and into darkness.

Tiny prickles of sensations were needling over the skin of Lydia's face. She was cold, but the prickles were somehow warm. She opened her eyes into a bright, swirling mist. She squinted, licked her lips. The prickles were minuscule drops of water. The mist was real. Inexplicably, a ragged teddy bear filled her vision.

Lydia batted it away, repulsed and confused. In its place came Seth's face, white and anxious, his hair plastered to his head with damp.

"Lydia!"

"What'd you do that for?" asked Lydia.

"It was the only way I could think of to see if it was really you."

"What?"

"I thought if you were Ms. Alton, you'd hug it or something. She was trying to take your body, right? Trying to be you?"

Lydia continued to look confused.

"You didn't hug the bear," said Seth. "It's her teddy bear, so I think that you are probably really Lydia."

Lydia started to sit up but thought better of it when the whole world tilted sideways.

"I'm wet," she said. Knowledge and language were coming back to her slowly.

"I know," said Seth. "Me too."

"Where are we?"

Seth pointed to her right, so she arched her neck to follow his finger.

Ms. Alton's house was barely visible about a hundred yards away. Lydia shuddered and looked in the other direction. There was nothing but mist.

"The ocean?" She poked a thumb toward it.

"Yeah."

Seth stood up and surveyed Lydia from head to toe. Lydia looked down at herself.

"Where are my clothes?"

Seth glanced at a garbage bag that was propped up against the golf cart. "I put everything in there. Your clothes were covered in blood." Seth swallowed. "Not your blood, I think. You're okay, except for your face. Also, I had to be sure you didn't have anything of hers."

"The blood was hers," said Lydia. "Is she . . . ?"

"Yes. She's dead." Seth glanced at Lydia, who blinked up into the mist. "We did everything we could to make it look, well, normal. Just a suicide. Dr. Kennedy is going to have some questions for us, but we have a story."

Lydia sat up, this time successfully. She was wrapped in a heavy winter coat and had on her own shoes, but they weren't tied. "Where is everyone? Is Marin okay?"

Seth blew out a breath. "I better start from the beginning." He looked around again. "Can you get up?"

Lydia thought about it. Everything was muffled and bright. She felt very dull, but safe somehow.

"Will you help?"

"Of course."

Seth managed to get Lydia into the golf cart, then started the motor.

"I hate this thing," said Lydia, flicking the golf cart with her finger.

"Sorry. I didn't think you'd want to walk."

"You're right. It's okay." Lydia bounced gently around in her seat as Seth drove. "Where are we going?"

"I'm taking you to my room, if that's all right."

Lydia nodded.

"It's about five a.m. No one will be up."

In response Lydia put her head on Seth's shoulder and closed her eyes.

They drove through the woods and past the library and the upperclassman boys' dorm without seeing anyone. Lydia followed Seth silently into his dorm and up one flight of stairs. It smelled different from her dorm—sharp and spicy; not entirely good, but not entirely bad, either.

Seth's room was dark and cluttered. The bed was unmade with maroon sheets and a dark green comforter half on the floor. Lydia sat down on it and looked up at Seth. He hesitated, then took the desk chair.

"So," said Lydia. "You were hypnotized and standing in Gaddify's office." She winced. "Is he dead too?"

"Yeah."

Lydia nodded and swallowed hard.

"So we were standing there," said Seth "and it was like when you nod off in class and then suddenly something catches your attention and you have to figure out where you are and what pulled you out of your reverie."

Lydia nodded, understanding.

"I could hear two voices coming through the intercom, not very clearly, but then she called you Lydia. So I knew one of them was you, and the other person was L., for Lazarus."

"I remember pushing the intercom button. Number three," said Lydia.

"That was us! We could hear you!" said Seth. "We heard what she said, so even though I had this idea in my head that you and Marin were insecure and jealous and lying, I *had* to believe you. The L. voice confirmed everything I knew from yesterday. That was the key. From there I could unravel everything Gaddify had told us in his office. It took us a minute, but we were all able to break free. I think since he was dead . . ."

Lydia nodded again.

Seth took a breath and went on. "So Marin was bleeding but conscious. Gaddify was dead. Proctor took care of Marin. Naomi pulled all the needles out. . . ." Seth went pale and glanced at Lydia. "Cora and I were listening to the intercom, trying to figure out where you were. She said she was the librarian, but then there was a sort of radio squawk and we lost you. I think she hung up to call for help for Marin."

"She called the physics lab. I thought maybe Pilar would figure out something had gone wrong."

"She did. Also, Gus and Sorcha burst in saying that Ms. Alton had called the nurse's office from the library." Seth got up and sat next to Lydia on the bed, holding her hands. "We figured out that L. was Ms. Alton and you were in the library."

"I thought Ms. Alton was my friend. I thought . . . ," whispered Lydia.

"I know." Seth looked stricken. "I'm sorry."

"Go on," said Lydia.

"Well, we got our story straight for Dr. Kennedy, left Proctor with Marin, and then took off after you. No one was in the library, but Cora knew where her house was. When we got to the house, we couldn't figure out how to get the stairs to the attic down from the ceiling. They're the trapdoor kind—"

"I remember."

"But the strap was pulled up. We were shouting your name and pounding on the ceiling, but Sorcha kept her head and figured out something, so that the stairs almost killed us all when they finally fell down out of the ceiling. We raced up and there you were."

Seth wiped his eyes and swallowed hard twice. "You were covered in blood, lying in the middle of a circle made of dirt and candles. Ms. Alton's body was all tangled up with you." Seth swallowed and swiped at his eyes again. "I dragged you out of that damned circle and it was like you came alive again. You breathed in this huge breath, a scream almost, so I knew you were alive, but I had no way of knowing . . ."

"If I was still me," Lydia finished for him.

Seth nodded. "I was ready to stab you, you know. If you hugged the teddy bear." He laughed limply. "The teddy bear."

Lydia's face twisted into a bit of a smile. "Good," she whispered. "That was the right thing." She touched his shoulder.

Lydia thought a minute. "So Gaddify and Ms. Alton are dead. Marin's okay. I'm alive. You're okay." Lydia sat up straighter. "We did it. Where is everyone? We need to figure out—"

"There's more," said Seth. He closed his eyes and sat with his head in his hands.

"Where is everyone, Seth?" asked Lydia again.

"I pulled you out of the ring. I was looking at you, so I didn't see exactly what happened, but when I looked up, Naomi was just walking really slowly into the circle. She took this little silver sickle out of Ms. Alton's hand and swiped it down over the front of her body. Then it got too bright to look. When my eyes cleared, she was handing the sickle to Gus, but she was different. Her posture was all crouched over, and she was smiling. Gus did the same thing. There was another flash, and then Sorcha did it and Cora did it." Seth was weeping openly now. "Pilar went too. She was crying, but it was the bravest thing I've ever seen. I knew it was my turn. I kissed you. . . ."

Lydia gave him a crooked smile.

"I stood up, and Pilar stepped out of the circle. She smiled at me. Gave me the sickle. It was so cold I almost dropped it, *burning* cold. But I didn't drop it. I stepped into that circle and I could *see* them, Lydia. All these famous people. They were *there* inside that circle. But then I saw a boy, a teenager. It was him. Seth Finn. Me. And he shook his head at me. I didn't understand, so I raised the sickle, and he stepped forward and blocked my hand. He didn't touch me, but I could feel him. My skin was tight, like a sunburn, and I could see he was saying 'no,' so I didn't. I didn't do it, Lydia. I am the worst kind of coward."

Seth made a sound that was half cough and half howl. "They're gone," he whispered. "And I didn't go with them."

Lydia held Seth's head in her lap and stroked his shuddering shoulders. After a long while he sat up and wiped his nose on his sleeve. "You must hate me," he said.

Lydia shook her head. "I don't." She touched his cheek and lifted a tear away. "I never knew Seth Finn. I only know that he was depressed. I think . . . I think he didn't want to come back. So I'm glad. I'm *so* glad that you are still here."

With that, she kissed him, runny nose and all.

Chapter 36

The students of Claybourne woke that morning and almost universally reported strange dreams. Many woke with their pillows and faces soaked by tears. Two out of three immediately removed their key bracelets from their wrists.

Later they would decide that the weird dreams were a product of some sort of premonition. After all, Dr. Gaddify had had a heart attack that night. Marin Blodgett had a concussion from trying to catch him as he fell. Even stranger, the librarian had gone and slit her wrists in her attic. The final bit of weird news was that Captain Whelk had quit that very morning, so none of the staff had arrived on time and breakfast was late. Expecting pancakes, the students were instead informed of a mandatory all-school meeting. When they all met in the auditorium, they felt unaccountably grateful that Cora, Gus, Pilar, Naomi, and Sorcha were there.

Two students were absent from the all-school meeting. Marin was in the nurse's office resting and being checked every two hours for signs of a concussion. Very few people noticed that Lydia Boswell was missing too.

Lydia had waited until everyone else was in the auditorium, then she walked quickly across the main lawn to her dorm. Her mouth was swollen on one side, and her ribs were too tender to imagine jogging. She was wearing jeans and a sweater that Seth had lent her, and they were too big. Lydia hurried upstairs to her room and closed the door behind her with deep relief.

She began to take off Seth's clothes; she had never wanted a shower so badly in her life. Seth had carefully cleaned the blood from her face, but the loop of Ms. Alton holding her bleeding wrist over Lydia kept playing in her mind. Lydia shook the vision from her head and then froze.

All of the hair on the back of Lydia's neck and arms rose. She turned slowly where she stood, but she was alone in her room. Or was she?

There on her desk were several things Lydia had never seen before. Clinging to the towel around her chest, Lydia approached her desk slowly. There was a small pile of bristles from a paintbrush. Beside that, a piece of floral fabric. A scrap of faded blue fabric so old that it was brittle. She touched each thing, and the knowledge of what they were arrived with her touch: bristles from Georgia O'Keeffe's paintbrush, a piece of Julia Child's apron, a scrap of a Union uniform. She picked up a NASA patch from Kalpana Chawla's astronaut suit, and the finger of a silk glove she guessed had belonged to Hedy Lamarr. A piece of paper with an old signature on it.

Naomi. Cora. Gus. Pilar. Sorcha. Marin.

"You kept your promise," whispered Lydia. "You said good-bye."

At that moment the light in the room changed from soft yellow to an intense white. Lydia saw faces then; famous faces, one notably tall, one notably beautiful, and one with a large mustache. One face so dear to Lydia that she couldn't bear to blink.

"You saved me, Matthew," Lydia whispered.

** *It is done.* ** They all spoke together in a voice that was hollow and jangling in Lydia's ears.

Lydia nodded.

** *The others are healed.* **

"The students?"

** *Every spirit who wanted to return has done so.* **

Lydia nodded.

** *Tell my sister that my bones are in the graveyard to the south of the apple tree.* ** Lydia nodded at the young man who must be Moses Johnson.

** *I love you.* **

This last was from Matthew, Lydia could tell.

** *Tell my mom.* **

"I will, Matthew."

The spirits all spoke together. ** *You will have the Sight now.* **

"Forever?" asked Lydia.

** *Use it well.* **

The light grew bright then. Lydia squinted as long as she could but finally had to shut her eyes. The skin all over her body got tight and hot, then cooled. She opened her eyes and knew she was alone again. She went to the window and looked out for a long time. Finally she gave a little shudder, turned, and went down the hall to the bathroom. The bathroom was damp, fragrant, and echoing. Lydia looked at herself in the mirror.

She didn't need Naomi to tell her.

Her eyes were bleached two shades lighter.

Hope A. C. Bentley

I had the kind of childhood that generally does not create great art since it was almost cartoonishly happy. My brothers and I had doting parents, wonderful friends and the run of an idyllic little village in Connecticut.

Most of my writing is a sort of wish fulfillment; what if there really was magic in the world? What if we had to go back to the pioneer days? What if we could bring back the souls of people we love?

I started Golden Light Factory because I love igniting curiosity in young people, and I believe that books have the power to do that.

I live with my hubby, three children and several chickens in an idyllic little village in Vermont.